COUNTERWEIGHT MANEUVER

By Richie De-Benham

www.richiedebenham.com.
Facebook: @RichieDeBenhamAuthor
Twitter: @DeBenhamAuthor
Instagram: richiedebenhamauthor
Cover design by Spiffing Covers. Printed by Amazon.
ISBN: 9781983086571

Author's Note

This is a work of fiction, but there are many real-life parallels.

The Brotherhood to which Hawk belongs has an existing counterpart. In 1904, occultist Aleister Crowley wrote *The Book of Law*, inspired by a supernatural messenger from the Aeon of Horus and proclaiming that humanity was entering a new Aeon. This text became the cornerstone of the spiritual philosophy Thelema, with its key belief in the True Will. Crowley believed that mankind was entering the Aeon of Horus, in which people would take control of their own destiny.

In the first chapter of this book, Hawk receives a message that the Aeon of Horus is fast approaching. It could be argued that, in fact, it has already started and is now amongst us in the present time.

Hawk later refers to the young lions of Tarshish. "Tarshish" is the ancient Hebrew word for Great Britain. "The young lions of Tarshish" is a name given by ancient Prophets that foretold that the future Britain would have other future colonies, or young lions, i.e. the USA, Canada, Australia, and New Zealand.

"Today a space shuttle flies overhead with an international crew. A number of countries have international space programs. During the space age we have increased our knowledge of our universe a thousand fold.

Today we have with us a group of students, among America's best. To you we say we have only completed a beginning. We leave you much that is undone. There are great ideas undiscovered, breakthroughs available to those who can remove one of truth's protective layers! There are many places to go beyond belief. Those challenges are yours – in many fields, not least of which is space, because there lies human destiny."

— Neil Armstrong, July 20th, 1994

Chapter 1

The early morning fog rolled inland from San Francisco Bay, carrying with it the low moan of a horn. It was hard to see much in the low light – the video was clearly taken on a smartphone – but behind the gray, billowing vapour, a dark, angular shape gradually grew more distinct within the dissipating wisps of the previous night.

"This video shows the Ultra Large Container Vessel, Cáifù, of the China Container and Shipping Company entering the Port of Oakland last Sunday. CCSCO has been an emerging force in international shipping since the 1980s and is now responsible for 90% of all incoming products from Japan, Korea, and, of course, China. Today, CCSCO is valued at over $148 a share, and is currently setting the global benchmark for swift and economical shipping in the fast-moving world of container transportation."

The Cáifù was almost fifty meters wide and over 600 meters in length, and piled high with carefully stacked container crates. It looked like a gigantic fortress powering its way into the bay, carrying with it vast quantities of electronic goods, ranging from luxury automobiles, textiles, and industrial machinery, to advanced photovoltaic technology, all backed by the growing economic and technological powerhouses of the Far East.

The video swung to the right and zoomed in on the Port of Oakland. Giant gantry cranes jutted into the sky in front of its massive terminals, while, stretching into the distance, thousands of containers filled the yard with a mountain of brightly-colored boxes in blue, red, and yellow.

In the water, a relatively small Panamax-class container ship with Free American Line markings on its side was moving out of the Harbor and into the bay. It was half-empty and listing ever so slightly to starboard, apparently due to its uneven load. The camera moved further out to reveal another FAL ship just ahead of the first, and then swung back toward the Cáifù.

Zooming out yet again towards the foreground, a line of Panamax container ships moved slowly out of the port, each vessel marked with the FAL logo, and appearing quite insignificant compared to the looming Chinese ULCV.

"While Asia's economic rise is widely acknowledged, this footage, taken by Bradley Wilcox, a freelance reporter, and his accompanying article in the Oakland Tribune, exposes a disturbing trend within the infrastructure of America's largest industries. Wilcox's article, 'Setting Sun', reveals that the Port of Oakland – the first port on the Pacific Coast to build terminals for ultra large cargo ships, and the fifth busiest container port in the United States – was totally unprepared for Sunday's delivery due to a failure of the port's antiquated logistics system. According to Wilcox, a backlog had suddenly developed, causing the system to malfunction. The Chinese vessels were given immediate priority, with twenty-five Free American Line ships forced to clear the port half-loaded. This is the first time an emergency evacuation of any kind has ever occurred in a US shipping port."

The camera moved over the line of FAL ships, then settled back on the Cáifù. Behind it, the shadowy images of yet more gigantic Chinese ships slowly appeared in the distance, all packed to the limit, all closing in on the port.

The image cut to the head of the Chinese fleet as it entered the channel leading to the outer harbor, this time narrowly missing one of the trailing outbound FAL ships and causing it to rock violently in its wake. Even from a distance, crates could be seen slipping away from their fixings, and unsteady containers moved across the deck of the smaller vessel.

Now the camera showed a clean-shaven man in a tan jacket, smiling: the name Bradley Wilcox flashed briefly along the bottom of the screen.

"This isn't just the result of an increased volume of imported goods from the Far East." His voice crackled. *"This is a direct result of the government's apparent failure to assist American exporters. It appears that in certain government circles they are deliberately trying to minimize corporate homeland grants so as to make it harder for our home companies to compete on fair and even terms. China's getting stronger and we're getting weaker. This is an indisputable fact."*

The picture changed back to the port, showing the slim, blond presenter standing beside a crane while dock workers moved busily in the background.

"The Port of Oakland has yet to comment on the article," she said, pushing windswept hair out of her eyes, *"but these images speak clearly: China is now leading the world in terms of technological innovation and economic growth, while the United States is currently a nation in decline. You've been watching Joanne King for KSF Bay Area News, signing out."*

***

Ronald Hawk watched the video end with a cold eye and passed the tablet back to his aide with barely a flicker of emotion. As advisor and confidant to the President of the United States, he had to appear in control, even though he was seething with rage.

"Tell the Press Secretary I've been held up and won't have time to go over the finer details of the Presidential announcement or the budget meeting."

Hawk's cell phone buzzed on the table and he picked it up, seeing the caller's traceless ID "LBM" revealed on its screen.

"You have the file," Hawk said, dismissing the aide with a wave of his broad hand. "Keep me informed of the board's progress."

The aide paused for a second, then gave a quick nod and left the room. Hawk waited until he was gone and then put the phone to his ear.

"Greetings, Brother Ronald. How have you been keeping?"

The voice was calm and spoken with a refined English accent.

"I realize that we haven't spoken for some time, but I assume you have also seen the Oakland media story."

"I've seen it," Hawk replied. "In fact, I was expecting some form of communication from you."

"The Brotherhood has convened and the decision to proceed has been made. Given your seniority within the inner cell, I trust that you are in full and final agreement and understand what needs to be carried out?"

Hawk smiled. It was high time something was done. "If the supreme council wills it, then I am in total accord, Brother."

"You need to be very clear about this, Ronald," the voice continued. *"The sacred Thelema has determined that the problem*

has escalated beyond mere trade imbalances. If we do not act now, our planet may never recover from the vacuous actions of the eco-pernicious Pacific Rim. The Aeon of Horus is fast approaching, and the time has come to purge from this Earth the undesirable factions ruining our society."

Hawk felt his pulse rise. "Then the Maneuver has been sanctioned?"

"By each and every member of the highest inner circle," the voice confirmed. *"It must be implemented and pursued without impediment or further delay."*

With that last line still sinking in, the caller hung up. Hawk sat there transfixed for several long seconds. He knew what the call meant and what he and his sacred organization were about to embark upon. Finally, after years of preparation, it was time.

He got up, pushed aside his espresso, and left the Cabinet Lounge, smiling politely at the mid-level government officials as he left. He walked down the hallway to the elevator, passing the marine stationed at the door with nothing but a cursory glance, and waited for the elevator door to slide shut behind him.

The iris-recognition software acknowledged his identity and he pushed the button to the tertiary-basement level.

He felt the merest tremor as the primary mechanism activated and the elevator began its sixty-second descent to the old basement war rooms, recently renovated at his own personal expense to be his strategic office.

While he waited, Hawk smoothed his graying hair and pulled his tie straight. He was the President's confidant and the mastermind behind the quarterly "Standard American Values Assessment."

The one thing the American people had come to expect of this President was "values," and that was largely because they had given up on anything else. Foreign policy, the economy, social services – it wasn't so much that the administration's policies on these matters were disastrous, but rather that the President was incapable of presenting them adequately.

This fact alone had reduced the public's expectations to shockingly low levels. And, to be frank, if it wasn't for Hawk himself, the President's approval ratings would look even worse.

Hawk had once harbored dreams of becoming President himself. But because his war hero father had died on that fateful day on Hill Eerie, young Ronald – only an infant at the time – had never had the benefit of a father figure to look up to. Now, years later, he realized that he had actually spent most his life trying to measure up to a man that he hadn't even known.

Yes, Hawk had his father's sense of high duty and moral purpose, but he hadn't exactly inherited his movie-star good looks, broad reassuring shoulders, or the perfectly-honed stately gaze that the general public had become so accustomed to in their perception of public figures.

Nowadays, Hawk spent most of his time strategizing for the President instead of accomplishing anything legitimate or tangible himself. Unfortunately, this primarily involved helping the President justify America's faltering world status, rather than talking about building something new and significant for the future.

And then there was an increasingly hard-to-control gutter press making all kinds of false and sensational accusations against the government – people like this damn reporter, Wilcox. It only made Hawk's job much harder.

"Another muck-raking moron," he muttered to himself.

When Hawk had first entered politics, after finishing a military career that included rising to the rank of staff sergeant in the Vietnam War, it hadn't been like this. Back then, the White House had carried real weight with the American people. Citizens took the time to watch the Presidential address live on television, instead of just reading about it and criticising it in the blogosphere.

The President shaped public opinion by what he said, and didn't say, in those days. Yes, back then there'd been a sense of real respect. But now the President, the most powerful man in the world, had to cower down before a tide of useless public opinion just to stay in favor. And all this coming after the efforts of people like Hawk's father – people who had sacrificed their very lives for this nation. Journalistic scum like Wilcox were happy to bury their country for a cheap editorial spread.

The elevator door opened and Hawk walked into his office. The lights activated automatically, flooding the room in a cool white light. He turned on the monitor in the corner and sat while he waited for the shielded browser to warm up.

The screen erupted in white static, then coalesced into a set of scales clutched in the talons of a bald eagle.

"Mother, please retrieve all web data on Bradley Wilcox," Hawk said. "Focus search on Oakland Tribune article 'Setting Sun.'"

Search engaged, the computer replied while searching for the data that Hawk required.

In the blink of an eye it was there on the on the screen.

The Oakland incident had gone from Monday morning political blog fodder to a full-fledged media maelstrom, something only the modern instantaneous news cycle could produce. Every pundit, blogger, critic, comedian, and average Joe in America had now gotten in on the discussion of their nation's certain decline. *Good Morning America* had a panel of experts on a half-hour segment detailing the high and low points of America's tenure as global superpower, complete with graphics that depicted the nation now at its lowest of lows.

Hawk watched the footage again and again on the screen. The Chinese vessels, low on fuel and toting billions of dollars' worth of electronics, cars, and other high-value cargo, were given priority while the much smaller American vessels couldn't even finish loading their cargo before being ordered to evacuate.

The article Hawk could handle – he knew better than anyone that the words of a journalist could always be discredited, disputed, picked apart, and watered down – but the film was about as damning as it gets, and it was now the lead video on the Huffington Post, the Daily Beast, Slate, the Drudge Report, and just about every single blog and news website in America.

The very thought that United States vessels were being ordered to evacuate a home port was more than Hawk could bear.

And for what? For the cheap consumer goods and silicon gadgets that were now making his fellow Americans a bunch of lazy, complacent, high-tech-obsessed denizens, too overweight to enlist in the military, and too stupid to continue the tradition of entrepreneurship and technological innovation that had formerly made the USA so great.

The scene also underlined the very real fact that Hawk was all too acutely aware of – that the great American corporations were fast losing ground against the voracious growth of the Far East. Well, now the Brotherhood had made its judgement, and with their decree, Hawk would bring this matter to a successful conclusion.

He picked up the phone on his desk and dialled his PA in the White House. She answered immediately.

"Barb," Hawk said, cutting her greeting short. "Get Blewitt and his people onto the Wilcox story. Yes, the one that's all over the news."

Hawk hung up before Barb could ask any further questions. He knew it would be difficult, but Blewitt would get it done. Truth was relative. But there were always other ways to manipulate it.

His thoughts went to the press conference that was due to start in twenty minutes, but he could do nothing but shake his head. It was supposed to signal the start of restoring the old school days of American social values which had been so quickly and cruelly cut short by the convenience of smartphones, computers, and the isolation of social networking. And now, thanks to a local tabloid reporter's Sunday scoop, the very notion of America's dominance was the laughing stock of the internet and the entire world.

Hawk knew something more than a Standard American Values Assessment was required to reinstate this nation's place as the indisputable champion and the greatest power on Earth. Today's news was a sign that things would only get worse, much worse.

But the sacred Thelema had at last initiated what needed to be done. He and the other members of the Brotherhood were the ones who would have to change the course of history, period.

He lifted the receiver again, dialled the White House internal line, and instructed the switchboard to put a call through to one of his personal aides.

"Jenkins," he said, when the young man answered. "I need ten copies of the proposal brought up to the Cabinet Room. Have them ready in fifteen minutes."

Hawk hung up and pushed the phone away. The next call would need to be fully encrypted and totally off the record.

"General Morgan," he said, speaking into the microphone on his computer.

The screen shifted to black and Morgan appeared on the screen. He was dressed in uniform, his thick black beard immaculately groomed.

"Mr Hawk, sir," he said, eyebrows raised. "I wasn't expecting your—"

"General, the Maneuver is go," Hawk stated. "Get Carrington."

Morgan's expression didn't change. "Sir, has the President been informed of this?"

"He will be," Hawk replied. "Now go to it."

Morgan nodded, and the screen immediately went dark.

Hawk switched off the monitor. It looked as though he might just make it to the meeting after all.

***

President Robert Moore was well into his itinerary by the time that Hawk arrived.

"Glad you could make it, Ronald," the President remarked. "I was told that you may not be coming. I thought you might be unwell or something."

There were some chuckles from around the room.

Hawk smiled politely. "Just a few minor issues, Mr President. I hope I can still be of some use."

"Well, the news isn't good, but when is it these days?" the President said, with an exasperated look on his unblemished face. "But we're setting a good standard for the next quarterly Values Assessment. That's obviously important with the election next year."

The President smiled at Hawk as he seated himself, then continued with his pointless exercise in feel-good statistics. "We've seen a rise in high school GPA consistent with the 2% increase targeted by the Responsible Education Act, and we've still managed to cut spending by 40%. Good news all round, I think?"

Hawk knew it was a load of bullshit. Cutting spending while also reducing grading requirements only made people more uneducated, but it made sense if one was already a product of the system. Christ, no wonder this great nation was now in such a state of terminal decline.

"Defensively speaking, a third of our air force is grounded, but the Korean military is looking stronger with each passing day—"

They looked stronger because the US was getting weaker.

"—and then there's the deficit. Well, there's no getting around the fact that there are some hard times ahead."

But not if you're the CEO of a foreign oil company, Hawk thought to himself, biting his lip.

Hawk looked to the door and saw his aide, Jenkins, on the other side of the glass. He motioned for him to wait there and poured some water from a jug on the table.

He had made some big plays in his time, but none like this. He had on a previous occasion casually mentioned some aspects of his proposals to the President, but he doubted Moore would even remember the conversation. The President would fall in line though, he was sure of that, just as he was equally sure that the others would also follow suit.

Hawk looked around the table. Most of the Cabinet were suck-ups and idiots, with many of them in the pockets of Big Oil, the NRA, and that GMC company that nobody was even allowed to mention by name anymore. None of them had the spine to stand up to Hawk – with perhaps one exception.

Christine Sheen sat at the far end of the table, a cool expression on her lined face as she watched Hawk. She'd been in the game a long time, through three administrations, and had survived by playing to the midfield. Furthermore, up until the present time Hawk had to admit that her policies had worked to some extent.

At fifty-six, with a PhD in Economics and Public Policy from Stanford University, together with several other honorary doctorates, Sheen was the only female member of the President's Cabinet. With a long list of previously published articles as the author and by-line creator, her subsequent reputation was rock solid.

Even though her principles and convictions were impressive, they were too fluid for Hawk to take seriously. Recently, however, she and Hawk had come head to head on several key issues, and Hawk knew she was going to be the one serious contender to his grand scheme. He locked eyes with her, but she turned her attention back to the President.

"Anything I've forgotten, Ronald?" Moore asked.

Hawk looked through the sheaf of papers in front of him and shook his head. "You've just about covered everything in the itinerary, Mr President."

"Then I think we should adjourn—"

"If you'll pardon my interruption, Mr President," Hawk interjected, "but there was just that one final matter that we discussed in detail last month. You asked me to bring it up before the next Standard American Values Assessment and, uh, that is today."

The President's mouth was agape but he closed it quickly. "I'm very sorry, Ronald, you are indeed correct. Please feel free to remind the assembled cabinet the finer points of the discussion? I must admit that I have been extremely occupied as of late."

"Absolutely, Mr President," Hawk said, smiling and getting to his feet. He waved to the door and Jenkins entered the room, holding a stack of gray-sleeved documents in his arms. The aide placed them in a neat pile in front of Hawk, then left the room.

Hawk took a swift drink of water and swished it around his dry mouth, then looked out across the U-shaped table at the rest of the hushed Cabinet.

"The matter that I – that is, the matter the President and I wish to address, is that of our country's current and on-going economic decline – its moribund stagnating economy, its lethargic education system, its crippled military, and this government's consistent failure to step up and meet these very real and serious challenges."

There were rustles around the room as people shifted in their seats and shuffled their papers. Hawk forced himself to smile. "The President and I recently discussed an option that would not only permanently solve these issues, but also completely reverse them. And with your permission, Mr President, I would like to present this option to our gathered and learned friends."

"Ah, yes, of course," President Moore said, attempting an expression of gravity.

"The United States is indeed undergoing a great crisis," Hawk said, scanning the eyes of his audience. "Now, I know that we've been here before, with people saying the US has seen its greatest day. They said it in 1958 when the Soviets launched the Sputnik. They said it in 1973 during the Arab oil embargo. They said it in the 80s and 90s when America's industrial towns started to fade away while the corporations commenced manufacturing overseas, and, most recently in this millennium, they said it yet again during the global financial crisis that sent our markets spiralling into decline while releasing shockwaves around the globe. But this time it's different."

Hawk began distributing the documents, placing them in front of each Cabinet member.

"I'd like to introduce you all to the idea of power as a three-dimensional chess board," he said, moving around the table. "The top layer of the game is military power among states. For as long as we can remember, apart from the bankrupt and failing Soviets, the US has had no real contender in military might. Now, as hard as it is to admit it, we do." He placed a document in front of Sheen. "The middle board is economic power. If any of you have observed the recent incident in Oakland, you'll have noticed that we have been surpassed in that arena, also."

Sheen coughed and cleared her throat while Hawk paused, but she only looked up, smiling apologetically.

"The bottom layer," he continued, trying to hide his irritation, "is the most important for our purposes. The bottom layer of the society that we occupy is governed by those things which are outside government control. The things that shape events which no one person or group of persons can be blamed for – pandemics, floods, natural disasters, unexpected acts, and pure, indifferent bad luck."

Hawk placed the final copy in the President's hand, and everyone's attention dutifully turned to the 150-page document laid out in front of them. Unlike most drab policy documents, this was marked with the highest security clearance possible – only to be viewed by the ten pairs of eyes in the room. "Counterweight Maneuver" was printed in bold type on the front page.

It read, in part:

In 1800, Asia was home to half the world's population and made half the world's products. By the start of the industrial revolution, its production had dropped back to one-fifth of the world's goods. However, in the present time, we see that yet again the vast majority of the world's manufactured goods are produced in China, Japan, and the Pacific Rim, but are now consumed around the entire globe.

Currently, China, India, Japan, and Indonesia are said to be collaborating on expanding and opening new state-of-the-art manufacturing plants to build highly advanced aeroplane and satellite systems, which will have serious implications for US aerospace industries and our long-term space programs.

China, until recently a fairly low-tech economy, has now miraculously turned full circle into a high-tech powerhouse that has overtaken the entire world in economic production. It has also been strengthening its People's Liberation Army for well over a decade.

In just ten short years, their defense spending went from $30 billion to almost $120 billion. This year, it's expected to reach $195 billion. If they maintain this current pace of defense development, they will totally outpace the US by 2035. China's urgency has only heightened since the US became engaged in costly wars in Afghanistan and in the Middle East. However, while seeing the high-tech and targeted forces that have been adopted to replace ground combat forces, the Chinese have also changed course.

No longer focusing on military prowess on the battlefield or with a face-to-face enemy, China's military strength is now focused on highly technological and precise attacks. As a military ideology, they have adopted a strategy called "Unified C4ISR." The four Cs are command, control, communications, and computers; ISR stands for intelligence, surveillance, and reconnaissance.

The US has also developed sophisticated counterintelligence that the Chinese have been working on, where we have also acquired A2/AD, or "anti-access/area denial" capabilities. However, the Chinese have recently developed a far superior technology, which allows them to pinpoint any ground attack or anti-ship missile system. They also have a growing fleet of modern nuclear submarines, with undersea cyber intelligence capability and highly sophisticated anti-satellite weaponry capable of destroying or disabling another nation's military assets from afar. Not only that, the PLA's document, "The Science of Military Strategy," plainly *states that "active defense is the essential feature of China's military strategy." It goes on to say: "if an enemy offends our national interests, then it means that the enemy has already fired the first shot, in which case the PLA's mission is to do all we can to dominate the oppressor by striking out first."*

After a brief period of reading, ten pairs of eyes looked up from the document and began darting around the room looking at each other. It was hard to tell what everyone was feeling, until Clint Addison, the Secretary of Defense, spoke up and said the obvious.

"Mr Hawk, we've known that this has been happening for quite some time, but our hands are tied. We can't declare any more wars. That would be disastrous for public opinion and you've heard the reports from our generals. Our military infrastructure simply can't handle another costly campaign."

"You're partially right," Hawk said. "War, in the traditional sense of the word, is both antiquated and out of the question. But this is about more than just military strength. This is about regaining the captive attention and respect of the American people and the wider world. We need to regain what power we've lost over the past decades to concentrate on competing with the high-tech industrial and manufacturing giants now firmly located in the Far East."

He took a breath to let his words sink in, and continued.

"If there's one fundamental difference between the citizens of the West and those of the East, it's in their attitude towards government. In the West, we believe that the authority and legitimacy of the state is a function of democracy. But citizens have become ambivalent about that authority – they barely even care if it's there anymore.

"In the East, the state takes on a more spiritual role. For over 2,000 years, the power of the Chinese state has not been challenged – the people accept it as the head of the family. The state is everywhere in China, its authority is ubiquitous. It is called the 'Way of the Han.'"

Hawk placed his hands on the desk and looked over those seated, his eyes finally settling on the President.

"The American people need us to step in. But it must be done in a way that is strategic. We cannot do this as a state actor."

There were murmurings from those seated. This was going to be crucial, Hawk knew, and he wasn't surprised when it was Sheen who spoke next.

"So what you're saying is that the US is now going to intervene, but *not* as a state actor. Isn't that called terrorism?"

"Terror is what will ensue when the US is no longer able to defend itself against the rest of the world," Hawk said, turning to confront Sheen. "In case you haven't noticed, Miss Sheen, China has no compunction when it comes to attacking our networks and manipulating our currency. A carefully placed computer virus can wipe billions off the stock market. It might not be as distasteful as a tactical strike, but the result is just the same: lives destroyed, businesses lost.

"When our economic dominance declines to the point where we no longer have the power to sway international agreements, when our people become so fat and lazy from sitting in front of a television screen that we can't put together the elite military that

America has relied upon so many times in the past, then you might notice that we've been the victim of the most subtle and heinous example of covert terrorism the world has ever seen."

There were more murmurs.

"Forgive me if I don't read this entire document now," Sheen said, talking over the others. "But what exactly will this 'intervention' entail?"

"Quite simply a Black Op," Hawk said, "under the direct command of myself and key military personnel."

"What do you exactly mean, Mr Hawk, by a Black Op? What are you getting at? Do you really think that a clandestine military option is preferable to forging economic and military alliances with these new powers?" Sheen asked. "We've made great progress recently, and opened up new markets."

"Excuse me, madam, but do you want the world to hear of America's weakness from the lips of its own leaders?" Hawk replied, frowning. Deep inside he was seething, but calm was required. He turned away, shaking his head. "I understand your ties to atheist China, Miss Shin."

He paused, waiting for those listening to realize he'd used her real name, not the adopted *Sheen*, and not by accident.

"Please remember that you are now working on the side that you picked."

There was some commotion in the room as Hawk walked back to his seat. He could hear several of the Cabinet members defending Sheen, but he'd made his point. He sat down, locking eyes with Sheen once again. She stared back with fury in her eyes, but he could also sense her fear.

The President was standing and the noise abated.

"Now, as Ronald has indicated, I am very troubled by these developments, but no decisions will be made without great care and deliberation. In the next few weeks, we will develop a specific strategy for how to deal with the task in front of us."

Hawk looked defiantly at those around the table. Had they never heard the ancient story of the young lions of Tarshish? The President could mince his words and offer all the pleasantries he liked, but the Brotherhood's plan was already in motion.

All Hawk had to do was make sure the American people never found out who was behind the events that would unfold. And once they had Oswald Carrington in their grasp, that would be very easy.

***

Oswald Carrington poured boiling water over the noodles, half-listening to the infomercial on the television.

"The new programmable Sani-Bot 3000 from Wèilái Guòqù will revolutionize your home."

"Simple crap," Carrington said, shovelling the still-crispy noodles into his mouth. "Basic, simple crap."

"What can it do, Dave?"

"Well, it's a vacuum cleaner, Bob, but it's capable of much more than that."

"It's a shitty trash can, Dave," Carrington said, laughing to himself.

He had finished his graduate studies at the prestigious Massachusetts Institute of Technology six months ago, but he still had no idea what he wanted to do with his life. His work on miniaturized robotic drones had gained him great acclaim at MIT, with professors from every department – astronautics, physics, bio-mechanical engineering, nuclear, and computer science – not just encouraging, but practically begging him to pursue a career in their given field.

In the end, he'd chosen a position at Apex Technologies, pursuing his favorite field: robotics. If he'd realized at the time that they were going to limit his work to simple drone technology, then he wouldn't have even lasted the two months he'd managed to complete.

"With this attachment, the Sani-Bot 3000 can clean in-between tiles, and it's precise enough to get between the individual keys of your laptop without disturbing the text on screen."

"Bullshit. Keyboards will be obsolete in two years."

The problem was that nothing could hold Carrington's attention for long enough. Not girls, not jobs, not hobbies – none of it was interesting enough on its own.

He'd been this way since he had been a very young child, and what with his parents having to work relentlessly to keep their brilliant offspring from getting bored, they were forever trying to stimulate his brilliant brain by setting him ever more complicated challenging tasks in order that he never stopped mentally progressing and thus losing his motivation in life altogether.

"And at $199 plus tax—"

Carrington turned off the television with a whispered curse, and placed the bowl of noodles on the table whilst retrieving a half-smoked joint from the ashtray. He lit it and took a long toke, feeling the comforting haze wafting slowly over his eyes and quietly tranquilizing his buzzing, hyperactive brain.

Fucking Sani-Bot 3000? He could build a better robot than that using an empty can of beans. And it wasn't even autonomous! It relied upon a primitive pre-programmed routine that gave it the illusion of semi-intelligence.

Well, Carrington had to admit that even he hadn't quite solved the true artificial-intelligence problem, but his insectoid Droniks used a highly advanced and sophisticated swarm-intelligence program to allow them to make extremely complicated decisions. They could identify friend from foe and easily incapacitate a fully-grown man. He had already proven that he could build the working prototype of one of those at college, but God knows how far he could have gone with the right backing.

Sadly, most companies were no longer interested in state-of-the-art technology. They just wanted to build cheap crap which they could then sell to fucking lazy morons, and none were willing to give Carrington full autonomy.

This was why, despite having possibly one the greatest inventive minds in the US, he was currently living in the basement of his parents' suburban Pennsylvania house and smoking copious amounts of marijuana, all in an attempt to stop really thinking about all the thinking he should be doing.

It had been weeks since he had done anything productive, unless you counted watching daytime television or hacking into the Pentagon archives and various celebrities' Twitter accounts, and yet he had no plans of changing that mind-set any time soon.

The clock said 18:15. Another hour until his parents got home and almost time for *Doctor Who*.

A beeping noise disturbed him from his thoughts. He walked through the kitchen to the living room, the joint clenched in his teeth, and pulled his battered laptop from under the cushions of the sofa, placing it down on the cluttered coffee table.

The beeping stopped as he opened it but the icon in the corner of the screen was pulsing red.

What the hell? Surely not intruders?

He tapped the icon and activated the Droniks he'd positioned throughout the house. A dozen square windows opened on screen, displaying the views from each of his twelve Droniks.

He frowned. Droniks 3, 4, and 5 were blank. He tapped the screen, then checked the software, but everything was working. He'd positioned 3 and 4 upstairs, guarding the balcony outside his parents' room, and Dronik 5 had been lodged in the chimney breast.

Carrington turned from the screen and glanced back in the direction of the kitchen and the hallway. Had he heard something?

He took a long drag on the joint, then thought better of it and stubbed it out on the remains of the pizza he'd had for breakfast. He picked up the laptop and walked quietly across the carpet to the cupboard, ducked inside it and sat down, the computer on his lap in front of him. He opened the Dronik file and activated the remaining drones. "Fucking wrong house to break into, buddy," he whispered under his breath.

Droniks 1 and 2 were folded into the smoke detector at the top of the stairs, 6 through 10 were hidden in the air ducts throughout the house, and 11 and 12 were on his desk downstairs.

He watched Cam 1 as it lit up and saw the top floor of the house slide into view as the drone quietly hovered out of its hiding place. "All clear," he whispered, activating its search-and-identify function. He then tagged 2, 7, 8, 9, and 10 for patrol.

The insect-like drones were all linked, all learning. The moment the threat was identified, the others would engage their combined combat function, and whoever was in the house – Carrington was pretty damn sure that *someone* had got in – was about to discover that his drones were far more effective than anything he'd previously used at MIT.

His breath caught in his throat as the power went out. The Wi-Fi was gone too. Something was definitely going on. His Droniks were operating on their own enclosed wireless system and running on miniaturized hydrogen cells. But now he had no way of reaching the authorities or anyone else – not unless he got up and physically fled the house.

The drones had already compensated for the darkness, and 11 and 12 had warmed up and were heading up the stairs from the cellar. Droniks 11 and 12 were packing a new invention that Carrington was particularly proud of. He called them Hornet Grifters, and while they were heavier and therefore slower, no burglar was going to appreciate the sting these things carried.

A pop sounded from his laptop – Dronik 7 had identified a threat! He stared at the screen. Dronik 7 was hovering by the door to his parents' room, and 1 and 2 were speeding their way towards it. He felt horror crawling up his back as the door swung inward.

Nothing there?

"TARGET LOST" was flashing on the screen and he overrode it with a punch of a key. His drones could never lose track of something once they had found it! They latched onto complex visual patterns, heat and audio signatures. They could hear a pin drop and tell you where it was dropped, how much the pin weighed, and even the composition of the pin. Any movement in that room should be showing up like a brass band, yet nothing was there.

Droniks 8 and 10 were still patrolling and he engaged their stealth function. The drones were already quiet, but now they were flying at one-tenth power – slower and lower, but with all the energy focused on detection.

There it was! The signature matched a footstep close by – a boot on carpet. Something was on the stairs!

A fizzing crack sounded, and Dronik 7's screen went white. Carrington stayed calm. He'd assumed that whoever had broken into the house was after money or jewellery. He hadn't even remotely considered that they could be after him, and even if that were the case, they'd soon be aware of at least the basics of his technology. No one, but no one, was as good as him. The tech didn't exist that could stand up to his incredibly advanced imagination.

The Hornet Grifters – Droniks 11 and 12 – had reached the ground floor and entered the kitchen. He set them to combat mode and watched as they descended to the floor, their cams aimed at the staircase and the entrance to the living room.

Droniks 8 and 10 were responding to the loss of 7, following the edge of the wall. There it was! Dronik 7 was on the ground, scorched and in pieces. The air above it was distorted by heat – whatever had hit it must have been a high-energy pulse. But then the distortion was moving and gone.

Carrington realized that something was indeed generating that heat signature, but it wasn't his damaged drone. Dronik 8 had noticed the heat source and powered up, buzzing into the room at speed, its weapon systems fully activated.

He engaged the tag-gas function and Dronik 8 released its payload, flooding the room with a mildly radioactive nerve toxin, designed to paralyze or at least slow down any intruder while painting it with a radioactive signature. Dronik 8 dropped and 10 was in, immediately latching onto the target.

Carrington froze. His drone had flown like a bat out of hell towards something, but he was so shocked he wasn't aware at first that both drones were done for.

The localized electromagnetic pulse caught the machines totally by surprise, frying both of them and wiping the images from their cams clean from his laptop in a blinding flash. Carrington, though, had seen something quite clearly against the blaze of light: a smooth mouth, jagged teeth, a compound eye, and a vein-like crest protruding from behind a metallic skull.

"What the fuck?" he mumbled to himself.

Quickly recovering, he shifted his concentration back to the Hornet Grifters. There was nothing on the stairs – not yet. Droniks 1 and 2 had moved into stealth mode in accordance with the survival algorithm he had programmed into them, and 6 and 9 were following the course of the air vent down to the living room. If anything got past the Grifters now he'd have at least some backup, and he'd use 1 and 2 as soon as he knew what was going on. He was certainly up against some very advanced tech, and whatever that thing was, it definitely knew what it was doing. Carrington needed to think differently now, more creatively. At that moment he realized, as terrified as he was, he was bizarrely starting to enjoy himself.

Something creaked overhead and he realized he was in danger of being outsmarted. He opened the cupboard door just a crack and cautiously peaked out, looking up at the ceiling. There was a strange humming noise reverberating through the house, flakes of plaster began to slowly drift down from above. Was it about to come through the ceiling?

Carrington folded the laptop closed and climbed out of the cupboard, sprinting for the kitchen just as the ceiling fell in with a gigantic cloud of dust. He didn't stop to see what had caused it and immediately leapt over the kitchen counter, falling heavily on his back, the laptop hugged protectively across his chest.

An eerie creaking, humming, screeching noise sounded from the living room as he saw what appeared to him to be a laser spike tracing the wall through the thick dust-laden air, almost as if it was investigating.

"Fuck. Fuck. Fuck," he said, as he pulled himself across the floor to the door of the basement. He heard an explosion – Dronik 1 had detonated to cover his escape – and the screeching rose an octave.

Carrington was already halfway down the basement steps, slamming the door behind him, when the Grifters also went off, releasing dozens of tiny, poison-packed, ambulating Goops: tiny marble-sized walking machines that were programmed to sting anything that moved. He tripped in his haste and fell face first.

His laptop went skidding across the floor but he quickly grabbed it back up before heading for the drawer beside his bed and the Glock 17 he kept there. He pulled it out and spun around, his back to the wall, the gun aimed at the closed door at the top of the stairs.

Nothing moved and there was total silence.

Suddenly he heard a strange high-pitched humming whine coming from the other side of the door, then silence again. Keeping the pistol trained on the door, he reached for his laptop and flipped it open. Twelve square windows of static reflected in his glasses. Every Dronik was down. Every single one.

"No way. No fucking way. Not possible," Carrington muttered.

The center of the door creased inwards, and the whole thing was pulled from its frame. A blinding blue and white flashing light shone down on him. He tried to pull the trigger, barely aware of what was happening, but felt the Glock pulled from his numb grip.

He caught a slight glimpse of thick compound lenses, and then a clawed hand was holding him down.

An alien voice like he had never heard before – hostile, deep, and distorted – croaked angrily in his ear, "*We have you now*," as a thick black hood was pulled over his head.

He could hear his breathing getting louder in his ears and subsequently smelled a strange chemical odor. A series of red lights flashed in sequence, up and down, inside the hood, as he felt himself being lifted, higher and higher, until the cold chill air declared he was outside.

Carrington struggled, harder and harder, but the lights were calming, soothing. He felt his muscles relax, felt his breathing slow, and the last thing he heard was a groaning noise so terrible he embraced unconsciousness.

Chapter 2

Bradley Wilcox calmly switched off his phone, weighed it in his hand, and threw it hard, barely missing the computer monitor and his close friend, Steve, who was seated directly in front of it.

"Another brush-off?" Steve said, frowning.

Bradley took a deep breath, then another, and then grabbed the microwave, forcibly tearing it from the wall and sending it in the same direction as the phone.

"Christ, Brad!" Steve exclaimed, leaping to his feet. "I know this is bullshit, but I'm here to help? Control yourself, man! Try to calm down!"

Bradley shook his head and turned to the window, facing out across the bay.

When he'd first gotten his local reporting gig at the Oakland Tribune, he'd been thrilled. A freelancer with some success writing investigative pieces for various publications, he had fallen on hard times while trying to help his elderly, frail parents, and needed a steadier income to recover his increased losses.

At first, the relatively small scope of what he was reporting on was exciting to him. He thought he would be able to delve into some meaningful issues and get to know the real characters of the community that he reported on. Soon enough, though, he'd felt totally stifled. His editor's requests that he only cover mundane city council meetings and ice cream shop openings just wasn't what he'd had in mind. It was an insult to the substantial body of work that he'd already accomplished in his career.

Listening to the funky sound of "Beggarman" by the rock group Smoove and Turrell, Bradley had decided that fateful day to take a leisurely drive down to the local port he so often frequented. Visiting this spot always had a mystical calming effect upon him, helping him to gather his thoughts in this crazy, uncaring world. However, having gone through his usual routine of sitting on the high ground with his binoculars overlooking the bay, he suddenly found himself wondering why there were so many cargo ships offloading on a Sunday.

As he stood there looking out over the bay, Bradley had remembered an astonishing statistic he'd learned while working a story about global shipping dynamics. In 2008, roughly 2.24 million cargo containers, each twenty feet long, had passed through this very port, which was one of the largest in the US.

Bradley scanned the horizon and saw more ships in the distance. He pulled out his smartphone and captured the arrival of the CCSCO fleet: massive container ships, one after another, were pulling into the bay. To his basic assessment, it seemed that the port, which was filled to the brim with a variety of smaller vessels, was not going to be able to accommodate the new fleet.

A traffic jam at one of the US's largest ports?

He panned back to the quayside: the American ships were all departing, half unloaded, crates still stacked on the dock.

He jumped into his beat-up Camry and raced down to the outer bay. The ships there seemed to be queuing and holding position. They weren't just small container vessels transporting corn or other lowly goods – these were gigantic ocean-going Asian vessels, the largest that modern engineering could design, transporting high-cost goods bound for the aisles and showrooms of corporate American retail outlets: automobiles, electronics, TVs, laptops, industrial machinery, and a plethora of other parts. With the high cost of fuel, there was no way they'd be able to turn back.

Knowing how much forward logistical planning went into the arrivals and departures at the port, Bradley was stunned. How could such a large mishap have occurred? He googled the number to Oakland Port Authority and called, hoping he wouldn't get an automated response.

"Port of Oakland?" a voice barked.

"Hello. My name's Bradley Wilcox. I'm a journalist working for the Oakland Tribune. I'm looking out at the bay and—"

"—and you want to know why the fuck a billion dollars' worth of Asian imports is being held up?"

"Uh, yes, that's exactly what I want to know."

"I'll tell you why. Ever since this government decided it was more important to ruin our own country and give the work to the Far East, our budget has been cut relentlessly, and now we're short-staffed. The guys that have remained are training under-qualified newbies. Mistakes are made. Shit happens."

"So what happened today, exactly?"

"Our logistics and IT system – the one that's been on the fritz for months – has finally failed. And the government have blocked a move to provide us with a new one, at least that's what I've been told us. Look, I gotta go."

"Well, thanks for talking—"

"One more thing."

"Yeah?"

"Whatever article you write, print my name: Tom Dalaney. I can't take any more of this bullshit. I'm outta here. I'm totally done. We're all fucking done."

Bradley had filmed until his memory card was full. Then he'd sped back to his apartment and written what he'd considered to be the best article of his career, 'Setting Sun.' He'd been complimented on the overall content by the editor and had been phoned by a local news channel who'd offered a lot of money for the footage. He'd also received lucrative contract offers from countless broadsheets, tabloids, and other magazines. But now the e-mail from The Tribune had undone all of that.

Bradley took several deep breaths to compose himself. "They're hanging me out to dry, Steve. That article got me national exposure – no, *international* exposure! – and now I'm being gagged because of some cheap crap about my source, about my fucking integrity? What proof do they have? What proof? This is America, for Christ's sake!"

"That's the whole point isn't it, Brad?" Steve said, typing away. "Look, I'm following the trace from The Tribune. Maybe we'll get to know who's behind this."

Bradley muttered an apology and took the half-empty bottle of bourbon from atop the fridge, pouring a glass for each of them. There were two advantages in using the small, crowded kitchen as his office. One was the view; the other was that there was always a drink within easy reach.

Steve was right, of course. The current administration was more concerned with matters of faith and appearances than education and economics. Two major wars and tax cuts for billionaires had made it clear that prior cabinets cared only about money, not the manufacturing companies of America. And now that Bradley's article had demonstrated just how bad it was getting, some schmuck was slinging mud and accusing him of "creative use of camera," a "hidden agenda," and "using a discredited source" from the port authority.

He passed a glass to Steve. "How could I have been more transparent?" he asked, downing his drink. "I had the footage, and a great source. I'm a patriot! What more could I have done?"

"The truth will come out one day, Brad," Steve said, sipping the whiskey with a grimace. "Now, give me a sec. It's another proxy, but I think I'm getting a bit closer."

Bradley turned back to the window. If he could just find out who was messing with him – someone high up at the Port of Oakland, he assumed – he might be able to get to the bottom of it, possibly take them to court. Then he could get his name cleared and maybe get his job back – not that he wanted to work for The Tribune anymore, the spineless dumb-asses.

"Whoa. Shit."

"What?" He turned back to Steve. "Have you found them? Who is it?"

Steve laughed nervously, finished his drink and got up. "You've really stood on some big toes this time, Brad. Quite a lot of them, it seems."

"Who? Who is it?" Bradley asked, forcing himself to stay calm.

"None other than the Federal fucking Government," Steve said. "Some guy called Hawk, specifically."

"Why would the government care about an article on the Port of Oakland?" Bradley said, his face portraying a puzzled look.

"Well, it makes the US look bad, doesn't it?" Steve replied, getting together his things. "Or maybe someone has shares in the port? Look, I've just followed a trace from the Oakland Tribune to a subsidiary branch of a company working for the White House. This isn't quite what I was expecting, Brad. I could get into deep shit for this."

"It's my computer," Bradley said, feeling dazed. He passed his friend fifty dollars for the work. "Go home, pal. You won't have to worry about anything. And thanks for your help."

Steve took the money and slung his backpack over his shoulder. "I'd stay out of this, Brad," he said, opening the front door. "Seriously. You're a good journalist. You can still get work, man, whatever The Tribune says. This kind of shit isn't worth it."

Bradley closed the door behind him and absent-mindedly reached for his glass. He didn't remember filling it, but the next thing he knew he was knocking back another drink while idly gazing at his TV. It was on the cooking channel. The grossly obese women coated in umpteen layers of makeup was demonstrating how to roast a whole suckling pig.

Signs of America's decline were everywhere: Foreign firms taking over. Home industries systematically shutting down. TV and advertising shows that used sublime alpha brainwave techniques, all designed to deliberately distract and placate the people while the country fell further and further behind, and then when it resulted in something like the travesty at the port, it was all quietly hushed up.

He poured another drink. At least the US still knew how to make whiskey. Maybe Steve was right – he could still get work that payed better than The Tribune. But his journalistic instincts told him he was close to something big, even though there could be a risk involved. What would happen if the Feds got wind of him? Would it go beyond him? Would they go after Steve?

The woman on the television was chit-chatting with a guest about nothing. Bradley couldn't even be bothered to feel angry anymore. He felt numb. He reached for the bottle and knocked it over. Fortunately, it was empty.

He sank back in the sofa, his eyelids growing heavy. *Is China the real enemy?* he thought to himself. *Or is our own government the problem?*

The pig was pulled out of the oven, a red apple placed between its charred lips.

***

Bradley woke up with a dry mouth, an acid throat, and a ringing in his ears. He wiped the sleep from his eyes and followed the buzzing to his cell phone which was lying in the corner of the room. It took him a moment to remember he'd thrown it there as his memory slowly came back into focus.

He got up, let the mild dizziness pass, then stumbled past the coffee table, retrieving his phone from the floor. The word "Withheld" flashed on its screen as Bradley answered it.

A female voice came over its speaker. *"Mr Wilcox?"*

Bradley cleared his throat. "Who's this?"

"You've left quite a trail behind you, Mr Wilcox. I take it that you didn't like having your article on the Oakland Port incident being discredited?"

Bradley paused. Had Hawk found him? "I… I didn't know…" he stammered.

"The question is, are you willing to do something about it?" the voice continued. *"I may have some answers for you – not all of them, but maybe enough to help you. Can you get to Washington DC in one week's time?"*

"DC?" Bradley echoed. "Uh, yeah, I suppose. Look, who is this?" What's your name again?"

"I would have preferred to meet you earlier, Mr Wilcox, but there are some further details to sort through. Be at the Kiyoko Sushi bar on Constitution Avenue, Friday 8th at 7 PM, Eastern Time. I think you'll find it worthwhile."

The line went dead.

Bradley looked at the time: it was 4 AM. He still felt hammered, which meant he had the hangover to look forward too. But because of that strange call he realized he might at last have a fighting chance. He poured himself a glass of water, drained it down quickly, then got another. It was time was to fire up his PC.

***

Oswald Carrington opened his eyes to total darkness. At first, all he could hear was his own breathing, harsh and loud in his ears. Then a series of stark white lights sparked into being.

He was lying on a flat slab, his arms and legs restrained with metal cuffs. The room was square; the walls, floor, and ceiling were of a smooth-silver like material, but there was no sign of a door. He vaguely remembered his abduction; the strange, hostile, alien face. He moved his wrists to test the cuffs, but they wouldn't budge.

What was this place? Where the fuck was he? It looked like a cell, pure and simple. Whoever had orchestrated this clearly had vast resources and highly trained men, but… alien? He doubted it.

"Hello?" he shouted.

There was a moment of silence, then a crackle of noise that settled into a low hum. Carrington waited as the hum became a rapidly oscillating series of shrieks and croaks, like the "voice" he'd heard back at his parents' house. Then silence.

A concealed door slid open and a man walked in. He was a hair under six feet, with wide shoulders and a solid, if not slim, torso. His graying hair was cut short and combed back, and his eyes, which were intense but calm, were focused on Carrington. He was wearing a black suit with a Stars and Stripes pin on the lapel. Carrington recognized his face from somewhere, but he couldn't place where. Perhaps from television?

"Mr Oswald Carrington," the man said. "It's a pleasure to finally meet you."

Carrington nodded, which was difficult given his current predicament. "You know, I would've made some coffee for you if you'd planned a visit. You didn't need to smash my house to pieces."

The man pulled a cell phone from his pocket. "I do apologize for your abduction, Mr Carrington. However, the nature of the work that

I'm offering will require a steady nerve. Let's just say that the abduction and your reaction to it is part of your evaluation. If you'll allow me time to explain myself, I'll make sure you get a cup of coffee." He pushed a button on the phone and the restraints holding Carrington silently slid back into the slab.

Carrington sat up, rubbing his wrists. He heard a sound to his left and glanced in that direction, but the room was empty except for himself and the man in the suit.

"You obviously need me for something," Carrington said, turning back to his captor. "But I don't know what my folks will think when they get home."

"Allow me to introduce myself, Mr Carrington. My name is Ronald Hawk. You may have heard of me?"

"The President's advisor?"

"The very same. And it is quite true that the results of your abduction will appear extremely odd, and not by accident. The media will probably be all over it by now." Hawk slid the phone into his pocket and gestured to the open door. "Care to join me for that coffee you mentioned, Mr Carrington?"

Carrington, his interest piqued, wasn't going to say no. He dropped his feet to the ground and let the dizziness pass, then followed Hawk to the door. He heard a clicking noise behind him, but again, when he looked, there was no one there.

"Many things are happening in the shadows, Mr Carrington," Hawk said, noticing his confusion. "Come with me and I'll show you where to look."

"Where am I?"

"A secret government facility, but please don't worry. These safeguards are put in place for your own protection. We wouldn't want you to know too much, would we, Mr Carrington?"

"I understand the cloak and dagger stuff, but this is crazy. And my abduction—"

"My office is very close, Let us talk there, where we have some privacy."

Carrington reined in his curiosity and followed Hawk out into a corridor. The walls were silver-colored like in the cell, and strips of purple light glowed along its length.

He followed Hawk to a door at the end. A man – a marine, judging by his posture – was guarding the door. He was dressed in a strange-looking uniform, and the slender weapon at his side was like nothing Carrington had ever seen before.

Hawk returned the soldier's salute. Carrington felt awkward as they passed, but the marine never even gave him a glance. On the other side of the door was a junction. He silently followed Hawk down a couple more corridors to another room.

Walking into the office of Ronald Hawk was exactly as one might imagine – like entering the underground lair of an autocrat. The room shone with the soothing haze of blue, white, and purple light but had not a single window. The walls were cluttered with certificates, military accolades, and pictures of past war heroes, some of which included Hawk's famous father. One photograph appeared to show a youthful Hawk in Vietnam, standing beside a younger version of the current President.

"Take a seat, please." Hawk gestured to a chair as he himself sat behind the desk. A tray with two cups of steaming coffee, a jug of milk, and a bowl of sugar lay between them. "I think you're going to be quite interested in what I have to say, Mr Carrington."

"I haven't committed to anything yet," Carrington replied, reaching for the cup closest to Hawk. "But you can call me Oswald."

Hawk shrugged in acquiescence. "You have every right to refuse the offer that I'm about to make, Oswald, but it's most important you understand that, whether or not you decide to move forward with this opportunity, the nature and content of our discussion today cannot be divulged to anyone, no matter what."

"There is the small episode regarding the damage to my parents' home and my Droniks." Carrington reached for a packet of sugar. "No disrespect, Mr Hawk—"

"Ronald."

"—but what am I supposed to say happened? Gas leak? Careless burglars?"

"You're a rather eccentric individual, Oswald," Hawk said, taking the remaining cup. "I have no doubt that the technology you were working on somehow caused the destruction of your parents' home, and whatever testimony you give is likely to be frowned upon at best. So you call those things Droniks? I like it." Hawk sipped the coffee and smiled. "You know, this coffee sells at ten bucks an ounce. It would cost more, of course, but the US Government staged a coup in the country of its origin back in the nineties purely to keep the price of coffee and bananas down. Do you see the unusual lengths to which our great nation will go just to make sure we can have a cheap breakfast? Of course, circumstances are rather more pressing these days, and further adjustments are now required."

Carrington felt himself going cold all of a sudden. He'd spent his whole life being underwhelmed by the intellectual prowess of practically everyone he met. But something about Hawk really scared him – his demeanour, the cold flash of intensity in his eyes, the fact that he happened to subtly hold the position of being one the most powerful men in the United States. For the first time in his life, Carrington felt intimidated.

"So what's this all about?" he asked, leaving the coffee untouched.

"Are you familiar with HSRCMDs?" Hawk asked.

"Highly Specialized Remote Control Monitoring Devices," Carrington quickly responded. "Yeah, sure. I designed several in a robotics course I took a while back."

"I'm well aware of your past work, Oswald. That is why you are here." Hawk reached under his desk, retrieving one of Carrington's badly damaged Hornet Grifters and placing it on the table. "Some improvements, but basically the same as those you worked on at MIT, am I right? Well, what if I told you I could provide you with unlimited resources for you to design a set of HSRCMDs on a scale that few people in this world could even contemplate?"

Carrington raised his eyebrows. "You abducted me to offer me a job building drones?"

Part of the reason he hadn't been able to commit to anything was because every past option presented to him was limiting in some way. A research grant would never cover his goal. A private sector position, even one at a top Silicon Valley powerhouse, would quickly get boring as soon as he realized his job was to create pointless technology for people to mindlessly play with. Carrington

42

considered himself somewhat a visionary, and nothing he'd been presented with in his life so far was capable of remotely matching up to his pioneering vision. Could this be the exception?

"What can you offer me that a hundred other companies couldn't?" he asked.

"In addition to unlimited technological and structural resources, you mean?" Hawk slowly placed his cup down. "Well, money, obviously, and anything you need for the ideal working environment will be provided for you. But then you require far more than that, don't you, Oswald?" He sat back in his chair. "We are going to change the world. The technological balance of this planet is about to shift and you, Mr Oswald Carrington, will play a part as one of its chief architects. First there was Newton, then there was Einstein, and now... you." Hawk gestured his hands towards him.

Carrington suddenly realized he was drinking the coffee and quickly put it down. "You need me to work on autonomous drones... and you're saying this will rival the deeds of the fathers of modern physics?"

"What I'm asking for in return is no small feat. The project, should you choose to embark upon it, will change our planet forever."

"Uh, very strange and weird," said Carrington. I like a challenge. But you still haven't told me what this job would entail."

"For reasons of your own security, I cannot reveal the full detail of what you'll be working on or how it will be deployed. However, let me assure you that it is of supreme importance, not only to the United States, but to the entire world. Now, you can decline my offer and go back to medicating yourself in the basement of your parents' home. You can do as you will, but should you try to go public with what you've seen, then – trust me on this – no one will ever take you seriously. You also needn't concern yourself with us. We'll totally forget you and leave you in peace."

"So you have others lined up?"

"We always have contingency plans."

Carrington pushed the coffee away. "Then may I suggest you use them," he said, standing. "You say I'll be doing work on a level with Newton and Einstein, and then tell me that you have a couple more geniuses waiting in the wings?"

Hawk blinked, took a deep breath and said, "Oswald, there is no other substitute. We have studied you in great detail and feel sure that you're the only person who could realistically pull this off."

Carrington turned to examine the photographs on Hawk's wall. The pictures of soldiers in uniform and of the United States flag. He saw one of a much younger Ronald Hawk in army fatigues. Well, whatever Hawk wanted done, he had to assume it was connected to the incredible technology employed in his abduction, and given Hawk's military background, whatever he was planning would probably be similarly spectacular. The key question was whether he could live with the consequences.

In terms of politics, Carrington was a self-proclaimed non-participant. He'd grown up watching his parents give their entire lives up to previous conservative administrations that could dismiss them for the slightest mistake or for the smallest failure in demonstrating the appropriate amount of loyalty. To his eyes, politics was no more than a farcical popularity contest. He never read newspapers either – just some blogs here and there – but he had garnered from his politically-motivated, liberal friends at MIT that Ronald Hawk's character could be boiled down quite simply: to a war-hungry, neo-1717 conservative agitator. Well, as far as Carrington was concerned, war was a symptom of over population and a by-product of thoughtless corporate greed. In a worst-case scenario, his Droniks could be used to commit mass murder, but the way things were going, would that be so bad for humanity and the world in the long term?

"What other conditions are there?" he said, turning back to Hawk. "And who am I working for? The government or you?"

Hawk noticeably relaxed and said, "You'll be an employee of the State, working directly under the President and myself. The only conditions are that you will be restricted to our main facility for as long as the project is underway and that you will conform to the terms of the Official Secrets Act of the United States. However, before we can proceed any further, we're going to have to do a few tests."

"I won't pass a drug test, if that's what you mean."

"Oswald, I don't care how many illegal narcotics you have taken in the past. All we require is that you allow your creative genius full rein. There is no margin for error. Understand?"

Carrington was already thinking furiously over what lay ahead. For the first time in months, he actually felt motivated and challenged by what was in front of him, and the fact that he was working directly for a visionary like Ronald Hawk made him feel much better about what he was doing. He was a big fan of anything that seemed weird or subversive, and this was the very definition of subversion.

"Okay," he said, reaching for his coffee. "Does it come with allowances?"

***

Carrington followed Hawk back out and into another branch of the base. By now he was pretty sure they were underground, although Hawk still hadn't told him where exactly, remarking casually that it was "a matter of global security." They'd passed more soldiers in silver suits and various unmarked doors. But despite the futuristic look, Carrington quietly speculated that this was essentially the bureaucratic arm of whatever top-secret facility they were in. Things would probably get even more interesting – at least, he hoped so.

They arrived at a door, larger than the rest and guarded by two heavily armed soldiers. Unlike the others, these wore tight-fitting helmets with strange-looking weapons.

"Just a quick scan," Hawk said, flashing him a reassuring smile. A beam of blue light instantly flashed over the two of them while the door silently opened to one side.

Carrington followed Hawk in and noticed the two soldiers were right behind him. They were in a small chamber with no other exit – an elevator, perhaps? There were no buttons inside, just the same high gloss stainless steel, but with a dull red light in the middle of the ceiling.

At this point, Carrington felt like he was inside one of those intense hallucinations he used to have while on psychedelic drugs back in college. But the serious expression of his minders indicated that this was no dream.

46

"Where are we going?" he asked hesitantly.

"You could say that we're taking the elevator to the stars," Hawk said.

With a sudden jolt, the elevator descended rapidly. Carrington counted the seconds in his head. A minute passed, then another. When a third minute had gone, he began calculating just how far they were going. If they were moving at the average speed for a fast elevator – say, twenty feet per second, which in this case felt like a very conservative estimate – in five minutes of travel time they would descend 6,000 feet, and who knew how far down they were to begin with. *What kind of stuff is going on in a structure over 6,000 feet underground?*

Among the flurry of thoughts going through his brain, one in particular baffled him: Hawk had said quite cryptically that they were taking an elevator to the stars, yet they were clearly moving downward. However, given his current state of disorientation, Carrington quickly let the thought pass.

The elevator slowly screeched to a halt and they stepped out onto what appeared to be an old railroad station concourse. Assuming they were still in the continental US, Carrington was certain there was no historical basis for a railroad so deep underground.

To his right, there was a twenty-foot-wide black tunnel, stretching into infinity, with white lights evenly spaced out along the passage as far as the eye could see. Overhead, a sturdy-looking double rail track with stabilising bars appeared to hang from the tunnel roof, also stretching ad infinitum.

"What the fuck—"

"You're about to take a ride faster than anything you've ever experienced before, Oswald," Hawk cut in, shaking a smooth pill into the palm of his hand from a curved, silver tin. "This will help oxygenate your blood and make coping with the g-force much easier."

Carrington looked at the pill in his hand. "What is it?"

"An advanced drug designed to help fighter pilots and deep-sea divers – not patented yet, but safe, believe me."

Carrington swallowed it with a sip from the bottle of water passed to him by one of the two unsmiling soldiers. "Aren't you going to take one?" he asked.

"I'm used to it, young man. Now please follow me, as we have to change into these special garments." He motioned towards a number of suits identical to those worn by the soldiers that hung from an incongruous clothes rail on the station platform. "The suits are absolutely necessary, believe me." He began dressing and Carrington followed his lead.

Next came the helmets, which reminded Carrington of something that an astronaut might wear. They had high-visibility visors and integrated earphones. "So we can talk to each other during the journey," Hawk explained.

Once fastened, a woman's voice came over the speaker in his ear. "Mr Carrington. Please sit down and let the automatic body restraint hold you in the seat. The buckle will fasten tightly. This is normal, so please relax and enjoy the journey."

"What are we riding on?" Carrington asked.

An eight-car monorail train silently and smoothly came into view and stopped dead at the center of the platform. He followed

48

Hawk onto the train, and sat beside Hawk at the front, the two soldiers climbing in behind them. His heart was beating fast and he forced himself to slow his breathing.

"Relax, Oswald," Hawk said. "This is the fun bit."

Without warning, their seats suddenly shifted down thirty-five degrees from a normal upright position, until they were looking slightly forward and facing the long stretch of the darkened tunnel. Carrington tried looking directly ahead, but it seemed to strain his neck too much. *That's intentional*, he thought.

The voice began counting down: *"Five... four... three... two... one."*

What followed next was not what Carrington would have termed "fun." As the train accelerated with what felt like the force of a jet aircraft, he was pinned back into his seat. The initial rush of air was almost deafening. His first thought was to try and calculate the wind factor but his mind was literally blown. He felt his suit inflating around his waist and legs, compensating for the g-force by restricting the flow of blood to his legs so he didn't pass out.

Once he'd acclimatised as much as was possible to the speed, Carrington reckoned that he had gone from a standing start to at least 250 MPH in just eight seconds. He estimated that the wall lights of the tunnel were at least 1,000 feet apart, but soon they were flashing past his head in a fraction of a second.

The female voice crackled once again. *"You're doing fine, Mr Carrington."*

Then he heard Hawk's voice through his earpiece. "First time going supersonic, Oswald?"

The bastard sounded like he was enjoying himself.

"Listen to the music, son. We'll be there in no time."

Carrington faintly recognized the song that began playing. He couldn't place the name right away – he just categorised it as one of those songs his dad would always play on Sunday evenings – but by the time he felt the train beginning to decelerate, he'd recalled what it was, and had to appreciate the ironic humor of playing "Going up the Country" by Canned Heat.

The seats tilted back to their normal upright position and the restraint relaxed its grip as they came to a stop at a platform almost identical to the one they had departed from.

Feeling somewhat giddy, Carrington stepped off the monorail. He removed his suit like the others and followed Hawk through a set of large stainless steel double doors.

It was like walking onto a film set.

There was a long, brightly lit corridor and a slew of doors listed with signs like "Design Room," "Earth Orbit Testing," "Flight Dynamics Coding," and "Living Quarters."

Walking to the very end of the corridor, they entered into a wider passageway. The structure itself looked like it had been built in the sixties, but the fittings and equipment were much more sophisticated than anything Carrington had used at MIT or any of the research labs he'd previously been assigned too.

The walk down this main passageway seemed endless. At one point, Carrington glanced to his right and saw a room full of technicians, engineers, and coders, each sitting with multiple screens in front of them, hacking away. The thirty or so young guys looked just like he did, but worse, with bags under their eyes, pale and pasty complexions, and scrawny physiques. He wondered if they'd all ended up here under the same terms that he had.

"Part of your department, Oswald," Hawk said. "But you'll have other people directing them for you."

They continued until they reached a door labelled "Medical Receiving."

"Just one those basic tests I mentioned," Hawk said. He looked happier and more awake than he had back in his office. Carrington just felt sick. "Once you've been approved, we'll get you started."

"I trust they'll take that ride into account," Carrington said, rubbing the back of his neck. "I feel like I've been kicked by a horse."

"You've had a trying day," Hawk said, nodding in sympathy. "The hood they used on you back at your house uses pacifying technology to knock you out. It can make you feel a bit rough, but the symptoms will pass. Just follow the doctor's instructions and you'll be ready for work in no time." He extended his hand and, after a momentary pause, Carrington took it. Hawk shook his hand warmly. "I'll see you once you've been checked out."

With that, he left. Carrington was about to object, but the two soldiers standing either side of him looked at him with blank faces, and a hand on his back maneuvered him gently but firmly through the door and into the room.

Inside, a petite female physician stood up from her desk. She smiled warmly.

"Mr Carrington, a pleasure to meet you."

She dismissed the soldiers, leaving the two of them alone in the small room.

"I had a physical last month, you know," Carrington said, looking around at the various instruments and machines. Most of them he recognized, but there were a few he wasn't sure about. "What exactly is the purpose of this check-up?"

"You look concerned, but really, there is no reason to be. What we're doing here today is just getting a baseline assessment of your abilities and brain function. Our technology is not too different from a CAT scan, though it will be significantly more comfortable."

"My brain functions extremely well, thank you."

"Of course it does," she said. "No doubt you'll set a new standard for our measurements. All you need to do is lie down on this bed here and we will connect some probes to your temples and forehead. It's non-invasive, but the sensitivity of the instruments makes it essential that you keep absolutely still for us to ascertain an accurate reading. I will administer a mild sedative in order that we can begin."

The physician's white coat and her calm and measured tone of voice immediately reminded Carrington of his favorite movie, *A Clockwork Orange*. Suddenly, the plight of its main character, Alex, seemed to be hitting a little too close to home.

"I won't need the sedative," he said, reclining on the bed. "I promise not to move." It was true. He felt exhausted.

"Our policy requires that everyone takes the sedative," the doctor said as she affixed cold plastic discs to his head. "It will be out of your system in a matter of hours."

"I really don't need it."

The doctor sighed as she began connecting the discs to a machine with what looked like thin fiber-optic cables. "One of the things you'll learn here is that it's best to follow policy. We're all here at the request of our government working towards a worthy goal. What's best for you is best for the project."

"I was told I answer only to the President and Mr Hawk," Carrington said, growing irritated. "I don't care about your policies."

The doctor leaned over him, still smiling. "You are quite correct, Mr Carrington. I apologize if I've offended you. However, your employment depends upon the results of this test, so, for now, you are, I'm afraid, completely at my mercy – just a little joke, there."

"I don't really care for your—" Carrington began, but a prick in the back of his neck made him flinch.

"There we go," the doctor said, her face blurring before his eyes. "Get some rest.

This will be over with very soon."

Carrington struggled to sit up, but it felt as if he was falling. The doctor's face was getting further and further away, and a comfortable warmth was spreading through him, slowing everything down until all he could see were flashing lights, blinking in sequence. He closed his eyes.

***

Carrington woke up beneath white sheets in a sparsely furnished, well-lit room. He had no clock and no idea whether it was morning or night, but he did know that he felt more rested and clear-headed than he had in years. Then he remembered the doctor and the sedative, and sat up, his hand straying to the back of his neck.

The door slid open and a man walked in carrying a covered tray. "Good morning, Mr Carrington," he said. "Breakfast for you."

"What time is it?"

"It's 8 AM. You've been asleep for around ten hours. I hope you slept well."

"That'll be due to the drugs I didn't want," Carrington said, irritably. "Where's Hawk? I want a word with him."

"You have a meeting with Mr Hawk in an hour," the man said. "Please eat, and have a shower if you like." He gestured to another door – the bathroom, Carrington assumed. "You'll find clothes in the cabinet – all your size – and a selection of movies, games, and books if you need any distractions." He placed the tray down on the bedside table and removed the lid, revealing orange juice, scrambled eggs, and white toast, exactly how Carrington liked it. Someone had researched him carefully.

"Were the tests good?" he asked, frowning at a sudden pain in his temple.

The man noticed his discomfort. "You'd really have to speak to the doctor about the results of the test, but from what I gather you have an exceptional brain and physically you're fine. They did say that you might experience headaches." He pointed to a curved silver tin, like the one Hawk had in his possession back at the train platform. "Take one of those if you feel uncomfortable."

"What the hell is it?" Carrington asked, growing irritable.

"Just ibuprofen," the man replied as he made to leave. The door closed behind him.

Carrington started on his breakfast, but with each minute the pain in his head grew worse. He shook a pill into his hand and

54

swallowed it with the orange juice. The pain rapidly diminished and he returned to eating with a renewed appetite.

Once he'd finished, he felt even more enlivened and took a shower. Then he chose some clothes from the cabinet. No jeans, unfortunately, but some slacks and a clean white shirt.

By the time someone arrived to take him to Hawk, he wasn't even that angry anymore. He was taken to a brightly lit conference room. Hawk was seated at one end beside an older man in a General's uniform. They were obviously finishing up.

"Oswald," Hawk called, waving with a free hand. He passed a data-pad to the General, who turned without acknowledging Carrington and left through a door at the back of the room.

Hawk stood to shake his hand. "I hope you slept well. The doctor told me you weren't interested in the sedative. Sorry about that, but the scan really is very sensitive and quite expensive to run. We've found that using a sedative just makes it easier all round."

"Well, she could have been a bit clearer," Carrington said, seating himself next to Hawk. "I feel fine, though. Did the tests turn up anything?"

"Only that we picked the right man," Hawk said, sitting back down. "The gentleman who just left – General Morgan – was very impressed. I'll introduce you two later."

Carrington shrugged. "I'm actually more curious about those technicians and coders you have working here. What are they all doing?"

"They're here to assist you, Oswald. They're intelligent men and women, all highly trained to do their jobs. However, they lack the real visionary leadership that we require." Hawk pushed a data-pad, identical to the one he'd given the General, across the table. "This is an abridged version of what your work will entail."

Carrington took the pad and scanned over the document, codenamed "Counterweight Maneuver." The text illustrated how the East had achieved economic dominance over the West, how ecosystems were being lost due to an amoral lust for power, how foreign governments were engaged in economic and cyber-terrorism against the West, and why, now more than ever, it was necessary for the United States to close the gap. Then he got to the part concerning him. It was brilliant, it was ambitious, it was… dark.

He swallowed. "You mentioned HSRCMDs before… this is what you were talking about. You want technology that can seamlessly launch an attack in multiple places throughout the world, without anyone being able to trace the source?"

Hawk nodded. "It's a contingency plan. In a worst-case scenario our technology would have to be deployed, but only if the US was under a direct and serious attack, obviously."

"And you have the kind of computing power and server space here to launch an attack of that scale?"

"We do. And there is far, far more. There isn't a facility on this planet that can match the technological and human capital that we have here."

"I just have one question, then: Where did this place come from? I mean, the US is practically bankrupt. How did you get the resources to build this place?"

"My dear Oswald. Have you ever heard of the Brotherhood of Thelema?"

56

Carrington shook his head. "Sounds like a cult," he said. "Or a religion or something."

"A society, Oswald," Hawk said. "We have pursued a singular goal for over a century, to raise mankind to a status where it commands its own destiny, one in tune with the universe itself. There are people within our government and in the upper echelons of US society who believe in the cause that we are working for here – elite academic minds, financiers, the military. I won't name who these people are, but they all agree on one common goal: a world guided by a dominant United States of America." Hawk lowered his eyes. "It might be better to think of yourself as working directly for an honorable and prestigious club, of which the President is himself a member, and whose ultimate aim is the salvation of humanity and our world."

Carrington looked over the document again. Hawk wanted a fleet of HSRCMDs – that was all he was required to do. He wasn't arming them or picking targets. And it was only a contingency plan. In any case, he kind of agreed with Hawk. America wasn't perfect, but at least there was some accountability. But where was it with China? A one-party system that made its own people mysteriously disappear, and with a bullish market in "medicine" derived from the rarest animals on Earth. Carrington's parents would have baulked at an all-out attack on the East, but wouldn't the end justify the means?

Carrington was pragmatic, and in the modern world it was clear that there would be no easy answers. And the challenge! He couldn't turn it down any more than Einstein could have when he had the chance to fight the Axis powers in WWII, even though he must have known that the nuclear bomb would be the end result.

"I'll be working from here?" he said, putting the pad down.

"Let me show you your office," Hawk said, grinning broadly. He led Carrington to a massive workspace which overlooked the room of coders he had glimpsed the day before.

When he realized that all those people were there to work at his disposal, Carrington felt a rush. He had a computer more powerful than any of the ones at MIT, and the machinery to build drones on a scale he'd only dreamed of. This was a working environment that definitely matched his abilities, and right now he felt a motivation that he hadn't experienced since graduating.

He let out a long, deep breath. "When do I start?"

From: *John Lane*
To: *Landon Marconi*
Date: *2/14/2025*
Re: *Financial Markets and the Rise of the East*

Hey, Landon. Just a quick memo per our conversation at the Pearl last night.

Rising costs have made the Oriental outfits appear to look more and more attractive and I can't see it changing in the foreseeable future. Our investments have grown by ten percent after shifting our economic branch to Hong Kong, and we've also made similar gains by switching our manufacturing to Asia.

To put it simply, these firms don't have the rigid environmental standards, the labor costs, nor the high taxes that the US constantly demands. Now, I know you're concerned about the ethical side, but our competitors aren't going to sit back while we take the high road, and the customers won't pay for it either, so, by all means, give me a better business model and I'll bring it to the board. Otherwise you might want to start looking for a new career.

See you at the golf club Friday?

Chapter 3

The weather in Washington DC was depressingly similar to the overcast drizzle Bradley had left behind in Oakland. He was standing outside Ronald Reagan International Airport in the rain, one week after the strange phone call, a single suitcase at his feet, and one hand raised as he jostled with others for a taxi. He managed to snag a yellow cab, and seconds later he was on 14th Street, heading for Constitution Avenue.

Through the rain-streaked window, Bradley watched the gray buildings pass. So much history, but what of the future? The seat of the US government, now a meeting place for corporate lobbyists and violent drug deals.

He watched the billboards depicting foreign cell phones, foreign cars, and superstores all built on the mountain of foreign aid and homeland debt. When he thought about it, the signs of America's decline were everywhere – it didn't take an article focused upon a port on the West Coast to demonstrate that. The only thing America had left was fast food and rock 'n' roll.

"You said the Kiyoko?" the cab driver asked through the thin vent in the plastic screen.

"That's right," Bradley said. He checked his watch: 18:30. "How far is it?"

"Ten minutes, tops. This your first time in DC?"

"Yeah."

"Better Sushi in the Sakura, you want my opinion. They got steak, too."

Bradley grunted a reply, and the rest of the journey passed in silence.

Ten minutes later, they were there. Bradley got out, took his suitcase from the trunk, and then paid the driver.

He turned to observe the Kiyoko. It looked clean, with colorful neon lights and a dragon fountain in the window. He saw a sign for Japanese beer. A drink wouldn't hurt, he thought, walking up to the entrance.

He stopped. A sound like breaking glass and rolling bottles had abruptly come from the alleyway between the Kiyoko and the Italian restaurant on the other side. Bradley glanced down it but, seeing nothing, shrugged and entered the restaurant.

Inside, Kiyoko was tastefully decorated in brass and oak panelling. And the joint was packed to the rafters.

He threaded his way past the throng of people waiting for tables and got to the bar. After five minutes he'd managed to procure a cold beer, and then scanned around for the mysterious woman that he was supposed to meet. Everywhere he looked there were businessmen laughing and talking, families eating, couples conversing in intimate booths. He spotted a small table, recently vacated, and sat down, pushing aside the plates and empty bottles.

A slim waitress with blond hair came over and glared at him as she removed the dirty dishes. Bradley smiled apologetically. He knew there was a wait, but he had more pressing issues. Hopefully they wouldn't ask him to move.

"Excuse me," a voice said. He looked up, but it was just some young girl passing his table, boyfriend in tow.

He turned back to watch the baseball on the television behind the bar. The Yankees and the Red Sox were playing. America's favorite sport. He'd always found it funny that it was called the World Series when, apart from the US, Japan, Mexico, and a couple of insignificant Pacific islands, nobody in the world gave a damn about it.

"Mr Wilcox."

He jerked his head around and saw an Asian woman in a long, light-blue coat and woollen hat, an expensive bag at her side. She took off the hat and sat down beside him, her eyes on the TV. "Such a distraction, television."

She must have been about fifty, very attractive, with dark hair and pale skin.

"You, uh, called me last week?" he asked, taking a slug of beer.

"Could I start you off with a beverage?" The waitress was back, this time a practiced smile on her face.

"Sparkling water, please," the lady said.

"I'll take another beer," Bradley said. He felt strange meeting like this – like he was a spy in an espionage movie. The waitress didn't even glance at him, but went off in the direction of the bar. "Crazy" by Gnarls Barkley erupted from the jukebox nearby. Bradley was glad of the tuneful distraction – it made him feel less conspicuous.

"Thank you for coming and for being discreet about our meeting," the lady said, placing her bag on the table.

"I started to doubt the whole thing even happened, to be honest, but I gather I've annoyed someone pretty high up," Bradley said. "Though I'm not entirely sure what I've done."

"Judging from what I've seen on your computer, I think you know exactly who it is you've annoyed," she said, "and why your career now lies in tatters. As for why, let's just say that your article touched a nerve in some very high places. This does, however, put you in a particularly useful position."

"Useful to you, you mean."

"One sparkling water, one beer," the waitress said, placing the drinks down.

Bradley handed her a ten and told her to keep the change. "Mind if I ask who I'm talking to?" he asked, once the waitress had left.

"You don't need to know who I am," the lady replied, sipping on her water. "Let's just say I'm close to our, um, mutual opponent. There are some changes coming in this administration, changes that he's behind, changes that will have terrible implications for America and the entire world."

"Could you give me some specifics?" Bradley asked. "And what has it got to do with my article?"

"You're a journalist, Mr Wilcox," she said. "A discredited journalist, but, nevertheless, I think you also possess the relevant investigative skills required to uncover what he's up to." She looked at her watch, then picked up her bag, leaving the water practically untouched. Bradley noticed a red and black USB drive on the table. "Follow the breadcrumbs," she said, "and good luck." She turned and left for the front door.

Bradley wanted to jump up and follow her, but he knew that this would draw attention, so he finished his beer as slowly as he could, stood up and pulled his coat back on, grabbing the drive from the table and slipping it quickly into his pocket. He picked up his suitcase and made his way to the front door.

Outside, it was getting dark, but the rain had stopped. He looked either way up the busy street, straining his eyes to spot her light blue coat. He heard a noise coming from the alley next to the bar – similar to that he had previously heard – and once again looked down it. Garbage cans were piled up beside the wall, and a single flickering lamp eerily lit the scene.

"Probably just a cat," he muttered under his breath. His suitcase was getting heavy and he decided it was time to find a motel.

He was looking for a taxi when he saw the black car with government plates pull up by the Kiyoko. His first thought was that it might be connected to the woman he'd just spoken with – and if she was indeed in the government, he'd soon source who she was once online – but when a tall man in a long black trench coat got out, eyes frantically scanning the crowd from behind dark glasses, Bradley immediately realized it could be something more sinister.

He ducked down the alleyway, pulling his coat tightly against the growing chill while at the same time dragging his suitcase along on wheels that had barely worked on smooth tiles at the airport, let alone cracked concrete. He'd follow the alleyway onto another street and get a taxi from there. Then try to find a hotel room, take a shower, and see exactly what was on this USB drive.

The sound of cars seemed distant despite the street being close by. He followed the alley, but the buildings on either side seemed to press down on him as it grew more enclosed. The rain started again, beating staccato against the trash cans, and Bradley began to wonder whether he'd made the right decision. The man in the car could have simply been going to get sushi. Or maybe he'd been there to pick up the woman in the blue coat after all.

An old apartment block loomed over Bradley to the left, while to his right a rusty corrugated iron fence was flapping in the wind. Ahead of him, a brick wall, coated in graffiti and stinking of urine, revealed a dead end.

A distorted groan sounded, long and low.

Startled, Bradley turned around, the suitcase still in his hand. *Was that a dog?*

It sounded again, the same as before, but rapidly changed into a high electronic shriek that cut through his skull like fingernails on a chalkboard.

Dropping his suitcase, Bradley covered his ears and started running back down along the alley. He very nearly ran headfirst into a jagged section of the iron fence as it was bent violently inward by some invisible force. He fell, panic rising in his chest, and pulled himself backwards along the ground as the fence was ripped from its foundations and sent spinning through the air high over his head.

He felt the hard wall against his back and stopped, eyes wide as he stared at the warped remains of the fence. He saw no movement in the darkness, and urgently strained his ears to listen beyond the beat of his heart and the patter of raindrops on metal.

Nothing.

He got to his feet, wiping his hands on his front. The fencing was warped and torn to the ground. Was this some fucking punk messing with him?

He'd almost convinced himself that some kids were playing a prank on him when the twin beams of white light blazed down from atop the remainder of the fence. Bradley watched it slowly buckle as a shape, barely distinguishable in the darkness, appeared to drop almost in slow motion onto the concrete.

He tried to focus on it, but the light was in his eyes and a croaking, snapping sound was in his ears.

Bradley was shouting for help, completely unaware of what he was saying and powerless against the instinctive need to escape. He started beating against a door in the apartment block just behind him. He tried the next and the next, all the while watching the light as it grew closer and the croaking grew louder.

The fourth door was unlocked and Bradley quickly ducked into the building, slamming the door frantically behind him and making for the stairs. He was running harder than he had done in years. His heart was pounding, his breathing coming in short gasps.

He was banging on doors as he passed, not really expecting any of them to open, until he reached the roof.

A padlocked door barred his way, but Bradley didn't stop, hurling all his weight against it. The door suddenly collapsed and he fell head first directly onto the uncompromising surface. He felt gravel tear through his palms, but instantly jumped up, still running aimlessly until he realized there was nowhere else to go.

He was eight floors up. He could see the roof of the Kiyoko in the distance, beyond the lanes jammed full of cars moving slowly on the wet street below.

The structure started shaking beneath his feet; a low vibration began moving up his body until his teeth were buzzing in his mouth. There was an itching sensation in his head, and he wanted to shove his fingers into his ears to make it stop.

Suddenly, all was still.

He raised his eyes to the overcast sky and saw the distortion overhead, elliptical in shape, blurring between darkness and transparency, sheltering him from the rain. He was fixed to the spot, transfixed by the sight above, as a circle of lights sparked into being, growing wider, and pulsing faster and faster until a dozen crimson orbs were spinning brightly overhead.

Bradley felt light, like he was dreaming. But a part of him knew he had to move, that he had to run. He saw the fire escape and hurled himself over the roof just as the lights coalesced into a ring of red energy arcing down onto the roof.

A violent surge of heat suddenly hit him in the back, and for a moment in time he was suspended over thin air, then he hit the metal fire-escape running. He stumbled down the angular, uneven steps, struck the rail and felt himself slipping over the side, stopping himself with a reflexive grab. He pulled himself back onto his feet and saw the flames above, while at the same instant, thick white smoke started billowing into the night sky.

Bradley waited for his rational brain to come back online, and got up. The building was on fire. But at least he had found a means of escape.

He looked at his hands – they were raw and embedded with fragments of gravel and glass. The back of his neck felt tight and sore, like he'd gotten too much sun.

Then he remembered the USB drive. He shoved a hand into his pocket and breathed a sigh of relief when he felt its smooth surface. He descended the fire escape as sirens howled in the distance, jumping the final few steps to the street below.

Bradley dropped down back in the alleyway just as the residents of the adjoining apartment building began piling out through the back door. He wasn't sure what to do. Would they connect him to what happened?

They'd never believe that some invisible UFO had hit the building, especially coming from him, a discredited journalist who'd just had a couple of beers.

Then again, maybe the facts would corroborate his story. Maybe somebody else had seen something.

He took a step toward the group, who were all staring up at the flames, oblivious to his presence.

Bradley felt something grab the back of his coat and was pulled back into the alley. His face was rammed into the brick, once, twice. Something spun him around, shoved him against the wall and lifted him off the ground by his shoulders.

A glistening transparency shimmered behind the clawed hand that now clenched at his throat. His eyes were wide as he fought for breath but the grip was strong and everything was growing dim.

He tried to talk, to ask: *Why? Why me? What have I done?*

For a brief second, he smelled a rancid stench and saw two large, pulsating, compound eyes and a distended jaw filled with thin, needle-like teeth.

A croaking noise that sounded suspiciously like laughter was the last sound he heard before he lost consciousness.

***

Hawk was watching Carrington on the monitor in his private room when the call came through. He opened it on the screen and saw Colonel Forge's chiselled jaw and iron-gray eyes.

"Colonel," Hawk said. "I trust our mutual friend didn't do anything stupid?"

"She made contact with the journalist, sir."

"And?"

"We let her go, as you requested. And the journalist won't be a problem either."

"Good." Wilcox, like Sheen, was a mere irritant, but an irritant could develop into a rash if it wasn't checked. "Then I think we can focus on the Maneuver. Thank you, Colonel."

Forge vanished and Carrington was back on the screen. He was leaning over the shoulder of one of the coders, pointing out something on a data-pad.

Hawk couldn't deny he was impressed with Carrington. On his first day alone, he'd written more lines of code, solved more engineering problems, and produced more perfectly sequenced schematics than Hawk's entire team of scientists had managed during their first week. And what with the mind boosters he'd been given, his intellect would only increase.

The big question was whether he'd toe the line the further down the rabbit hole he went. Could Hawk trust him with the true scale of the technology they had at their disposal? Would Carrington's vision match Hawk's?

He poured himself a scotch and sipped it as he watched Carrington going about his business. He'd deal with those problems if and when they arose, but for now, the Counterweight Maneuver was on point and on schedule.

Hawk smiled to himself. Father would have been very proud indeed.

Chapter 4

Bradley heard a voice speaking and became aware of someone shaking him. He felt an ache at the back of his head, opened his eyes and saw her leaning over him – blond hair, full lips, blue eyes.

He realized it was the waitress from the bar about the same time as his hearing came back, and then the pain in his head hit him with the force of an ice pick.

"Oh God!" he hissed, struggling to sit up.

"Are you okay?" she said, helping him to a seating position. "I'll get a paramedic!"

"Wait," he said, gripping her wrist tightly.

Bradley was still in the alley on the ground, with people moving around him – residents milling about, firemen appraising the damage, cops taking statements – but they weren't interested in him. He looked up and saw the flames burning overhead. The drizzle that had soaked him appeared to also affect their movements.

"Did you see it?" he said, looking around wildly. "The… thing that did this? It had teeth, and… and big eyes!"

Her frown deepened, and she politely disengaged his hand from her wrist. "You could be concussed. Come on. There's an ambulance just over there."

"No! No, damn it!" he snapped, hauling himself to his feet. He glanced over the crowd, looking for compound eyes.

It could still be here, watching me. Then he remembered the man in the black suit standing outside the Kiyoko.

"I have to go," he said. "Shit, I've lost my suitcase."

"You don't look okay to me," the waitress said, shaking her head. "Maybe some debris hit you. There was an explosion—"

"I was attacked!" Bradley said, pointing up at the still burning building. "How do you think that happened?"

"Gas, I suspect," she said. "Listen you need to get looked at."

Bradley sighed. "I'm okay – just dazed. I have glass in my hands, some bruises and burns, that's all." He looked up at the night sky, at the smoke, and the stars barely visible through the glare of the city. "Someone's after me."

"Right," she said. "The thing with teeth."

Bradley shoved his hand into his pocket and took out the USB drive with a sigh of relief.

"Is that important?" the waitress asked, with a puzzled look.

"What? Oh. No, not really." He looked back past the crowd, saw the bent piece of fence lying on the ground, and shuddered. "Where's the nearest internet café? I have to... e-mail someone."

"You don't have a phone?"

"I think it's damaged," Bradley said, wincing at the pain in his hand as he carefully replaced the USB stick.

The waitress looked at him strangely, her red lips pursed. She gestured at the bag on her shoulder. "I have my laptop with me, if there's something you need to check."

Bradley frowned. Was she in on this somehow? Was she with the man in the long coat? "I need a... secure line, you know? I'll, uh... thanks for the help."

He started walking back towards the street. He heard her heels on the sidewalk behind him and kept his eyes focused ahead.

"You know, you stole one of my tables from me," the waitress said, catching up with him. "Just sat down, didn't care about anything."

"Sorry about that," he said. "I was meeting someone."

"Yeah, I saw. Christine Sheen doesn't usually turn up without prior notice."

He looked at her. "Is that who she was?"

"So you didn't even know who you were meeting?"

"Well, no, but—"

"This is getting better by the minute," the waitress said, smiling. "When you helped yourself to my table I thought you were just another ignorant jerk, but you're more than that, aren't you?"

"I'm a journalist."

"So I wasn't far off," she smiled. "My name's Shana. Shana Grey."

"Bradley Wilcox," he said. "You may have seen my latest report on TV?"

"No, sorry," she said, keeping step with him. "Listen, you owe me more than the small tip you left me. There's a bar near here, nice and private. I'll help to get the glass out of your hands and clean you up. You can buy me a drink and maybe, just maybe, I'll let you use my laptop."

Bradley didn't think she was going to leave him without a fight, but if he was honest with himself, she wasn't unattractive. She was very forward and obviously not afraid to speak her mind, but then he'd always gone for women with fire, occasionally to his detriment.

"How far is it?" he sighed.

"Two blocks," she said, her smile growing even wider. "I like vodka, but I gotta tell you I'm not a cheap date."

He touched a hand to the back of his head and winced. Maybe a drink would help.

She took him to the bar – a small hole in the wall set in the basement of an old building below a real estate shop. "It's called the Mouse Trap, get it?" Shana said, talking over the music playing on the jukebox as she led him to a table in the corner. "Because it's an internet bar."

"Yeah, I get it," Bradley said, sitting down and looking around. They were the only ones there. "Is it getting ready to close?" he asked.

"It will in a few, but I know the owner, so don't worry about the time." She pulled the light over from a table next to theirs and put her bag on the table. "I have tweezers and a needle. Let's see those hands."

Bradley held his palms out. "Why are you so interested in me?"

"Hmm, it's not every day I meet a guy who claims to have had a close encounter with bug-eyed monsters. Let's just say you kinda fascinate me." She didn't meet his gaze, keeping her eyes focused on his hands. "You meet with Christine Sheen, and then you're involved somehow with that crazy stuff by the apartment." She leaned in with the tweezers, extracting a sliver of glass. Bradley's hands were so sore he barely felt it. "And you did get very excited about that drive in your pocket."

Bradley almost snatched his hands back. "You work for someone, don't you?" he hissed.

"Yes," she said, looking at him like he was a complete idiot. "The Kiyoko's owned by a Japanese firm, so I guess I work for them. When I'm not studying at Howard, that is."

Bradley looked at her for a moment, then relaxed. "Sorry. It's been a rough day."

A woman with tattoos and a long, black ponytail came over. "Hey, Shana. What you need?"

"The gent's buying," Shana said. "Bradley, Su. Su, Bradley."

"Hi," Bradley said with a nod. "I'm not fussed what we drink. Vodka, I guess."

"Better make it a bottle, Su. You okay to stay a little longer?"

Su gave Shana the thumbs-up and left for the bar.

"She doesn't sleep much," Shana said. "Ooh, I'm gonna use the needle for this one."

Su came back with a frosty bottle of Vin Gogh and two shot glasses.

"You don't need a chaser, do you?" Shana asked.

Bradley cursed. "You don't have to stab me!"

"There are some small bits left. I'll have to dig a little deeper. You want a coke or something to chase this vodka with?"

"Maybe a beer," he said, wincing at the burning in his palms. He noticed Su was looking at him with a bored expression, and added, "Whatever you have is fine."

"So what's on the drive?" Shana said.

"Nothing important. Look, I appreciate your help, but I'd like some privacy when I check it."

"Oh, of course," Shana said, smiling. She left his hands for a moment and poured them both a shot. She passed him a glass. "To mystery."

"There's too much of that already," Bradley said, taking his glass. "Let's drink to transparency." They both drank. The vodka was clean and cold.

"Transparency's dull," Shana said, filling the glasses again. "I mean, you're a journalist. You wouldn't have a job if there weren't things hidden away from everyone. Secrets are much more fun."

Bradley agreed with her on that. They downed their drinks, and he gave his hands back to her. This time, the needle didn't hurt at all.

"What do you study?"

"Computer science, mathematics, algorithm analysis, matrix coding, etcetera."

"Your face doesn't fit that stereotype."

"Was that a compliment or an insult? Remember, I have the needle."

"In that case, neither," Bradley said, smiling. The vodka was helping, and he had to admit he liked the girl. He realized he was looking directly into her eyes, and turned to examine a model galleon ship fixed on the shelf next to their table. "Looks like it was hand carved?"

"The boat?" she said, dropping his hands to the table and picking up the bottle of Vin Gogh. "I mean, I wouldn't call myself an expert on the subject, but I think you could be right." She splashed vodka over his hands and grinned, obviously taking some delight in his pain. "Just some disinfectant."

"Your face would make a pleasing ship's figurehead," he said, wincing.

"Heh, I'm not sure if you're complimenting me or not."

"It's a compliment. Your face could launch a thousand ships."

"Well, I've never been complimented like that before," she said, laughing and pouring another two shots. "But thank you, I guess."

Su brought over two beers, and with another shot in front of him, Bradley realized this could turn into a tricky night. He took a slug of beer, watching as Shana pulled a smooth silver laptop from her bag.

"Do you want to check that drive before we do another shot? You're looking a little glassy-eyed there."

"I'm fine," Bradley objected. "Just tired, that's all. I always am after a flight. Can't stand airports."

"Well, let's check out this USB drive of yours before the vodka kicks in."

"It's probably just some files on shipping manifestos, or—"

"Come on. Let's plug it in."

"It's not anything interesting."

"If it's boring crap, why don't you want me to see it?" She leaned across the table, her eyes narrowed. "You don't know what's on it, do you? Just like you didn't know who you were meeting."

Bradley wanted to argue further, but he knew she wouldn't buy it. He'd stumbled onto something massive, something he probably shouldn't be involving others in, but Shana seemed capable and her laptop was open, right in front of him.

"Okay," he said, grabbing the drive from his pocket and wincing as his palm caught against the material of his coat. Shana took it and slid it into the USB port. Bradley leaned over and turned the screen towards him. "But I'm opening it."

She pouted but didn't argue.

Bradley looked over the screen and saw the drive pop up in the corner. He traced the cursor over the icon and double-clicked, feeling excited despite all that had happened. At least now he may get some answers.

The screen went white and a black window appeared at its center. Shana leaned closer over the table.

"This isn't a file. It's opened a connection to another server. Shit, it's a virus!"

Bradley waved a hand in an attempt to hush her up.

A complex geometric pattern appeared in the window, turning, spreading, and growing. It stopped, and then the shapes were moving and spinning as a female voice said, *"Hello, Mr Wilcox. How are you? I can see you've picked up a friend."*

"Who's this?" he said, looking over to the bar, where Su was bobbing her head to the music and staring mindlessly at her phone. "Is this Christine Sheen?"

A moment's silence, then, *"You work quickly, even for a journalist."*

Bradley shrugged and glanced at Shana, who was smirking at him. He wouldn't have had a clue about Sheen if it hadn't been for her. "So what's this about?" he said, looking back at the screen.

"Whoever's next to you had better be aware of the risk she'll be putting herself in."

"Risk?" Bradley snapped. "I was attacked just after our meeting. Why wasn't I informed of the risk?"

Another moment's silence.

"I'm sorry, Mr Wilcox. I had no idea they'd be onto us so soon. This makes what I'm about to say even more urgent. Something very strange is happening at the highest level and it needs to be exposed. Your female friend is involved now, whether she wants to be or not."

"As long as I don't miss my mid-terms, I'm fine," she said.

Bradley cursed under his breath.

"This connection is secure," Sheen said, *"but I cannot always be reached. There is a mailbox where you can leave and also receive messages from me. I advise that you check as often as you can, and for God's sake do not lose this drive."*

"What the hell do you expect me to do?" Bradley said, trying to suppress his frustration. "I thought you were going to give me answers, not enlist me in some damn political game."

"Look through the files on this drive. You'll find one with an address. The 88 Motel. Get there and you'll find what you need."

"And then?" Bradley's voice was raised; Shana put a hand on his arm. He looked up and noticed Su watching from the bar. "What am I supposed to do then?" he asked, in a hushed tone.

"I need evidence, Mr Wilcox. I can set you on the right path, but you will have to go and find it."

"I'm a journalist. You know that, right? I'm not a spy!"

"This is big, Mr Wilcox, very big" Sheen said. *"You'll be performing a massive service to your country and to the entire world. It could expose those who ruined you. It could clear your name. This is the most momentous story anyone will ever have. Ever."*

Bradley sighed. "Look, at least tell me who I'm up against. Is it this Hawk guy?"

"He is not the man you think he is," Sheen said. *"Stay well below the radar, and do not inform the authorities. They've come for you once already."*

The line flashed white and the call ended. Bradley stared at the screen. He was supposed to go somewhere on this and risk everything he had, simply based upon a vague warning of some catastrophe in the making.

Shana poured two more shots, her eyes staring into the distance. "I wasn't expecting anything this crazy," she said.

Bradley grabbed his coat and stood. "Yeah, thanks for the help, but this isn't something you should get involved with."

"What?" Shana grabbed the coat out of his hands and threw it back onto the seat. "I heard everything. I'm already involved. Besides, I'd give anything to miss those damn mid-terms." She sat back down and started typing.

"What are you doing?" he said, still standing, his hands clenched into fists.

"Looking for the motel," she replied. "Don't you want to find out what Sheen means? This is a chance to expose those who ruined you – not that I know what happened, but you can fill me in on that, right? Hey, Su, can we get the tab, please?"

"Thanks for your help," Bradley said, taking his coat back again. "I'll pay the tab, but then I'm outta here."

"Wilcox, can you afford *not* to have me along?" she said, standing and staring back at him.

"What do you mean?"

"One, I know too much, and two, this drive contains some of the craziest stuff that I've ever seen. Top-of-the-line software. Do you know anything about military-grade encryption?"

"Well—"

"Sheen's given you the key to a billion safes and God knows what else. You understand how to use that kind of technology, right?"

"No, but—"

In the pause, Bradley noticed that "I Want You" by Cee Lo Green was playing on the jukebox.

"Pay Su and try to leave a better tip than you did me," Shana said, staring at him. "Maybe we can get a cab to this 88 Motel?"

She went back to typing. Bradley walked towards the bar and paid, still slightly shaken. Well, if he was going to have company, at least it would be attractive.

***

Oswald Carrington finished the last line of code and pushed the tablet away, rubbing his eyes. The clock said 01:00, which meant he'd been working on the new algorithms for five hours, but rather than feeling tired, he was still coming up with new ideas, still aching to solve problems, and that was despite all that he'd achieved over the last few days.

He'd started to upgrade Hawk's Droniks, then soon discovered a problem with the nuclear fusion parameters and immediately improved their running efficiency by making a revisionary calculation. There was also the matter of coordinating the Orbital

Insertion Vessels. He'd overhauled the original mathematical designs with an improved and enhanced network, and it had already showed much promise.

Carrington got up and walked over to the window overlooking his staff. They were all bent over their screens, working hard with only three breaks a day and a regulated sleep schedule.

He'd spoken with a few of them and had been quite impressed by the depth of their knowledge, but none of them seemed very interested in small talk, wanting only to concentrate on the mission at hand. Their relationship to each other was almost robotic in nature, only caring about the one thing that they had in common, which was: think work, and only work.

He realized he felt hungry and left his office, heading down the corridor to the dining area. A marine in a silver suit was guarding the door, but Carrington was already so used to them he barely noticed its presence.

A couple of people were in the room sitting down, but Carrington had no interest in talking. He walked to the far end where a food dispensing machine stood. He tapped in his order – a grilled cheese with salad and a Coke.

The large widescreen television in the corner was showing a wildlife documentary, but when Carrington tried to watch, imaginary lines of code scrolled before his eyes. Damn, his brain just wouldn't switch off.

The phone buzzed in his pocket and he took it out. "Mr Hawk," he said as the machine turned his sandwich over.

"Oswald. I thought you'd still be up. How's the project going?"

"Fine, just fine. You, um, need something?"

"Do you have a TV near you? Turn to channel 236. I thought you might like to see how effective the new cloaking tech is."

Carrington took his Coke from the machine and walked over to the TV. He picked up the remote lying on the table beneath it and changed the channel.

The news instantly flashed up. Washington DC was glowing in the night. The camera angle came from a helicopter: it was passing over an apartment block, the roof of which appeared to smoulder in the light drizzle.

"What am I looking at?" he asked.

"They're looping footage from a news chopper. Check the feed at 10:38:20 and tell me what you notice."

Carrington murmured a response and turned up the volume on the remote.

"The blast occurred just after 10.30 PM. Reports indicate several injuries to those on the upper floors, but fortunately no one is thought to have been killed. Police are now looking for the man seen in this image."

Carrington saw the figure of a man running across the roof, then a flash of white light, and flames were rising into the night.

"No suspect has yet been found, though experts are in the process of searching the surrounding buildings."

"We caused that explosion?" Carrington asked.

"An OIV was situated directly above that building," Hawk said, "and nobody even suspected it. With your improvements, our abilities will be greatly enhanced. You're part of an elite team, Mr Carrington. Keep up the good work."

Hawk hung up. Carrington took his food to a table and sat down, taking a big bite of his grilled cheese.

So Hawk was impressed? Well, Oswald Carrington hadn't even begun yet.

Wèilái Guòqù Unveils New Robotics Contracts
by Li Jinhai

Robotics is entering a new and exciting phase in the development of human society, and Wèilái Guòqù is poised at the forefront.

Familiar to most as a producer of entertainment and sanitation automata, Wèilái Guòqù is increasingly active in the defense market, producing components for the Chinese military and with contracts stretching to Europe and Africa.

Despite recent gains, the United States government has made repeated legal suits towards Wèilái Guòqù and its parent company, Zhěngtǐ Incorporated, filing for copyright infringement, and multiple claims of corporate espionage have also been levelled, with some claiming the company is nothing more than a front for the Chinese Government. Zhěngtǐ Inc. CEO, Teng Hung, has been quick to dismiss these claims.

Chapter 5

Hawk waited in the parlour, a cup of black tea and a segment of lemon balanced on the saucer in the palm of his hand. A man in a black suit and wearing an earpiece stood at the door to the President's rooms, his hands folded, a blank expression on his face.

Right now, President Moore would be speaking with Secretary of Energy, Mark Leary, and that damn mouthpiece for the oil industry, Secretary of Commerce, Terrance Sullivan. Hawk knew they'd be trying to undermine his words, trying to change the President's course. They represented corporate interests – money and nothing more. What they didn't realize was that they would soon be paying a heavy price for their greed and lack of thought.

Hawk took the lemon and squeezed it into the tea, placing the rind back on the saucer. He blew gently over the cup, savoring the delicate scent of Darjeeling in his nostrils.

He'd acquired a taste for it when studying in England during his university years. Back then, he'd been untutored, unenlightened, and short-sighted, but the following decade had brought considerable knowledge. By the time he'd met Robert Moore in Saigon, he'd already realized just how foolish men were, how easily they could be led and manipulated. Now, fifty years later, nothing had changed but the stakes: Hawk was still here, his dream very much alive, and ready to bend humanity's path to the correct course.

He lifted the tea to his lips and drank it in one, placing the empty cup on the table beside him. The man in the suit placed a finger to his ear and stepped aside as the door opened. Hawk stood, straightening his cuffs, and walked past him without a glance.

He followed the short corridor and saw Leary and Sullivan coming the other way, each carrying a briefcase. Sullivan looked straight ahead, his face white behind his short beard, while Leary smiled the practiced smile of a pathological liar.

Hawk kept his face neutral, his breathing calm, but his eyes were locked on Leary's, tracing the whites of his eyes. Leary's gaze was cold, dead. There were too many like him these days – corporate slaves to money and power, with no essence of their own. Hawk passed them without a word.

The door to President Moore's personal chambers was guarded by two men immaculately dressed in jet black suits and matching ties. One man opened the door for Hawk, while the other simply stared like a robot.

Hawk entered and saw Moore sat on his settee, a thick file in his hand. His leg was jiggling rhythmically, but he stood up when he saw Hawk.

"Ronald. How are you?"

"I'm feeling well thank you, Robert."

Moore went to his desk and placed the file in the drawer, then walked over to the liquor cabinet. "Whiskey?"

"That will be fine."

"It's been a long day. I hope whatever you want to discuss won't take very long."

"I hope so, too, Robert. As the Chinese would say, we live in interesting times, and that leaves little room for talk."

"I agree." Moore passed him a glass. "Sometimes I wish things were as simple as they were during the Cold War. Nam was hell, but at least we knew who the enemy was back then. These days it's terrorism, cyberspace, and the economy. Who knows where to look?" He laughed nervously as he sipped his drink.

"Greed and envy have always been the problem, Robert," Hawk said, taking a small sip. "Shameless greed has now overtaken the planet, corrupting the very fabric of our nation. Our great ideological supremacy has been downgraded and corroded, tainted by the very cup that it has drunk from."

"Do you really think that?" Moore said. "Your perception of the world is so very different to the views of other people."

"Other people are in denial, Robert. I can see things that you tend to overlook… it's easier for me to see this when one is spared the big chair," Hawk said, smiling.

Moore grunted in acknowledgment and sat back down on the sofa. Hawk loosened his collar and joined him.

"I take it certain individuals are suggesting we alter course."

Moore let out a long sigh. "What we're doing—" He paused to drink, then continued. "What we're doing could be construed as criminal, Ronald."

"We've discussed the risk."

"Yes, but I don't know if you've fully considered the price of this endeavor. So many lives could be lost." He finished his drink and looked at the empty glass. "And if we're found out, I'll go down in history as being the biggest genocidal maniac of all time – far worse than Adolf Hitler."

Hawk placed his drink down and took the President's empty glass, getting up to refill it. "We were in dire straits back in Nam, remember that?" He took the decanter and poured a generous amount into the empty glass. "We'd lost half our men and were carrying three with us, all seriously injured. I told you we had to push on."

"Yes," Moore agreed. "You were right, way back then."

"If we hadn't continued, the advance would have failed." He passed the whiskey back to Moore.

"I lost most of the platoon, Ronald."

"And you received the medal of honor for it." Hawk sat back down and retrieved his drink, downing it in one. "People in our position sometimes have to make the big calls, Robert. Lesser men have no business making big decisions."

Moore looked agitated. "But Vietnam was a fiasco. Something America will have to bear for the rest of its days."

"And yet who knows what Asia would look like today if we hadn't taken up the torch that had been left by the French." Hawk leaned closer to Moore. "The Counterweight Maneuver is a tool to thwart a perceived enemy, but do not think for one minute that a real enemy doesn't exist. The constitution of our country was allowed to borrow money, and this borrowed debt has now reached close on sixty trillion dollars, with most of it owed to China and the Far East. Given that our biggest competitors are now our creditors, how exactly do you propose that we are ever going to pay for what we owe and continue to set the main agenda for this planet?"

President Moore looked at him silently, apparently thinking his question rhetorical.

"We can't," Hawk continued. "We've fucked ourselves, Robert, and we have no chance of ever paying it off. We have to start afresh, like we did after World War II, and this is the only way out."

He carefully gauged the President's expression, and pressed on.

92

"Don't you see, Robert? The Maneuver is as it sounds: the counterweight, designed to tip the scales back in our favor. We will be saving millions of lives, saving our homeland, and saving the world. You will stand in the history books as the man who changed the entire course of history and, ultimately, won. You understand that, Robert? You are the man that will alter the entire course of mankind's destiny on this planet."

Moore was frowning, but Hawk knew he'd hit the mark. The President placed his hand on Hawk's shoulder.

"You sure you know what you're doing, Ronald?"

"Mr President," Hawk said, looking him in the eye. "I know exactly what each side is doing."

The conversation turned to baseball and the next meeting of the G8, but Hawk knew he'd achieved what he'd come for. All that remained was to give the final orders and make sure the rest of the Cabinet knew how serious the situation had become. Sullivan and Leary could be silenced, and, once the situation had developed, Hawk would take further measures.

Hawk wished the President goodnight and left, walking back along the corridors and out to his car. He waited as the driver opened the back door, and settled into the seat, taking out his phone.

"Barb. Put me through to the secure connection." He waited for the tone. "General. It's time. Ensure this goes off without a hitch."

He tucked the phone back in his pocket and watched the lights of DC as he left the White House grounds. Tomorrow, the world would wake up being a very different place.

***

The taxi stopped on Glebe – a dimly lit street off the freeway – and Bradley paid the driver. The 88 Motel was an old building with a neon vacancy light flickering in the window.

Outside the office door, a battered soda machine stood beside an ice dispenser coated in grime, and a man wearing a torn plaid shirt was leaning against it, smoking a cigarette.

"Lovely place," Shana said. "But I'm not sure about coming in with you."

"I did warn you," Bradley said, getting out of the cab. He gave the driver fifty dollars.

"Don't leave, okay? We'll be right back."

The driver took the bill and nodded.

Bradley looked at Shana as they made for the motel. "We should keep moving, stay one step ahead of anyone following us."

"Well, you're not paranoid when they're really after you," Shana said.

They reached the office. The man hastily put out his cigarette and opened the door. He smiled a gap-toothed smile. "You guys looking for a room?"

"Unless you're selling real estate in Hawaii," Shana said, walking past him into the office.

"Yes, a room," Bradley said, following her in. The office smelled of smoke and mold. "There should be one ready for us."

"Oh, yeah," the man said, walking behind the desk. "Paid over the phone. I'll need ID, though."

Bradley slid his driver's license across the counter and waited while the guy punched keys on an ancient keyboard.

"Cool. Room 7. You and the lady have 'til 10 AM," the man said, passing him the key with a wink.

Bradley forced a smile in return as he took the key.

They left the office and walked up the lot to Room 7. Bradley unlocked the door and pushed it open. The room was clean but for a musty smell, with an elderly-looking AC unit rattling below the smeared glass window.

"How nice," Shana said, looking around. "What are we looking for, then?"

On the bed was a cardboard box, tightly fastened with tape. Bradley immediately tore it open and looked inside.

"A briefcase," he said. It was metal, heavy, and tightly fastened, but there wasn't a lock or any clasps to open it.

"What's in it?"

"I don't know. It doesn't open."

"Here, let me see," she said. Bradley passed the case to her and Shana looked it over. "Can I see that USB drive?"

"What good will that do?" he asked, taking it out.

Shana grabbed it from his hand and turned the case over. "Sheen wouldn't have given you a case that didn't open. The drive must have something to do with it."

He watched as she examined each surface, and jumped when a slot in the side popped open.

"See?" Shana said, excitedly. "Moving the drive closer to the case opens a secret USB port built into it. This must be the key."

Bradley was about to say something, but Shana shushed him and inserted the drive. "Cross your fingers," she said, grinning.

There was a click, the drive glowed bright green, and the case cracked open. Shana laughed in triumph. "Wilcox, I told you before you are lucky to have me along."

Bradley mumbled his thanks and took the case. Inside was a state-of-the-art combat jacket and a thick manila envelope.

"So what did Sheen mean?" Shana asked. "About your career being ruined?"

"I wrote an article which someone then used to discredit me."

"You mean somebody wanted to silence you?"

"Yes. An important somebody." Bradley tore open the envelope and looked at the multiple portraits of Benjamin Franklin. "Holy shit!"

"How much is there?" Shana exclaimed, leaning over him to gaze at the thick sheaf of bills. "It looks like thousands! Wait, there's something else in the envelope."

He shook out two small round metal devices. "Hearing aids?"

"Earphones," Shana said, taking one and shoving it into her ear. "Nope, nothing yet." Bradley pushed the notes back into the envelope. "What's that?" he asked, looking at the jacket.

"Kevlar, maybe," Shana said, shrugging it over her shoulders. "There's another USB port just under here." She took the drive from the case and plugged it into the port on the jacket. "Hmm, much more portable than a laptop. It's all about access these days."

The jacket flashed and LED icons sprang up along the length of her left arm, projecting a light that gradually correlated into a computer screen.

"Is that a hologram?" Bradley asked.

"Fucking incredible," Shana said, her eyes wide. "There must be a hard drive built into this thing. Look, every icon is a different program – calculator, media player, internet… and documents." She tapped the screen on her arm. "You'd better read what's on the screen for yourself, and put that earpiece in. I have a feeling it might be useful."

Bradley looked at the crystal clear text on the screen that had projected out of thin air from the jacket, and pushed the device into his ear, then listened in amazement to Christine Sheen's voice as it read the following letter:

Mr Wilcox,

The United States government has been subverted by a group of powerful individuals – the same group of individuals responsible for your own career difficulties – with Ronald Hawk, chief advisor to President Moore, pulling the strings.

His project, codenamed the Counterweight Maneuver, has been set in motion, but the crucial parts have been kept secret even from the Cabinet in order to maintain unaccountability. This is where you come in.

Hawk owns shares in multiple companies, none of which have links to any businesses pertaining to the operation, but recently uncovered documents have given us a starting point: Chen Future Materials, 43 Chelsea Industrial Park, Detroit.

The money in this suitcase totals $25,000 and should be sufficient for your needs. Further information will be revealed to you as you progress. I apologize for the lack of details upfront, but due to the many risks that are involved, the less you know, the safer you will be.

This computerised combat jacket has been designed to function with the USB drive that you've been supplied with and will allow instantaneous communication, as well as access to a wide variety of other programs. The software is many years ahead of anything else developed on Earth, so see to it that these items do not fall into the hands of others.

The powers we fight are extremely dangerous and they will do everything to stop us. Good luck and be careful.

C.S

"Ronald Hawk?" Shana said with a frown as she read along. "I think I've heard the name."

"He's in the Cabinet, but he keeps a low profile," Bradley said hesitantly. "I did some research on him. He carries a lot of weight with the President, so they say."

"What the fuck is the Counterweight Maneuver?"

"I don't know," Bradley said, irritated. "You know as much as I do now, and that isn't much."

"Why didn't Sheen tell you back at the Kiyoko?"

Bradley shrugged, then he remembered the man in black on the street. "Maybe she was being watched," he said. "You read the document. The government is in on this. They could have a satellite trained on us right now, for all we know."

Shana looked around. "Do you think they're watching us?"

"I hope not," Bradley said, shoving the envelope of money into his coat pocket. "But I think we should leave now."

He reached to take the jacket, but Shana hugged it close to her chest. "I thought I could familiarize myself with this. Besides, it will keep me warm. You wouldn't know what to do with it anyway, would you?" she said, smiling. "Go on admit it. I've got to be good for something on this trip."

Damn it, she was probably right. "Don't you dare lose it," he said. "And stay close."

They left the motel, taking the delivery case with them, and caught the taxi driver as he was about to pull away. Bradley got into the back seat, passing him a hundred-dollar bill through the slotted security glass. "That's for waiting. Now, how much to Detroit?"

The driver looked at him, wide-eyed. "Detroit? Man, that's an all-night drive and I need to get back here tomorrow? Buddy, that'll cost like a grand at least!"

"Fine," Bradley said, pulling the curtain across the glass for some privacy.

"Detroit?" Shana asked, buckling herself in beside him.

"It'll cost less than two plane tickets. We can be there in eight hours or so. And it's the best way to keep a low profile. We really don't want anyone following us."

Shana looked at her phone. "It's 10.30 PM."

"Sleep on the way," he said. "We have to move fast."

The taxi pulled out onto the road. Bradley felt the same excitement he used to feel, back when he first started investigative reporting. It was risky, but they now had a purpose, a destination and a lead. They were on their way and he felt confident they could evade Hawk and possibly discover what was going on.

He felt Shana's hand on his arm and looked at her. "What is it?"

"I need to use the bathroom."

The metal plating creaked under Colonel Forge's feet as he stepped up the entry ramp and into the ship's interior. The lights raised as the computer registered the chip in his armor.

"Come on, come on," he muttered. "You've flown on aircraft before, haven't you?"

The others got in behind him – Fitz, Conrad, Miller, Jonns, Thompson, and Dennis. They were all elite troops, the best of the best. Each of them had survived countless tours in a variety of conflict zones, each of them had killed many times, but, most importantly, each of them was loyal.

They could be counted upon, they could be relied upon. The funny thing was that they were all crapping themselves right now.

"Where's the engines on this thing?"

Forge turned around, his eyes scanning them. "Who said that?"

Miller raised a hand, looking Forge in the eye, unblinking. "Sir. I was just wondering just how this thing flies, sir."

"The technology doesn't concern you, Captain," Forge said. "All you need to know is that we're standing on very unstable hydrogen fuel cells. If something does go wrong, you can kiss your ass goodbye because there's nothing we can do about it, so let's just hope that the brains who designed this thing knew what they were doing. Now, you've had plenty of time to work with the C-7 armor, so get ready. You'll soon learn how this bird flies."

The troops immediately began tightening cuffs and engaging the safeguards that would make their armor airtight and battle-ready.

Forge admired the smooth metal plate, the curved horns projecting from the shoulders and elbows, the barbed gauntlets, and the slim-bladed fingertips. They certainly looked unearthly, un-human, but more than that, they looked ready for a fight.

Forge tested the ID monitor in the coupling of his left wrist, then bent to retrieve a rifle from the rack on the wall. The EP rifle was heavy and bulky, capable of burning through a tank or hitting a cruiser from 2.5 miles, and it weighed a ton, but with the C-7 exoskeleton it was as light as a Beretta.

"Colonel Forge."

He saw the pilot at the hatch and saluted. "This is Flight Lieutenant Strunkey," Forge said. "He'll be making sure we land in one piece."

Strunkey nodded to the men, quickly sweeping past Forge, and then locked the door to the flight deck behind him.

Forge waited for the men to get their rifles off the rack before pointing to the seven empty seats.

Hanging over each of them, a helmet was supported mechanically. The compound eyes and grinning sharp teeth were hideous, frightening. Forge loved them. When they made landfall, truly they would look like unearthly monsters.

"Get seated, gentlemen," he said, still looking at the helmets. "We'll be ready to go once all helmet sat-feeds are primed and synced."

Each of the men sat in their chairs and slid their rifles into the grips between their legs. Restraint harnesses engaged and there was a whirring hiss as the seats connected to the armor, powering up their systems and downloading final updates to the software.

Forge watched each of the men carefully. Due to the extreme secrecy surrounding the Maneuver, every one of Hawk's soldiers would receive their baptism in the fire of conflict.

It didn't matter how many hours a man logged in an F-35, no one was ever prepared for a high-speed insertion through the atmosphere in one of these machines. You did it, you survived, and occasionally they had to wipe your armor clean afterwards. Still, the fear of dropping to Earth at twenty G was nothing compared to what those on the ground would feel when they climbed out.

The hydrogen engines hummed to an eerie crescendo while Forge felt the mildest of vibrations. He saw the soldiers around him taking deep breaths and blinking away sweat.

"One quick orbit around the moon, then a seriously fast descent through Earth's atmosphere," Forge said, "but the armor will cushion the impact, so you'll barely feel it. Just stay calm and keep your minds firmly fixed on the mission. Things will get hot once we land."

A few of the men were nodding. Miller was praying.

The vibration increased as the pilot activated all cells. The helmets descended smoothly and Forge saw each soldier's face change into that of an alien – cold, hideous, and evil. He felt the smooth padding cover his face and his vision changed. Each trooper lit up, a sat-link appeared in the corner of his right eye, while technical data began streaming over his left.

The seal around Forge's neck clicked tight as he felt cool air suddenly envelope around his nostrils. "The Orbital Insertion Vessel is fully enclosed, airtight, and sheathed in holo-graphene armor," he explained to the men. "Intel will come through your sat-link. It will connect soon."

He waited for the sat-feed to link, and General Morgan's face appeared in faint outline. Forge knew he'd be appearing in each of the others' helmets, too, with the obligatory pre-recorded pep-talk.

"Honored men," Morgan said, his eyes cold and unblinking. "You've trained long and hard for this mission, each of you hand-picked and deemed worthy of the task that lies ahead. Do not shirk your duty, do not fear. You are the vanguard of the new world order. Be proud of this moment, be proud of your country. But most of all, be totally invincible."

The feed cut and Forge looked over his fellow soldiers. "This is the first strike," he said, as the screeching, hooting noise of the scrambler sounded in his ears. "There will be more, many more, but you're the first. Don't let me down."

The click of the OIV's release sounded, and the lights dimmed as the hydro-fusion engines powered up.

Forge briefly felt a sense of inertia. His sat-link showed them rapidly leaving the stem of the space station behind them, with the moon getting closer and closer with each passing minute.

It took a lot of preparation to send a mission. The OIVs had to loop past the moon in a wide elliptical orbit in order that the unsuspecting world nations wouldn't doubt their extra-terrestrial origin, but the slingshot brought them in so fast that their range of attack was limited. Future missions would require longer journeys from the space station.

They passed the moon, and the pilot altered course with skilled manipulation of the ship's fusion propulsion, pulling the ship around until they were heading back towards Earth.

The suits kept them cool and fully shielded until the mass of Earth's gravity hit – they'd have died in ten seconds flat without the exoskeletons – and now they were accelerating, dropping very, very fast. Forge felt the rush of heat, the excitement of soon-to-be-fulfilled bloodlust. The ship's cloaking had deactivated once they'd successfully rounded the moon, and from that point onwards every advanced nation on Earth was in a position to detect them.

A countdown on his helmet's screen declared they'd land in twenty seconds. Forge cycled through the audio-connections to his men, hearing the usual bullshit prayers.

Once they'd landed they'd be ready, but if any soldier was foolish enough to lose it or be captured, they'd soon discover that the batteries in their backs doubled as fusion explosives – the technology had to remain a secret. No DNA could ever be recovered – with the one exception of the small bag of moon dust and pebbles that each man carried. This was to be deliberately scattered at will for the Russians to analyze as proof that the attack was indeed extra-terrestrial.

Ten seconds.

Forge felt the deceleration and opened the intercom. "We hit the ground running. Remember the brief. Head for the building and let nothing slow the advance. Keep moving, keep shooting, and show no mercy."

Five seconds.

"Rifles."

Each of his men pulled the rifles from their grips, artificial muscles compensating for the still-increasing g-force.

Three. Two. One. Contact.

Forge let his instincts take over as the restraints pulled back and the ship's ramp opened. Daylight blazed into the interior of the OIV as he dropped through the hatch, knowing his men would be right behind him.

Gray concrete buildings towered over them, walls blackened by two centuries of rapid industrialisation, with traffic blaring and moaning around them.

Forge dropped to the sidewalk, noting the cracks the force of his landing sent through the concrete, his rifle raised up before the nearest civilian had even managed a scream. He pulled the trigger, watching the searing ray of compressed energy burn through the crowds heading home from work, and saw identical beams on either side as his men advanced with him.

The hum of the OIV above shuddered as the holo-graphene plate bent into cloaking mode, hiding the ship from sight.

"Miller, Conrad, take the right," he said, hearing the screech through the helmet's filters.

Miller lumbered off across the street, and Conrad ignited his armor's thrusters, landing atop a car which collapsed under his weight. He fired a pulse into a crowd of people. They fell like scorched mannequins.

Now that they were down, the men were enjoying themselves – Forge had known they would. Each of them had been conditioned to be a remorseless killing machine. The power that the suits conveyed was awesome, and their mandate was pure. He'd felt the same when they'd dealt with that journalist back in DC, but that had been a small, covert operation. This was terror, pure and simple.

People were running now, and he could hear sirens faintly in the distance. Things were going to get interesting.

"I have security forces in sight," Miller sounded in his ear.

Forge could see the target down the street – the Bank of Moscow – and inside, some of the highest security vaults on Earth. He signalled to Miller and Conrad to deal with the police, and called Fitz, Jonns, Thompson, and Dennis to him.

The police car rounded the corner and screeched to a halt. Forge saw the driver's wide stare, his lips moving into a radio, utter disbelief in his eyes. Miller raised his gun and the stare got wider, then the car erupted in blue flames and debris was scattered all over the street.

Thompson's voice crackled in his ear. "Colonel Forge, I've found the entrance."

"I have a better way in." Forge activated his gun's over-charge and aimed it directly at the bank's thick walls. The vents on the gun glowed red, then popped open with a hiss, as he emptied a concentrated beam of high-impulse energy into the masonry. The bricks disintegrated into molten slag running down onto the street near where Thompson stood, hunched over in his exo-suit.

"Don't think like a human," Forge snapped. "We are not human, got it?"

Thompson muttered an affirmative and followed Forge in, trailed by Fitz, Jonns, and Dennis.

Forge heard the whine of a bullet and felt the barest impact on his chest. He looked down the corridor and saw the security guard, a

106

feeble-looking man with a revolver in his hands, frozen, horrified at the sight. Jonns grabbed the man by his neck and snapped it with a careless twist of his claw. More security guards appeared, coughing violently in the dust of the bank's new entrance, but when they saw Forge and his men, they turned tail and ran. Surprisingly intelligent for money-obsessed sheep.

"The building's schematics say the vault is twelve meters south and four levels down," Fitz said.

"Take out the floor," Forge replied, vaporizing a man in a suit who came staggering out of a nearby office. "We don't have long until the Russian Bear arrives, and I want to be back up here to greet them."

Fitz aimed his gun down the hall and waited for the charge to build. He fired and the floor collapsed in on itself as flames and smoke rose in a ball of heat.

Forge dropped through the hole, then through another, landing in a blackened crater in the second sub-level of the bank. He felt something soft beneath him and realized there were bodies, burned and still. The others dropped down beside him.

"That way," Fitz said.

The alarm was shrieking, and Forge adjusted the audio levels as they made their way down the hall.

"Miller. What's the status topside?"

"More police and security, sir," Miller replied. "And helicopters. Conrad just took one out."

"Alert me when the military arrives," Forge said. A security guard jumped out, shotgun in hand, but Forge cut a neat groove

107

through his head, watching as the man's skull slowly fell apart. "And keep an eye out for the media. This is a demonstration, after all."

A demonstration and an introduction, he thought, as the dead guard slumped to the floor.

They reached the vault. It was a meter thick and built of titanium. It might exhaust his rifle's power-pack getting in, but they'd already taken that into account.

Forge placed the palm of his hand against the electronic lock and let the virus enter the bank's mainframe. If it worked like Morgan had told him, not only would the vault open, but they'd also have a window into the entire banking network, and from there it could spread across their entire system. It had been designed by some genius recently recruited by Hawk – Carrendon or Cassington or something – as if they didn't already have enough geniuses.

Lights on either side of the door began to flash and a dull tone sounded deep within the door as thick bolts unlocked. With a groan of heavy hydraulics, the door gradually opened.

"Way, way too easy," Fitz said.

Forge smiled. It wasn't over yet.

Lights had automatically switched on inside the vault. There were shelves stacked high with gold, and cabinets filled with everything from diamonds and other precious stones to contract notes worth billions. None of them mattered.

Forge checked the Geiger counter on his wrist while memorizing details of the object they had orders to locate. A metal chest at the very back.

"That's it," he said, directing Dennis to recover it.

"What's in it?" Dennis asked.

Forge took it from him and tore the lid from the case with ease. A metallic rock fell to the ground – a dense, irregular, unearthly lump of metal that had been pulled from the ground in Russian-held Tunguska many decades ago. An unremarkable-looking piece of material, not even terribly radioactive, but extremely valuable because of its unprecedented creation – valuable because it was of extra-terrestrial origin. He lifted it in his free hand.

"Time's up. We need to exit now."

They headed back to the hole and jumped out, hastening their rise with a quick burst of their thrusters. Forge reached the hole in the wall just as Miller contacted him. "They're here, sir," he said. "Tanks and troops. A hell of a lot of troops."

"This is where things get hot," Forge said. "Go back to the extraction point. Vaporise anyone and anything you see."

They hastened off, backing up to the street where their UFO would be hovering invisibly. Forge walked out onto the cracked concrete, stepping over bodies and burning vehicles. A massive crater was burning furiously, and further off he could see twisted rotors amidst the wreckage of a helicopter. Rifles crackled and he saw Miller and Conrad further down, exchanging fire at a mass of vehicles and flashing lights.

A deep thud sounded and a building opposite the bank collapsed. Forge looked towards the noise and saw a T-90 tank moving over the burnt-out shell of a van.

"Orders, sir?" he heard Conrad say.

"Keep their troops back," Forge said. "I'll deal with the T-90."

The Russian soldiers were trying to gain ground, shooting their automatic weapons from the safety of the tank and from the protective corners of the surrounding buildings. Forge made straight for them, channelling extra-energy to the servos in his legs, his rifle in one hand and the meteorite segment in the other. He cut down a dozen Russian soldiers with one devastating sweep of energy fire, and reached the tank before it had any chance of pointing its barrel towards him.

Forge stored his weapon and the meteorite safely into his suit compartment, then roared a challenge, hearing his cry distorted into an inhuman shriek. With one mighty effort, he reached under the turret and maximized the energy-flow, lifting the top half of the T-90 clean off its hinges and proceeding to fling it through the air like a giant Frisbee.

The massive chunk of metal flipped, then spun wildly across the ground, tearing men to pieces and embedding itself in the other tank that had pulled into view.

Forge unlatched his rifle and emptied it into the newly arrived T-90, watching its armor glow red hot and hearing the screams from within, quickly stifled. The soldiers were running away in panic, the helicopter overhead pulling back. He saw a man with a camera huddled down in the gutter, his lens still focused on the alien Forge, his face screwed up paralyzed with sheer terror. Forge shouted, "Spread the fear, media parasite!"

His words were rendered unintelligible by the scramblers in his helmet – the world would certainly have fun trying to decipher it. Then the humming groan of the UFO sounded above, and Forge launched himself upwards on his thrusters, feeling the ship close around him. The others were already inside and they lifted fast.

Forge placed the lump of rock in the compartment at the base of the OIV's central column, and fell into his chair as the acceleration threatened to drag him to the floor.

"Thank you, gentlemen," he said, feeling the welcome rush of combat. "I can't wait to see what the paparazzi make of this."

The men were laughing and talking. Forge let them enjoy the moment. The world would now be in disbelief and wondering what had happened, yet this was only the beginning.

This was the future, the future of war.

Chapter 6

Bradley blinked away the sleep and watched the headlights streaming past the window. He lifted his eyes and saw a beautiful nose, lips, and eyes looking directly into his, then he realized his head was on Shana's shoulder, and he sat up.

"Sorry. Didn't mean to fall asleep on you like that."

"I was asleep, too," she said, pushing her blond hair back from her face. "I hope you behaved yourself."

"Yes, you were quite safe," he said. "I was dreaming, actually."

"Was I in your dreams?" she asked.

"How far out are we?" Bradley said, ignoring Shana and addressing the driver through the cab's security window.

"About an hour," the driver called back. "Gonna have to stop for more gas soon."

"I've never been to Detroit," Shana said.

"I heard it's a shithole," Bradley replied. "Cars, factories, guns. Debris all over the place. It seems like the whole world's going the same way."

"I've heard there are some nice parts though," Shana protested. "You should see the world more positively."

"Positively?" Bradley replied. "The planet's being consumed by globalization that demands ever-increasing sacrifice, while everyone pretends it's all okay. It's total madness."

"You're very cynical," Shana said, activating the hologram screen on her arm. "Anyway, I've figured out some of this drive. It's basically a complex algorithm, very original. It can get into most programs using a creatively designed set of smaller algorithms, and it operates on every frequency. The genius of it lies in that it's so different to typical computer viruses, it's essentially invisible within modern networks – it can attack with impunity and can also defend itself."

"Similar to a skeleton key," Bradley said, shifting in his seat.

"Yes, and much more," Shana said, staring at him like he was a complete idiot. "It can hook onto a signal and connect us to Sheen pretty much anywhere in the world. God knows how many other applications this technology could be used for."

"What's that? A toy or something?" the driver asked, squinting back at them.

"Yeah, new iPhone app," Shana said, lowering the projection to a flat picture with a button on her cuff.

"Can it get internet?" Bradley said. "Because we really should check the news."

She tapped the screen a few times, frowning. Bradley leaned across as they scanned the front page of BBC News: *Terror attack in Moscow blamed on foreign insurgents.*

There was live footage of the event streaming to them crystal clear on the screen, and each of them put in an earphone to hear the audio. A reporter stood with Moscow's skyline behind him.

"Authorities remain tight-lipped about the bewildering incident in the Russian capital, confirming only that a serious attack has caused major damage in central Moscow. No footage has been released and no eyewitness accounts exist as yet, but a pall of thick black smoke now hangs over the city and the whole area has been cordoned off. There is a heavy military presence, but no further

shots have been fired since the incident first occurred at approximately 5.45 PM."

"Could this… could this have anything to do with the Counterweight thing?" Shana asked her voice shaky. "Does Hawk actually have the audacity to attack Russia?"

Bradley scanned the page, and then checked some other sites, but all were similarly devoid of real information. "Could be anyone," he said, slowly shaking his head. "Unfortunately, nothing's been released by the Russian government yet. So much for glasnost."

"It must be terrorists," Shana said, looking at Bradley.

He reached over and gently squeezed her hand. "Probably just your standard maniacs coming out of the woodwork."

"Good. I really don't want to find out if those aliens of yours actually do exist."

Bradley studied her face, examining her eyes for some trace of deception. "We only met a few hours ago. Why do you want to come with me?"

"I don't know," she shrugged. "When you came into the restaurant, I could tell there was something different about you – you looked so… well, so damn nervous."

"And I thought I was as cool as a cucumber."

"A frozen cucumber," she said, smiling. "But when I saw you in the street on my way home, and you were knocked to the floor, I knew something spellbinding was happening, something very strange and important. It was at that moment I thought that I needed to protect you at all costs. It all happened so quickly?"

"It's not too late for you to get out. You can go back to DC."

114

"No, no way. I'm coming," Shana said. "You'd be screwed without me. Anyway, you're right. We just can't ignore what's going on out there."

Despite his initial misgivings, Bradley was relieved and grateful she'd decided to remain with him. He knew he needed Shana's technical abilities. True, she was indeed a comfort to him and extremely beautiful, but more than anything it meant he wasn't alone and that someone had his back. They were heading into the unknown, possibly into danger, but now at least one other person would know.

Shana rested her head on his shoulder and closed her eyes. "Come on," she said. "I have a dream I need to get back to."

***

The meeting began with the President's usual optimistic evaluation of the state of America. He briefly touched on dismantling welfare programs in the face of a still-growing deficit, and then moved quickly onto the state of the current financial markets.

Hawk watched those around the table, noting Terrance Sullivan's white face, the way he kept mopping his brow with a handkerchief, and his constant glances in the direction of Mark Leary. Leary had an ever-present half-smile on his freshly shaven face, and was directing his mild gaze at each speaker in turn.

Christine Sheen wouldn't make eye contact with Hawk, which he was more than gratified to see, and her comments were confined to objecting to the planned austerity measures. She seemed reserved, but he'd have a word with her later, just to be sure. Leary's political

115

manipulations required immediate attention, but Hawk didn't want to turn his back on Sheen for a second. She was the most talented person in the room, barring himself, of course.

President Moore cleared his throat. He focused on his old friend, the commander-in-chief.

"I think we should first speak on the most recent events in Moscow," Moore said, rubbing his chin. He looked at Hawk. "Certain cabinet members are worried about how your... *pet project* is about to affect our most important financial and industrial institutions."

Hawk paused, and then sighed. "Mr President, this is a matter of national security, and ultimately global security. What exactly has a corporation's profit margin got to do with America's well-being?"

"These companies have invested heavily in the United States, Mr Hawk," Leary said, shifting in his seat. "The attack on the Russian capital has already wreaked havoc on the energy markets."

"Russian energy companies have taken the biggest hit," Hawk replied. "In fact, I believe the Moscow incident has actually raised share prices for American oil and gas firms."

"But the industry is nervous, and that can spread like a virus across all world markets," Leary said. "You've yet to divulge the full details of your plan, and Russia has been very sparing with the details of what happened in Moscow. So when and where will the next incident, as you call it, occur? Will it be one of our allies, one of our own investments? And what exactly *did* occur in Moscow, Mr Hawk?"

"When you speak of 'our' investments, Secretary Leary, you actually mean the companies that are paying you. I've heard that

116

you're keen on opening our energy sector to foreign firms. Those firms wouldn't happen to be based in the Far East, would they?"

Leary's smile faded. "I read the document you gave us last week, Mr Hawk. It talks of re-establishing American economic dominance, bringing the good times back. But I can't help thinking that this Counterweight Maneuver goes a lot further than that. We'll be changing the world and reversing the march of time. You want us to backtrack on all the progress that we have made, which will not be for the common good or for the betterment of the American economy. What you're talking about is bringing down the current model."

"The current model is totally fucked," Hawk said.

He looked over at Moore in an attempt to gauge his mood and approval, but the President just sat back, watching the proceedings while waiting for further guidance. Christ, if Hawk was running this thing, he had no choice but to now take full control. Leary represented a fossil-fuel driven slide to economic and ecological suicide – his kind had all the money and a vice-like grip on Congress. Humanity would be done for unless Hawk did something.

"An economy is a fine balance," he said, "but your brand of irresponsible capitalistic greed only tips things in one direction, pulling everyone along with it on a massive drunken borrowing binge, while leaving nothing but a huge bill and a mountain of debts that future generations will never be able to pay off." He leaned toward Leary, placing both hands on the table. "But as you've so astutely pointed out, Secretary Leary, the Counterweight Maneuver will balance out your perverse dreams of corporate excess by giving the world a real future with the United States of America leading the way once again."

Leary spluttered while the others looked on, frozen. They understood now that there were real implications, that – for once – this wasn't some self-aggrandizing scheme that would simply grind to a halt and gather dust in the governmental machine.

"Ronald," the President said. "Perhaps we can postpone the next... incident? Some further discussion regarding this matter may assist in clearing up the finer details."

Hawk sighed. "I expected some jitters before the doors opened, but as you all know, the curtain has been raised. It is far too late to back out now. Each person at this table is complicit in what has been done, and what is about to be done – even you, Secretary Leary."

"This nation answers to its people," Leary snapped. "And I represent many people with severe concerns about this administration."

"Corporations are not people, you greedy sycophant," Hawk said, his lip curled in distaste. "You don't care about anyone, least of all America – or the planet. You only want what you can take. You're a parasite, a drain on the host. This is why the Maneuver is so necessary."

There was silence for a few moments, then Moore cleared his throat. "Ladies and gentlemen, we are not going to solve this issue speedily, so I am declaring this meeting over."

The others got up quickly, especially Leary and Sullivan, who left before Hawk could conceivably reach them. Hawk made straight for Sheen.

"Miss Sheen," he said, noting her recoil. "I would like a word in private, please."

"We can make an appointment."

"Now, Christine."

He led Sheen out and down the hall to an empty office room. She followed him in, but he noticed she made sure the door was left open.

"Yes?" she said.

"I obviously know of your objections to my plans," Hawk said. "Not that you're alone, of course."

"And your colorful descriptions of a world without capitalism won't sway me," she said, moving to leave. "The sentiment is wonderful, but your methods leave a lot to be desired, Mr Hawk."

Hawk blocked her exit with his arm. "I know you made contact with Bradley Wilcox," he said.

Sheen abruptly stopped and turned back to him, her face pale.

He had her attention now. "Wilcox has been dealt with and won't be bothering anyone anymore, so for your own good I would advise that you work with me from now on, not against me."

"And if I choose not to?" Her voice trembled.

"The plan has now been executed," Hawk said. "There's no stopping it. However, if you want to rock the boat, then feel free to follow Leary's example and see where it gets you."

"I'll try to behave, then," Sheen said.

"Miss Sheen. You won't just try to behave, you will behave," Hawk said, his voice low. "I'll be watching you."

She left, a dark look etched on her face.

Hawk took out his phone. "Barb. Put me through to General Morgan."

Morgan's voice was suddenly in Hawk's ear. "Sir?"

"Any further word on the irritant in DC?" Hawk asked.

"Wilcox was seen leaving the scene, clearly shaken and in the arms of a woman," Morgan said. "He managed to escape the explosion, but he won't be a problem anymore."

Hawk wasn't so certain. "General, I want you to keep an eye out for him. If he resurfaces, make sure he disappears, only this time permanently. We don't want any more loose ends."

"Affirmative. One thing," Morgan said. "Government agents were seen near the Kiyoko bar. You know anything about them?"

"Probably with Sheen," Hawk said. "Bodyguards."

"They arrived separately to Sheen and remained after she'd left."

Hawk cursed quietly under his breath. Had some other agency suddenly stumbled onto his scheme? Had someone in the Cabinet, besides Sheen, made a play against him? "I'll look into it," he said. "Be ready for further orders."

General Morgan grunted, and the line went dead. Hawk left the room, making for his office. Time was of the essence and he had people to deal with.

Tiger Populations and Folk Medicine
by Simon LeVille

Increasing development coupled with consumer demand has pushed tiger populations to near extinction. At the beginning of the twentieth century, there were an estimated 100,000 tigers in the wild, but today fewer than 1,500 wild tigers remain throughout the world.

While deforestation and loss of habitat is the main culprit, certain cultures value tiger parts for their supposed aphrodisiac and anaesthetic properties. Although there is no evidence to support these claims, tiger farming is a growing business, with semi-tame cats bred in captivity in an attempt to profit from such beliefs. Some experts believe that this could mitigate the effects of illegal poaching, but others think it cruel and a contributing fact to the illegal trade.

Leading conservationists believe that there will be no tigers left in the wild by the year 2030.

Chapter 7

It was 10 AM when the taxi reached the edge of Detroit, and they were surprised at just how busy the streets were with traffic and pedestrians.

"Detroit usually this hectic?" Bradley asked. "It's like LA at rush hour out there."

"I heard some weird news on the radio," the driver said. "Terrorists or something in Russia. People probably a bit nervous. You never know which city will be next, you know?"

"Yeah, I saw the footage," Bradley said. "Looked crazy, even for terrorists."

"The world just gets crazier," the driver said with a shrug. "Where did you say you wanted dropping?"

"Forty-three, Chelsea Industrial Park."

The driver checked his GPS system and turned onto another street, honking his horn and yelling at the people in his way. "I ain't never seen so many people on the road as today," he said. "It's like everyone's trying to get home at once."

"You really think it has something to do with the attack in Moscow?" Bradley asked, watching the slow-moving cars.

"Yeah, maybe," he said. "But shit happens every day. People might hunker down in front of the TV for a night, but then it's back to business as usual. Fucking weird city, that's what it is. Get off the road, ya dumb fuck!"

Bradley let him concentrate on driving and looked at Shana, who was checking her phone. "The Kremlin is saying that there was a sophisticated attack carried out by unknown foreign forces," she said. "But that's all they've got. No images, no film." She shook her head. "YouTube's down, everything's running slow. Something really bad must have happened if the media's being blocked. Something worse than bad."

Was it Hawk? Surely it had to be. But what the hell would he ever need in Moscow? And what was behind the internet slowdown?

"We'll find out what we can at the factory," Bradley said, taking Shana's hand and squeezing it. "The President will have to make a speech at some point."

They drove in silence, watching the streets jammed with cars, listening to the horns and the shouts. It reminded Bradley of a plane flight he'd been on once before. The turbulence had been terrible – really, really bad. People had thought they were going to die and were crying, begging others for reassurance – even a lie would have helped – but, for some reason, the stewards never said anything. Usually they warned you when the slightest bump was going to happen, but then, when the cabin had gone dark and the plane had sounded like it was about to shake itself to pieces, there hadn't been a single word. Even Bradley had thought they were going to crash.

Detroit wasn't panicking yet, but it would be if there wasn't any news soon. "How close are we?" he asked.

"Half a mile," the driver said. "Gonna cost a bit extra 'cos of the time. Sorry about that."

"It's fine," Bradley said, checking his wallet. He'd never had so much cash on him.

They reached the industrial sector, which was much quieter than the main roads with only a few trucks coming and going. Bradley motioned for the driver to stop before they reached the address, and

124

they got out. He tipped him generously and followed Shana along the sidewalk.

"It's just past that," Shana said, pointing at the venerable hulk of a former steelworks. "Should be the next along the block."

They walked, taking in the dull functionality of the buildings and the parked trucks. Bradley had always hated these places, so dirty, so artificial. He saw a high fence and a large white sign that said, "Chen Future Materials." There was a small brick-built hut at the gate with a single security guard sat on duty.

Shana made to approach him, but Bradley stopped her. "He hasn't seen us," he said, taking her hand. "Let's keep it that way." They walked into the neighboring lot, making their way quickly past the parked cars and skips full of junk, until the hut was almost out of sight.

Bradley looked through the fence at the large, gray Chen building. There were windows, all shuttered, and doors padlocked closed, but the smoke from chimneys and vents at the back revealed the factory was still running.

"How do we get in?" Shana asked. "Look, cameras."

Bradley looked where she was pointing and saw a staircase leading up to a fire exit with a camera trained on it. He strained his eyes to see the door and realized there was no padlock, just some kind of keypad.

"You said the USB drive had some sophisticated software on it," he murmured. "Can it open that door?"

Shana pressed her face to the fence, looking at the door. "Keypad," she said. "Simple, providing we can get to it."

Bradley noted the fence was free of barbwire and followed it with his eye to where an old brown Ford was parked up against it. "We can get in over there."

"You climb a lot of fences in your career?"

"Quite a few when I was younger," Bradley said, "and only got caught once."

They got to the car and climbed up onto its roof. Bradley cupped his hand, inviting Shana to step into it, and hoisted her up onto the fence.

"Try to be quiet," he whispered, looking back to the front where the silhouette of the guard was visible through the misted glass of the hut.

Shana clung to the top, then dropped to the ground on the other side.

Bradley pulled himself up and over with a grunt and landed on the gravel. He checked the nearest door, but it was securely locked. "That's the only way in," he said, looking up the steps. "We'll have to be quick with that damn camera watching us."

"Let's get a bit closer," Shana said, moving towards the stairs. She quickly tapped a key on her jacket. The hologram instantly flashed from her arm, forming into a screen from thin air. "I might be able to connect to it from here."

Bradley looked over her shoulder as she cycled through some tabs, getting to an icon marked with a key. "I'm checking frequencies," she said. "Found it. Oh, this gets even better."

"What?" Bradley asked. The numbers and abbreviations on the screen were completely indecipherable to him.

"This thing has a scrambler on it," she said, beaming.

126

"And?"

"It can interfere with that camera, for a start. I'm keeping this, right? Once we're done and everything, we'll tell Sheen it got lost."

"The cops will be confiscating it if you don't hurry up!" Bradley hissed. Shana waved her arm closer to the door. Bradley saw the panel light up green. "What are you doing?

"Shhhh. I'm concentrating."

He forced himself to be quiet and watched her as keys flashed in sequence: *7, 8, 0, 8, 1, 4, 7.* Suddenly, there was the unmistakable sound of a bolt being drawn, and the door opened just a crack.

Shana traced her finger over the screen to another icon. "And... run. Just fucking run!"

Bradley sprinted up the steps and through the door into a dark hall. Shana followed, closing it softly behind them. She raised her arm to the camera in the wall. "We'd better be quick," she said. "Anyone watching the screens will soon notice if the cameras keep losing feed."

Bradley looked each way along the hall. There were multiple doors, all unmarked, and it was hard to see anything in the dim light. "I don't know where we're supposed to be going."

"We could try the back," Shana said. "I saw vents at the back, lots of them. Must be the factory floor."

They walked slowly down the hall, looking out for the red blink of cameras, until they reached a door at the very end. Bradley could hear machinery now. They were on the right track.

"Where is everyone?" Shana said. "We saw the guard at the gate, but you'd think there'd be someone in here keeping an eye on things. The machinery's obviously working."

Bradley slowly pushed open the door. The noise rose in pitch, and he smelled the unmistakable odor of worked metal and oil.

He glanced in quickly, ready to duck back at any moment and make a fast run for the exit, but he saw no guards, no cameras; just conveyer belts moving in unison with massive robotic machines that were processing large slabs of a dull grayish metal.

He was startled as a huge pile of metal dropped into a mechanised cart with a loud clatter.

"Relax, Brad," Shana said. "I think the place is totally automated. Look, that material's brought through on that conveyer and dumped into there, then... what is that, a crucible or something? It's gigantic, whatever it is."

They watched the cart moving along the belt towards a scorched, rectangular bowl at the center of the factory floor. The cart abruptly stopped at the bowl and tilted the metal into it. A flash of flame arose around its blackened edges, then a lid quietly descended over the whole apparatus, sealing the top with a hissing, groaning noise. The cart was then lifted back onto the conveyor, where another cart had just entered and was being filled with more of the same material.

"It's graphite, I think," Bradley said, remembering an article he'd read in *New Scientist*. "Pure carbon."

He walked down the metal steps to the factory floor, feeling the scorching heat on his face. The crucible opened with a pop and he heard the hiss of steam escaping through the gap between it and the lid. He walked its perimeter, making sure to keep a safe distance, and saw, about halfway down one side, a thin material being extruded onto another conveyor belt. A chemical was being sprayed

128

over it, perhaps to cool it. He followed it further down to where a guillotine was chopping the substance into square panels and neat segments which were then dropped into waiting boxes, each marked with a special barcode.

Shana put her hand over a strip of metal. "It's cool."

Bradley picked it up. It was almost transparent and weighed next to nothing, and when he bent it between thumb and forefinger, it instantly popped back into shape. "Looks like it could be graphene or something similar," he said, half-smiling. "You know, the new miracle material."

"Yeah, I've heard of it," Shana said, taking a picture with her phone. "You get a sample, and I'll grab a photo of the marking on those boxes. Maybe it will mean something to Sheen." She was pulling at a box from the side of the machine when the mechanism suddenly cut out and the lights died. "Oh," she said, looking at Bradley. "I guess it's quitting time."

Bradley shoved a piece of graphene into his pocket. "Or you may have just set off a hidden alarm," he said, his voice sounding loud in the now quiet room. "Let's go before…"

He stopped talking. Somewhere further up the stairs, a high-pitched whining noise was getting louder.

Bradley's thoughts went back to the attack at the apartment building, the invisible thing hanging over him, the strange alien language in his ears. He was barely breathing, looking up the stairs for the slightest movement. Then he heard a sound from beside him and saw Shana's phone flash.

"*Shana!*" he hissed.

Pricks of white light flashed on and he was blinded as two – no, three – *things* floated down the stairs. He caught a glimpse of metal glinting in the air and shoved Shana back behind the conveyer belt. They moved as quietly as they could, keeping the machinery between them and their pursuers. Whatever those things were, they weren't friendly, and having experienced Hawk's agenda first-hand, Bradley was damn sure they didn't want to be caught.

They reached the back of the factory, but the wide doors were padlocked shut. Bradley couldn't help but think that, for all the technology imparted to them by Sheen, a set of bolt cutters would have been handy.

"What are they, flying cameras?" Shana whispered.

A light rounded one of the big machines and Bradley saw what did indeed look like a medium-sized camcorder built around a small turbine. It dropped under an overhead conveyer belt and hovered across the factory floor, spinning its "eye" back and forth.

He felt Shana tapping his arm. "Give me your phone," she whispered.

Bradley placed a finger to his lips and willed her to be silent. Whatever those things were, they seemed to go for sound more than anything, and so far they were on the wrong track.

"*Phone!*" she hissed, louder, holding out her hand.

One of the lights turned towards them. Bradley felt panic, even as Shana's hand was in his pocket, grabbing at his phone. Another of them was on the other side of the factory, coming their way.

Bradley realized they were caught in the middle. He was preparing to run, thinking he should have cursed at Shana for giving away their hiding place, but then his phone's alarm went off and

Mozart's 25th symphony was playing at full volume. Shana kicked the phone across the floor and all three of the flying objects headed after it.

Shana sprinted for the stairs, with Bradley right behind her. They reached the steps as a burst of electricity erupted from the front of the leading drone, frying the phone to dust. Bradley ran through the door at the top, uncaring of the camera in the hall.

A voice stopped them.

"You! Get on the ground now! Both of you!"

A man in uniform was standing by the door they'd just burst through, a flashlight in one hand, a pistol in the other. "I said, *get fucking down*! The police are on their way, so don't try anything stupid!"

Bradley was breathing hard, unsure whether this guard's appearance was a good thing or not. He looked over his shoulder and saw the door still open a crack.

"I think we should do what he says, Brad," Shana said, her hands raised.

He held up his hands and got down on his knees. The guard's radio crackled and the man lifted it to his mouth. "Two of them," he said. "Situation's under control."

Bradley heard the door open with a clap and felt the buzz of small rotors pass swiftly by his ear.

The guard seemed shocked, but managed a shot, knocking one out of the air, before the remaining two discharged their weapons directly into him. He writhed in pain as continuous crackling blue and white tendrils of energy coursed through his body.

Bradley watched in horror as the attack ended, and the guard fell to the floor, wisps of smoke rising from his charred body.

Shana was pressing the screen in her jacket sleeve urgently as the two remaining drones spun around, their glowing red eyes focusing once more on the two of them. Bradley closed his eyes, but only heard a whining sound as crackling tendrils of blue and orange blossomed in the air, then two thumps. He opened one eye, wincing in anticipation of an attack, and saw the two remaining spy drones on the floor, both inert.

"I found the wavelength they were operating on," Shana said, her voice shaky, "and made them attack each other. Thought it might be worth a try."

Bradley stood up. He felt numb. The smell of burnt flesh reached him and he almost gagged. He could hear sirens approaching in the distance and felt even more nauseous.

"Come on," he said. "We have to go. Sheen has some questions to answer."

Bradley kept his eyes on the drones as they walked past, but Shana reached down and picked up the one that the security guard had shot down.

They stepped over the dead man. Bradley tried to avoid looking directly at his face, and saw the gun on the floor. He held his breath as he picked it up. It was hot to the touch.

Then they were outside, and the fresh air reinvigorated Bradley as he ran down the steps, sprinting for the front of the building. He looked both ways on the road. The sirens were getting damn close.

"Over there," Shana said, pointing to a warehouse on the other side of the road.

They ran until their lungs were almost at bursting point, following the fence until they were at the back of the yard. Then they scaled a brick wall and found themselves in another parking lot. Bradley made sure the safety catch was securely on the gun and slid it into the back of his jeans, covering it with his jacket.

"Look." Shana pointed at a black Lexus. "Top of the line, modern, unstealable."

Overrated, Bradley wanted to say, but he was too horrified to speak. A man was dead. What the fuck had they uncovered?

Shana was next to the car, pressing a hidden indentation on her sleeve. The car's locks popped open. She smiled, but her eyes were red. She was holding it together, but only just.

Bradley couldn't let her do all this alone. He got into the driver's seat. The engine started and he laughed, a mix of nerves and exhaustion, but absolutely no humor.

"Sheen's jacket must be worth millions," he said.

"This thing must be worth a fair bit, too," Shana said, her voice shaking a little as she hefted the damaged drone in her hand. "All of this stuff is so far ahead of our time. Makes you wonder what else we peasants aren't being told about."

Bradley drove out of the lot, accelerating until they were going close to seventy. When they reached the open road, some of the traffic from earlier had cleared, and he forced himself to slow down, just to keep to the speed limit.

"Where are we going?"

"Out of Detroit," Bradley said. "We'll have to ditch the car and get a motel, maybe."

"Hopefully what happened in Moscow will distract them from us," Shana said. "Maybe the police will have other things to worry about."

But it wasn't the police Bradley was worried about.

***

Hawk was in his office below the White House. The monitor was switched to a shielded multi-party line and bathed the room in a pale blue and white glow.

General Morgan's face filled one third of the screen, with Colonel Forge and Oswald Carrington occupying the other two segments. The signal was coded and sent in bursts through a scrambled closed-network. With technology many years ahead of anything else on the planet, Hawk was confident their conversation was secure.

"Gentlemen," he said, smiling broadly. "Thank you for attending at such short notice."

"Everything going okay, Ronald?" Carrington asked, sipping from a coffee cup.

"Just perfect, Mr Carrington," Hawk said, suppressing a tug of irritation at the young scientist's lack of formality. "Given the complex nature of our mission, the Maneuver was built with flexibility in mind. I have called this meeting to deal with a recently discovered problem."

"The journalist?" Morgan said, raising an eyebrow.

"No," Hawk said. "Although we should be mindful of Mr Wilcox, this particular issue concerns individuals within the Cabinet.

134

It's come to my attention that Secretary Leary has been involving himself in more than unethical business practices."

"So our Maneuver hasn't quite caught their imagination yet?" Forge said.

"Quite," Hawk said, taking a Havana from the box on his desk. He lit it with a match, puffing gently. "Fools can sometimes serve a purpose, however. Leary's lapdog, Secretary Terrance Sullivan, is representing the US Government at the upcoming economic conference in Shanghai."

"They're still talking business?" Forge said, frowning. "The attack on Moscow should have caught their attention. We made a hell of a mess down there."

"The media's being controlled," Hawk said. "There's panic, for sure, but the tycoon in his ivory tower is always the last to notice."

"They can't suppress this forever," Morgan said, his eye twitching.

"Quite," Hawk said, savoring the complex flavors of the tobacco. "And the Shanghai meeting provides us with an ideal opportunity to ensure that the next attack is seen for what we really want to accomplish – an act of war, plain and simple. It's time these unaccountable corporations recognized their days are numbered, and with so many important representatives present, they've presented us with a perfect opportunity."

"What needs to be done?" Morgan said.

"I want Sullivan taken alive, with no other survivors," Hawk said. "I also want China to know it is no longer untouchable."

"For sure it can be done," Forge shrugged. "The OIVs are ready, the men are trained."

"The Remotes are functioning beyond their specifications," Carrington said. "They're ready for deployment whenever you give the word."

Hawk felt a surge of pride. He'd chosen well, and with such a cadre of loyal and disciplined men, he couldn't fail. "Prepare the strike, Colonel," he said. "And liaise closely with Mr Carrington. This will be the first time our upgraded Droniks will face well-trained security forces. I don't need to tell you the technology must not fall into enemy hands."

"I'll personally lead the assault, sir," Forge said. "They won't stand a chance once we're done with them. Do we deploy the moon dust again, sir?"

"Yes, Colonel. And I'm gratified to hear that you will be leading the charge," Hawk said.

Morgan and Forge winked out until only Carrington's face remained.

"Something else, Ronald?" Carrington asked, wincing as if he had a headache.

"How are you feeling?" Hawk said. "Your most recent medical states that you're still having migraines."

"Oh, minor stuff. My work hasn't been hindered."

"Your work has been exemplary," Hawk replied. "Just be sure to let the doctors know if it gets worse."

Carrington nodded. "Other than that, everything's going well."

Hawk put his cigar out in the stone ashtray. Carrington seemed okay, but it was probably time Hawk went up there to make sure he was still functioning at a safe level. The nootropics he was taking worked better than anything on the market, but their side-effects were undeniable, making the line between genius and madness about as narrow as you could get.

"How are your new facilities?" Hawk asked. "Quite a view up there, huh?"

"It's incredible," Carrington said, growing animated – well, who wouldn't be excited after witnessing the scale of this thing? "I've read documents on the feasibility of the space elevator concept, but I had no idea it was already possible. It's a modern wonder, and just as miraculous that you've actually managed to keep it a secret."

"I would like to come and inspect the production line, Oswald," Hawk said. "As much for a chance to get out of DC as anything."

Carrington leaned closer to the camera. "Bring up some more creamer and I'll put the kettle on."

Hawk grinned. "Then I'll see you soon. Keep up the good work."

Carrington's face vanished. Hawk called for his aide to have his car brought around. The Maneuver was accelerating fast and soon the rest of the world would have no choice but to accept it. The old world was done with, now a new age was about to dawn.

Chapter 8

Colonel Forge leaned over the pilot's shoulder, checking the controls on the dash. They were holding level, only 100 feet from the building, yet completely invisible to everyone on the street below – the protestors, the cops in riot gear behind their barricades, the media boxed in at one end of the street, and the cordoned-off crowds. He could see the glass tower of the Tianjin Main Bank on the OIV's monitor, jutting high above its concrete lower levels.

"Keep us stable until the signal," Forge said, heading back into the drop-chamber.

Fitz, Conrad, Miller, Jonns, and Dennis were buckled in, along with Bryant and Coca, two senior technicians from Hawk's R&D department who were riding along with the new Dronik devices that Carrington had developed.

"You ready?" he asked. "Things could get very hectic real fast, so tell me now if you anticipate any problems."

"No problems," Bryant said, pulling a pair of goggles over his eyes. "I'm interacting with the Droniks through VR. You can follow on your helmet feeds so you'll have multiple perspectives of the entire action."

The others were already wearing their helmets. Forge took his from its place above his seat.

"My men will be quick and clean," he said, pulling his helmet on. "I expect your side of the operation to go just as smoothly."

"I'll be backing him up and managing the signal," Coca said. "These new Remotes are reliable and effective. Your men won't have much trouble."

Forge opened the Dronik feed in the corner of his visor and watched white and black static transform into a gray image. Then six other small screens appeared below, all showing the perspectives of each Dronik as they hovered towards their targets.

Right now, Jiang Ming-Tun, the Chinese Finance Minister, Chong Bo Wang, Chinese Minister of Industrial Development, Charles De Lai, the London-based President of the Global Finance Union, Terrance Sullivan, the US Secretary of Commerce, and the CEOs of the twelve biggest banks on the planet, were all gathered for a meeting on Shared Continental Prosperity – in reality, a discussion on how to further weaken the industrial base of the United States, while widening Sino/Russian global influence, with a lucrative trillion-dollar payoff at the end. The building was protected by 200 cops and the finest security money could acquire; however, they were about to discover that their defences were worthless.

"Droniks 18 and 19 are new models," Coca said. "The head designer calls them Hornet Grifters. They'll cover the ground levels and deal with any resistance from below while Droniks 13 through 17 take care of everyone in the meeting room – with the exception of the target, of course."

"Then we drop in, extract Sullivan and blow the building. I know the mission." Forge hated working with scientists – they had no sense of urgency. "Just give me the salient points and tell me when to fucking hit them."

"Our Droniks are approaching the room via the ventilation system," Coca said. "They'll be in position within two minutes."

"Just do your job," Forge said, reaching for his rifle, "so that I can do mine."

***

Terrance Sullivan finished his second scotch and sat back, smiling at the men around the table while they all spoke on various matters relating to profit and expense, ways on how to widen the global market, and how to gain a much bigger share of the emerging economies. They were all following the money, as Leary would say – all of them hell-bent on cutting the cash cow to ribbons with no thought for anyone or anything else. You could either watch from the sidelines or join in.

At fifty-five, with a senior position in the worst administration in decades, a fortune fluctuating around $93,000,000, and a wife and two kids that didn't want anything to do with him, Sullivan saw no reason why he should sit back while everyone else enjoyed themselves. And with Leary leading the charge, he saw a great chance to join the table.

Bob Tipper, the CEO of the International Exchange Bank, was talking.

"We're looking at bringing oil through the state of Alaska, refining it down south near the Mexican border, and then shipping it with Hainan Transport to Asian markets," Tipper said. "We've been offered a sizable tax incentive to carry out the refining process in the state, and the environmental cost can be covered by the taxpayer. The market will respond and we can jump-start further operations in Asia and the emerging economies."

Chong Bo Wang slowly turned his face towards Sullivan.

"Mr Sullivan." He spoke English with a heavy Cantonese accent. "Are you sure the American public will accept this?"

140

Sullivan replied in a high, cocky tone. "What with the imported drugs and the chemical-based junk food we've have been feeding them for the last few decades, the American people will accept whatever they are given, Mr Wang."

The Minister for Finance, Jiang Ming-Tun, stood. "We've gone over new markets, the wildlife problem, investment opportunities, American debt, and the fragility of the Euro-zone, but what about the main item on the agenda?"

Ming-Tun held out a hand, palm up, to Sullivan.

"Secretary Sullivan. Would you care to outline your government's proposition?"

Sullivan sat up in his chair, but didn't stand. He felt warm and comfortable after the scotch. Leary had briefed him fully, and this should go easily.

"Gentlemen," he smiled. "The President of the United States has charged myself and the Secretary of Energy, Mark Leary, to revolutionize the US energy sector. We have a severe energy deficit and it's growing by the day. The nuclear option is the one we want to pursue, but the taxpayer is loath to pay for it, so we plan to open the sector to foreign private companies."

There were murmurs from around the table.

"In addition to nuclear power, the new fracking revolution will be made accessible to all your corporate enterprises, and with the additional legislation and taxation that we will push through, I guarantee that you'll have no competition from domestic US firms."

The murmurs rose and Sullivan felt his pulse quicken.

"I'll be happy to discuss the venture with any interested parties, but please bear in mind that the professional fees for myself and my esteemed business acquaintances do not come cheap. However, the good news is that your profits will be huge. And let's face it, energy costs are not about to come down anytime soon."

A tapping noise suddenly had everyone looking at each other. Sullivan could hear it over the whisper of the AC and looked around for the source of the noise.

The lights flickered, and clangs sounded from all around them. Sullivan stood, along with everybody else, and the light quickly returned. He suddenly wanted another scotch, but thought he saw something glinting on the floor – a thin metal grate. As he watched, the vent opened, and what appeared to be a metallic insect perched on the edge, a jet-black lens situated where its head should be.

Someone cried out, but before Sullivan could react, the thing in front of him had sprung into the air on slim, articulated legs, and was hovering over him. He fell back and rolled over, getting to his feet, gasping fast breaths as cold fear clutched his heart.

He saw thin blue arcs of electricity streaming through the room, men falling in contorted shapes, wreathed in smoke. He heard gunshots and thought he saw security through the frosted, explosive-proof door, but the door wouldn't open; it was as if the room had been locked down from inside.

He glanced around for another way out and saw Ming-Tun's forehead momentarily illuminated by a thin blue light. Before he could say a word, the pencil-thin beam violently erupted from the back of his head, and Ming-Tun's body stood there for a second as his head melted into falling ashes.

Sullivan saw that he was the only one still standing and staggered back in horror as the terrifying metal creatures hovered around him.

He closed his eyes and realized two things. One: Leary must have suspected something could happen at this meeting, which was why he hadn't come. And two: He was now well and truly fucked.

***

Coca gave the word, and Forge breathed a sigh of relief.

The center of the OIV opened and Forge dropped through, guiding his fall onto the concrete block of the bank's lower levels with precise bursts from his thrusters. He landed on the lower section roof alongside his five men, with the meeting room just two stories down. Conrad burned a hole in the roof and they climbed in, cutting their way through two more levels.

Forge checked his feed and opened the comm to hear Coca talking.

"*I think security may have seen your drop-off. It's like a swarming ant hill down there.*"

"What about the target?"

"*Secure, but police are on their way. The Grifters will engage on sight and detonate when all other options have been exhausted. No trace will remain, except bodies and carbon ash.*"

Forge followed the others at a jog. They reached the first room on the correct floor and Jonns sent the door flying off its hinges with a casual back-hand.

They piled in, quickly executing the surprised office workers before continuing to a wide corridor with portraits of former investors on the walls.

At the far end, three security guards were trying desperately to open the doors to the meeting room. Dennis and Miller instantly vaporized them with quick bursts from their EP rifles.

Forge blasted the door to smithereens, and stepped over the fragments of glass and metal into the room. He immediately spotted Sullivan crouched down in the corner, and walked up to him. Forge simultaneously opened his mouth, revealing fast-revolving, razor-sharp teeth, while pressing his face towards Sullivan.

Jonns grabbed the politician by the neck and Sullivan gasped for air. "Have you ever traveled in a UFO, Earth creature?" Jonns grunted through his mask.

Sullivan whimpered and went loose. Jonns slung him over his shoulder.

"Keep him secure," Forge said, checking the feeds from the Grifters. "And re-engage your voice-scrambler, for Christ's sake."

The flash of gunfire appeared to be all around, then everything went quiet. Forge felt a tremor underfoot, accompanied by a tremendous booming thud.

"Sounds like the foundations are about to go," Forge said. "Time to exit."

They ran back down the corridor and through the room, leaping back through their entry holes up and onto the roof.

A beam of light was in his face – no, two beams – and he recognized helicopter gunships in the distance. He zoomed in on them and switched to thermal imaging, making out the heavy guns on their sides.

Forge was about to order his men to fire when he saw the Droniks speed away on the air, like mini sentinel missiles, heading for the incoming helicopters. He noticed them zip back and forth through the aerial vehicles, then red and blue flashes of electrical discharge hit the machines like a sledgehammer and both fell helplessly out of control. Man, those things were more useful than he'd ever imagined.

The OIV rippled into view as the holo-graphene plate shifted, and Forge signalled Jonns to get Sullivan up there before someone saw. He followed, and felt the metal zipping around him as the Droniks hovered aboard with them.

"Make sure Sullivan is still unconscious and restrained in his seat," he said to Jonns, before running through to the cockpit.

The pilot had brought them up to a safe altitude as small-arms fire rattled up at them.

"Drop the device," Forge instructed the pilot. "Then cloak and get us out of here."

He ran back to his seat and buckled in, feeling the vibration as the ship gained altitude.

"Switch your feed to Nine, and you'll see what a low-yield fission explosion looks like," he told his troops as they strapped themselves in.

The feed showed the Tianjin financial district with the bank at the center. Then the building rippled like liquid and fell in on itself, the glass tower collapsing into a shower of flickering shards, before a brilliant flash of yellow and red sent smoke billowing up into the air. The OIV bobbed crazily as they ascended on the edge of the shockwave.

"We're cloaked," Forge said, pulling off his helmet. "We'll drop the prisoner off and take the direct route back." He looked at the Droniks clinging to the walls of the OIV. "These are real nasty fuckers. Are they aware?"

"They don't like fucking swearing," Bryant said, grinning as he pulled off his goggles. "They aren't sentient, but they're as close to AI as you can get. The command algorithm is incredibly complex, yet simple in its implementation. I've heard the head designer is making improvements all the time. Just think of what these things can do."

Forge watched the Droniks as they clung silently to the wall of the ship, deactivated, for now, and thought of how far this technological rabbit hole really went. Would those things end up watching him?

He sat back, enclosed in his armor, and suppressed the thought. They were changing the world, after all – nerves were to be expected.

146

Transcript of Last Radio Communication with INS Kolkata

00 00 03   INS K   *Ready to begin test.*

00 00 07   Control   *Clock has begun. The package is in place. All signs looking good.*

00 00 12   INS K   *Begin the countdown, starting in—*

00 00 15   Control   *Uh, hold on, Kolkata. Unknown signatures on our scope.*

00 00 18   INS K   *Confirm hold, Control?*

00 00 25   Control   *Confirmed, Kolkata. We have multiple contacts inbound.*

00 00 30   INS K   *We see them. What are they... they've targeted us. Have they targeted us? Confirmed, Control! We're under attack!*

00 00 35   Control   *Protect the package at all costs! Fighters are scrambled, but attackers are moving too fast! We have no idea what they are, but—*

00 00 40   INS K   *Wait, they've gone! We have no contact, repeat no conta—*

00 00 47   Control   *Kolkata? Kolkata, you're not showing up on our scopes? Kolkata?*

Transcript ends

Chapter 9

The man lay dead on the carpet, his eyes rolled back in their sockets, smoke rising from his burned and charred skin, his hands frozen, fingers stretched out towards the revolver on the floor next to him. Bradley reached for the gun, but he couldn't pick it up, and then the dead fingers twitched and the corpse's eyes rolled forward, staring straight at him.

Bradley jerked awake. He slowed his breathing and looked at the stained yellow ceiling above, then over at Shana who was asleep beside him, still fully clothed, as was he.

After the crazy robots at the factory and the mad drive from Detroit, they'd arrived at the motel totally exhausted. They'd been unable to get Sheen on the drive, and had spent the evening trying unsuccessfully to get any news on the ancient TV.

They'd eaten tacos from the fast food joint across the street, finally leaving a hastily typed message with Sheen concerning the graphene and the serial number on the box. They'd eventually fallen asleep around 11 PM.

Bradley looked at the clock: 7.20 AM. At least he felt rested.

He was careful not to wake Shana as he got up and reached for his shoes. They'd need supplies for wherever they were going, and he'd seen a gas station no more than two blocks from here.

He quietly crept to the door, lifting the key from the table on his way out.

The sky was cloudy, the sun low in the sky. Cars passed him on the street, and Bradley pulled his collar up as he walked. He got to the corner and saw the Lexus parked at the far end of the next street. Hopefully it wouldn't be noticed.

He continued on to the gas station, passing under the yellow glow of its neon sign as he entered the shop.

A bald man with a mustache stood behind the counter, stocking cigarettes. Bradley mumbled a greeting and picked up a couple of toothbrushes, toothpaste, shower gel, and shampoo, then went over to the fridge for some water. He grabbed some energy bars, peanuts, gum, and a carrier bag to hold everything.

Walking to the checkout, he emptied the bag onto the counter, glancing down at the Kansas City Sun's front page: *Moscow burns in terror attack.*

"Strange shit, man," the clerk said, glancing at the paper as he scanned each item. "And they still haven't said what exactly happened. I've heard rumors, though."

"Rumors," Bradley said. "What rumors?"

"The internet," the man shrugged. "I haven't seen it, but I know people who know people who are saying… yeah? Well… something about… aliens."

"Aliens?" Bradley asked, paying with a twenty. "Do you really go for that?"

He took the bag and left the store, eating a raspberry-walnut cereal bar as he walked. He turned back up the street and looked back to where their car was parked.

Shit.

He found himself walking mechanically back toward the motel before the image of the three men standing around their stolen car had properly registered. He rounded the corner and started running, sprinting for the motel. They'd looked very much like the men he'd seen at the sushi place, but who were they? Had Hawk sent them?

Bradley reached the door and unlocked it with a furious twist of the key. When he walked in, he was surprised to see Shana sat up on the bed, the screen of her jacket sleeve glowing and Sheen's voice emanating from it.

"Sheen called while you were gone," Shana said. "I've already sent her pictures of the graphite stuff and the serial number. Are you okay?"

"We need to move!" Bradley said, running over to get his coat and other things. "There are men by the car and I think they'll be here soon!"

Shana's eyes grew wide, and she grabbed her shoes.

"Have you found something, Sheen?" Bradley asked as he packed. "Do you know what the graphene is being used for?"

"I don't know, but your discovery could well change that," Sheen said. *"What I do know is that the graphene plates were being sent to Las Vegas, Nevada. A scientist, specializing in light-bending and the effects of light distortion. His name is Jerry Pullins. I'll send you all the details. Head there and I'll be in touch if I hear something. But you need to hurry. Hawk's plan is gathering pace."*

Sheen didn't have to tell them twice. Shana thanked her and ended the call. Bradley retrieved his gun from under the bed and stowed it in the grocery bag before following Shana out the door. This was the second motel they'd left from in a hurry, and he wondered when and how this thing was going to end.

"The main road is over there," Shana said. "We could get another taxi?"

151

Bradley looked over his shoulder. "One of them is behind us and walking this way," he whispered. "Just keep walking and pray he doesn't notice us."

Shana took his arm and they started walking – quickly, but with no sense of urgency. Bradley wanted desperately to look over his shoulder again, but he was too scared. They reached the junction and he finally risked a glance as they crossed the street.

He felt the blood drain from his face. The man was right behind them, his face expressionless and his gray eyes looking straight ahead. Bradley thought of the gun in the bag. If this Fed was onto him he'd have to use it.

Or should I just let myself be arrested? How far would Hawk go to shut me up? He could have us both executed and no one would ever know.

Bradley forced himself to calm down and casually walked arm-in-arm with Shana further along the street. Then he saw something that lifted his spirits.

"Bus," he said. "Head for the stop over there."

They crossed the street and got on board. Bradley watched the man in black while Shana paid the driver, and then they headed towards the back.

"He didn't clock us," Bradley said, sitting down. "Thank goodness for that."

Shana sat opposite him. "I think this bus goes to the rail depot. Hopefully from there we can get a train to Flagstaff and then travel on to Vegas."

"We could take a plane, but I think we would have a further problem."

152

"You mean… you won't be able to get that gun through," Shana said, frowning.

"If you'd seen what I had, you'd think a gun was a good idea," Bradley said. "We won't be able to get that broken drone thing on board, either. And the plane's easily traceable. If anyone's looking for us, they'll find our IDs in the system."

"So how do you want to travel?"

"Get another car?"

"You want to steal another one?" Shana said, incredulously. "And you're packing a piece? You've really embraced the lifestyle, haven't you?"

"I didn't say we would steal it… and remember, this wasn't my idea," he muttered. "But this *is* my story. I uncovered it, and assuming we can figure this all out, I want to live to see it published." His mind went back to the dead security guard. "I don't know what will happen if those guys catch up with us. We certainly can't take any more chances."

"I do pick some strange men to hang around with, don't I? Not that I'm complaining." Her eyes met his and her hand gently caressed his leg. "There are worse people to be stuck with."

Bradley felt his face grow warm. "Thanks," he said. "I mean—"

"You're welcome," she said, moving her hand onto his. "Just don't get us killed. We'll figure this out somehow."

Bradley hoped she was right, but even with Sheen's help, the odds were firmly stacked against them.

The bus pulled into the train depot – a dozen coach lanes with accompanying shelters in the shadow of the station. A couple of buses were parked and a few people were waiting to board them as they pulled to a stop in Lane 3.

They got off, and Bradley zipped up his coat against the sudden chill as he followed Shana over to the main building and into the ticket office. He looked around while he waited, trying to spot anyone suspicious or unusual.

A woman's face was visible on the TV through the window of a nearby café. The subtitles declared she'd been close to the incident in Moscow:

"There were loud explosions, then sirens. I heard some weird squawking, like it was through a megaphone, and a strange language of the like I have never heard before. I didn't see anything, though. We were all quickly moving in the other direction."

So there was still precious little on the media. But he thought of the squawking the woman had mentioned, and the strange "voice" he'd heard back in the alleyway when the alien thing had knocked him unconscious. Was there something more to this? Had aliens really landed on Earth?

He saw Shana waving at him from the ticket office and hurried over. "How long until we leave?" he asked.

"There's a train leaving in an hour," she said. "Platform 8, just over there."

"Nothing sooner?"

She shook her head.

The hour passed slowly as they sat on an uncomfortable wooden bench just outside the train station, with each second stretching out further and further the nearer it got to the departure time.

154

Bradley must have dozed off, because the next thing he knew the train had pulled up to the platform. Then he saw the black car and the man standing next to it.

He grabbed Shana, shaking her awake. "They're here!" he hissed. "The Feds!"

Shana looked to where he was staring. The man was leaning against the car, sunglasses on, like he was casually waiting for someone. In the lane behind him, another man stood smoking a cigarette.

"And there's another one over by the taxi rank," Shana said. "How the fuck did they find us?"

"They must have traced the stolen car to Kansas City, then looked at possible escape routes. Or maybe that guy *did* see us getting onto the bus."

"They could be watching us with drones."

"If they were, they'd be on us right now," Bradley said. "But I can't see a way to the train without going past them."

Shana got up. "Walk with me," she said. "I'll be able to distract them. Trust me."

Bradley was about to walk with her, and then a weird thought hit him – what if she was with them? She'd just turned up and immediately gotten on board, and she'd figured the USB drive out damn quick. She could have been leading him all along, bringing him here to his fate.

"I don't think so."

"We can get past them, Brad," she insisted. "Why are you looking at me like that?"

"Give me the drive," he said, holding out his hand.

Shana looked anxiously at the men. "Why?"

"Because, suddenly, I'm not sure I can trust you."

Shana looked at him, furious now. "Listen, Wilcox. When I said you were lucky to have me, I wasn't joking. You think you'd have been able to get into that factory, stop the drones, steal a car, and escape? Don't get paranoid on me, Brad. You know you couldn't do this alone."

"And how come you're so good at it?"

"Intuition plus a dash of creativity," she said, clicking a button on her wrist. "And it's about to save your fucking ass."

Bradley heard the screeching wail of a car alarm blaring loud and close, then more alarms in the distance. He put his hands to his ears and saw the men running back towards their flashing and shrieking vehicles. Everyone had stopped, distracted.

Shana was halfway to the platform when he'd started to run, and for a brief moment Bradley thought he'd lost sight of her, but he glimpsed her blond hair as he reached the front of the first carriage. He climbed on breathlessly, showed the conductor his ticket, and walked past the few other passengers to the roomette compartment at the rear of the carriage where Shana was sitting, panting, and looking out the window.

"You decided to trust me, then," she said as he approached.

"What did you do?"

"I used the drive to set off their car alarms, of course. I also locked their cars in anti-theft mode – they'll soon discover that when they try to leave."

156

"So you aren't working for them," Bradley said, shoving his backpack onto the seat while sitting down himself. "But who *do* you work for?"

"You asked me that before."

"Well, I'm asking you again."

She swore under her breath and leaned back in her seat. "I don't know who those men are, but they may spot us, so calm down, will you?"

The carriage door closed with a firm clunk as the sweet sound of the departure whistle reassuringly echoed in their ears, and then the train began to slowly pull away from the platform. They kept their heads low as they passed the black car nearest the tracks, but Bradley caught a glimpse of one of the men looking around suspiciously and talking on a phone. Clearly, the distraction had worked.

They left the station behind as the train picked up speed. Bradley let out a sigh of relief, noting that Shana looked less agitated, also.

"So, *now* are you going to trust me?" she asked.

"I'm warming to you," he said.

"Warming to me? Well, thanks very much. That's real nice of you." Shana was looking out the window, not making eye contact with him. After a pause, she said, "I don't know too much about this Hawk guy. Do you really think he could be connected to the attack on Moscow?"

"We know he's connected with the graphene plant in Detroit," Bradley said, feeling exhausted as the adrenaline faded. "But is he acting alone, that's the real question. I don't think even a man of

Hawk's stature could finance something like this without having additional help."

Shana rubbed her eyes and looked back out the window. Bradley cursed under his breath. This was much bigger than just a news story, his reputation didn't matter anymore. He needed her and he needed her big time. Maybe she was on the level. Maybe there was more to her than just a lustful fascination in him.

"Do you want me to leave, Brad? Because I'll leave if you don't think I'm being totally honest with you."

She was still avoiding looking at him, and he sighed. "I'm sorry. You've helped me so much. It's just that I don't know who to trust anymore."

Her lips were still pursed when she turned her gorgeous blue eyes on him.

"You are so damn beautiful," he said before he could stop himself. She raised her eyebrows, and he looked away, annoyed at himself. "Sorry if I offended you."

She sighed. "Wilcox, there's something about you, you know?" She leaned over and kissed him on the cheek. "I'm going to trawl the net for something on Moscow. There's got to be something."

Bradley sat back, watching her work as the gentle swaying motion of the train coupled with the clack of the rails gradually calmed him. He felt his eyelids lowering and let sleep take its course.

***

A light flashed on passing each tenth mile, and at 22,369 miles long, that was a lot of candle power.

The elevator had only two levels – one, known as Tombside Station, far below the Cerbat Mountains in Arizona, and at the other end, spinning silently with the Earth's rotation, the gigantic Orbit Station. The whole thing was completely invisible to anyone on Earth thanks to the light-bending properties of its holo-graphene-coated titanium construction.

Hawk closed his eyes as he hit the 10,000-mile mark, thinking of the infinite black depths that Earth floated within, and the carbon titanium shell keeping him safe as he ascended inside this invisible machine, a high-speed projectile elevator heading for his nest at the top – the space station he had tethered to this very planet.

Despite his incredible intellect, Carrington had been as amazed as anyone when he'd been moved from the lower laboratories to the more extensive facilities up in Orbit, and even Hawk still felt a flutter in his stomach when he came here. Without a shadow of a doubt, the elevator would be one of the wonders of the modern world if the world could see it, but Hawk's mission was far greater than mere self-aggrandisement. Arrogance and greed was what had gotten the planet into this mess.

A tone sounded in his earpiece and Hawk's eyes flicked open. He reached into his pocket and switched on his phone. "Barb. Yes, put him on. What can I do for you, General?"

"*We have an issue, sir,*" Morgan's voice sounded.

"And what would that be?" Hawk replied calmly.

"*There was an attack on the graphene plant in Detroit. Two of our Mini Lazer Drones were fried and one is missing. We're working to retrieve the memory on the remaining two, but it's proving difficult.*"

"Send the memory cores up here," Hawk said, his mind racing. If anyone could get that data retrieved, it would be Carrington. "Has the factory been secured?"

"*Yes, sir,*" Morgan said. "*But government grunts arrived shortly afterwards. Strange thing is, they were pursuing a person of interest, name of Bradley Wilcox.*"

So Sheen's dog, Wilcox, hadn't gotten the message after all. Hawk didn't know whether to laugh or curse, so he did neither. "Who did the agents answer to?"

"*We detained the men and debriefed them as best we could,*" Morgan said. "*I managed to trace their orders to your friendly asshole, Mark Leary. I thought you'd want to know sooner rather than later.*"

Leary? "Thank you, General. Monitor Secretary Leary's agents. If they're after Wilcox, we can follow their trail and kill two birds with one stone."

"*And the graphene factory?*"

"Clear the site and switch production to one of our subsidiary companies, just to be safe. Now, if you'll excuse me, General, I have a meeting with regard to leading-edge technology that your men will soon put to the test."

"*Very good, sir,*" Morgan said. "*I'll keep you informed of any developments.*"

The line went dead just as the elevator cleared the 20,000 mile mark. Hawk took a deep breath. Even with the world on the brink of war, Leary and his bitch, Sullivan, were still trying to twist the President to their cause. At least Sheen had been acting out of some naïve moral obligation to humanity, but Leary was in it purely for the money. Petrochemicals had bought him yachts and homes in the Caribbean, but he and his kind would still carry on pushing their shameless agenda even as the world dried up and died around them. People like Leary were the sociopathic dark side of humanity – they had no place in Hawk's new world.

He slowed his breathing and focused on the flashing levels. He'd fix this broken society. He'd fix the whole sick fucking planet. Everything was in place, and now a patient and attentive mind-set was required.

Leary and Wilcox he could easily deal with – Sheen, too, if she interfered too much. Hawk just hoped the President would realize which side to choose.

The elevator reached the final mark and stopped without the slightest jolt. The doors opened onto the main gallery, an open space with a walkway curving around its gigantic circumference. More levels circled above and below, while transparent glass layers separated the various compartments which also acted as bulkheads in case a sudden loss of pressure was experienced. Massive reinforced Plexiglas windows were set into the walls, through which he could see the blue sheen of planet Earth gently curving far below. Hawk took a moment to absorb the beautiful panorama – its deep blue oceans, white cloud trails, and the green and brown continents. This was what he was fighting for, the beautiful, fragile, yet thoughtlessly abused Earth.

Two marines in silver exoskeletons arrived and saluted him.

"At ease," he said, smoothing his shirt with his hands.

The joints in their armor clicked rhythmically as they fell into step behind him, following him along the walkway to where it sloped down to the lower level. As he walked, he looked down to the vast cavern of floors below, where the Gallery gradually narrowed to the tether of the elevator's Earth cable. At this moment, the entire thing was spinning with the Earth, the counterweight pulling it taught and holding it at a precise altitude. From here, it was relatively simple to launch a wave of attacks upon the Earth via circumnavigating halfway around the moon, and what with the holo-graphene coating, the whole thing was totally invisible to the eye, to radar, to laser – anything just short of a physical collision, while the airspace was monitored incessantly. God, it was a beautiful thing, but nothing compared to the planet it had been built to protect.

Hawk entered the observatory, catching Carrington momentarily leaning over the rail, looking at the planet through the transparent floor beneath them. Above, the broad brim of the elevator hung, barely visible as its responsive panelling bent the light around it.

"My dear Ronald," Carrington said, straightening up. "How's life down there on the surface? Has the weather suited you?"

"It's the current climate that concerns me, not the weather," Hawk said, turning to dismiss the marines. "How are you doing up here, Oswald?"

Carrington pulled a tin from his lab coat's pocket and threw a couple of pills into his mouth. "No weather to speak of, nor much in the way of climate. No gossip, either, but the scenery is awesome, just awesome."

Hawk walked to the rail and checked his watch. "You've been very productive, Oswald. I knew you were the best man for the job."

"I've barely started," Carrington said, looking again at Earth. "The research on nuclear fission and my improvements to your

162

HSRCMD program have given me a lot of ideas." He pointed down at America's western coastline. The entire world was the target, now the next blow was about to be struck. There was a flash on the west coast. "San Francisco," Carrington said. "Maximum panic, minimum mess."

"Bang on schedule," Hawk said. "Now, let us get onto the real point of business."

"Come up to my office," Carrington said, closing the observatory's shutters with a wave of his hand. "I'll make you a brew."

They walked back up the walkway to where multiple elevator-platforms were situated, allowing access to the various upper levels of the Gallery. Hawk stepped onto the nearest elevator with Carrington following closely behind. As they rapidly ascended through the manufacturing levels to the launch bays and main control room, Hawk heard the muffled thump of machinery. "How's production?"

"With the new 3D printers? The Droniks are way ahead of schedule. The OIVs are also coming along, and I have some radical new designs that will go into effect shortly." Carrington was tapping his foot and gnawing on his lower lip. "How long will this project take?"

"Depends," Hawk said. "My advisors say three months, although I'm inclined to say four – people consistently surprise you. But don't worry, Oswald, you won't be stuck up here forever, and if things go according to plan, the Earth will be a much better place for you to return to than when you left it."

They passed the launch bay doors and reached the main control room. Carrington led Hawk into a large expanse where various personnel sat at control terminals. The terminals all faced towards a massive screen which depicted the space station's many levels and planned OIV flights, while simultaneously monitoring the elevator's Earth orbit.

The programmers looked up at Hawk's entrance, but quickly returned to their work.

"We can see the new orbital fighters from here," Carrington said, politely shooing a young woman from behind her desk.

He adjusted the screen and toggled through cameras until it showed an enormous metal frame with a pillar at each corner. Material was being extruded from a rapidly moving arm, building the frame for an OIV.

"The eight printers have seriously increased productivity and efficiency," Carrington explained to Hawk. "The ships are coated in holo-graphene armor before the hardware is installed and tested. It's intensive and complicated, but we could double production by manufacturing the electronic segments at the Tombside station and lifting them into orbit."

Well, increased efficiency would certainly offset the added risk.

"I'll have my engineers get straight onto it," Hawk said, admiring the image on the screen. "The quicker we complete the Maneuver the better. It's a shame we can't use this science back on Earth. Technology like this would certainly make the world a better place, but I suppose it would eventually get hijacked, and used to enrich the gluttonous political elite. Nobody down there could ever be trusted with it."

164

"I've already put your machines to good use," Carrington said. "The new Droniks are assembled. The software's taking somewhat longer, but I think you'll be impressed."

"I know you won't let me down," Hawk said, patting Carrington on the back.

"There's one detail that I am curious about."

"Oh?"

"The attack on Moscow," Carrington said. "I monitored the entire mission. I understand that it was a first strike, and I can see why you wanted to infiltrate the Bank of Moscow's network, but why the meteor fragment? What use is it?"

"The fragment was found in Siberian Tunguska back in the 1920s," Hawk said. "Something exploded over that area in 1908. You may have heard of it?"

"I have indeed. Fascinating stuff, but hardly worth stealing."

Hawk gestured to Carrington that they should head back to the elevator-platform. "There are two types of value," he said, as they walked. "Monetary and spiritual. Monetarily speaking, the meteor isn't by most people's standards worth much. However, within the upper echelons of the scientific and religious communities, it has incredible Earth-changing and spiritual applications."

"What do you mean, exactly?" Carrington asked. "And how come you know so much about it?"

"Let's just say we have seen a similar piece before," Hawk said, "and we know exactly where to look. The Ruskies never knew what they had."

Carrington looked at him, then laughed. "Christ, Ronald. I wouldn't even want to know what other secrets you have locked inside your head. Let me show you around the workshop. I'll introduce you to the latest generation of Droniks."

"Unfortunately, I have to return to DC," Hawk said, stepping onto the elevator platform. "I have a couple of ongoing issues with certain members of the Cabinet. But I would be eager to see your new designs in action."

"Understood," Carrington said, taking out his tin of pills. "I'll keep you updated."

"Thank you, Oswald. Oh, and I have a pair of damaged drones coming your way. I need the images from their databanks."

Carrington popped two pills into his mouth and nodded. Hawk watched him as he descended out of view. Things were running smoothly and Carrington's work was more than impressive. Hawk just hoped the kid's brain would last the course.

***

Officer Tom Banks had been riding his motorcycle through downtown San Francisco when the explosion happened.

The flash had been blinding, the energy released so powerful that cracks had appeared on the surrounding buildings, setting off car alarms and security systems. He'd waited for the ringing in his ears to pass, then got to his feet, hearing the screams and the blaring alarms. Al Qaeda, it had to be!

Banks attempted to contact HQ on his radio but no one was answering, and the mass of people around him weren't stopping. He tried to direct people to get to the nearest hospital, but even with his

166

badge out and his hand firmly on the grip of his gun they still wouldn't listen.

He'd gone back to his overturned motorcycle and had started to pull it upright when the shadow passed over him. When he looked up again, he wasn't able to explain what he saw.

The gun was violently pulled from his hand and a croaking voice snapped in his ears, then what appeared to be a weapon flashed and he'd felt the entire world pass through him on a searing dagger of heat and a final rush of adrenaline. His last thoughts were that they were under attack, but by something of which he had never experienced before.

***

When Bradley awoke, Shana was sitting opposite him, her face caught in the glow of the hologram screen. She noticed he was awake and lowered her arm.

"Sleep well?"

"Better than that taxi," he said, yawning.

"I was about to wake you," she said, moving the projection closer to him. "I found something."

Bradley looked at the website that was displayed on the hologram. "What's this?"

"It's from a video feed I found – Ukrainian, or something. I downloaded a clip before the site was taken down – which it was, very quickly."

"The site was shut down?"

"Watch the video and you'll see why."

Bradley watched the video while the faint rustle of static came over his earpiece. It was a gray street, filmed from almost ground level. A tank was burning in the near distance, and behind it shapes moved very quickly.

Then the camera focused on what looked like a man – or was it a man? – leaping forward with what appeared to be a segment of rock raised in one hand with some kind of futuristic weapon gripped in the other. Its oscillating screech was audible over the crackle of distortion, then it leapt out of shot and disappeared into thin air as the camera followed it upwards towards the sky.

Bradley's mouth fell open.

For a brief moment, a disc-shaped object seemed to appear, with smooth nodules lining its surface. It lifted on a circle of energy and vanished into the sky with a groan that set his teeth on edge.

"I've seen one of these things before," he said, "back in DC. Well, I didn't *see* it, precisely. It was somehow invisible, but I could sense its presence as being very close to me in the rain."

"You saw a UFO?" Shana said. "First it was just an alien, now there's an entire spaceship?"

"I didn't think you'd believe me," Bradley said, looking at the screen frozen on the blurred outline of the alien. "You were hardly pushing me for questions about the alien, were you?" He sat back. "Whatever's going on, this technology is far in advance of ours. Mini drones, the weaponry, an alien ship – they totally outclassed the Russian forces, and the media's been locked down, presumably due to the fear of the global chaos such news would create. Christ knows where the next attack will be. Things could really go downhill when that happens."

168

"But it's Hawk, right?" Shana said. "He's doing this, not aliens."

"Maybe aliens have control of his brain. Maybe they control Washington."

Shana rolled her eyes and looked away. "I really didn't believe you when you said you saw an alien back in that alleyway in DC."

"I don't know if they're aliens, but something incredible is happening. The technology is way out of this world, like that damn UFO thing that flew off. I mean, how the hell does it work? Where has it come from? And what about the way that thing jumped?"

"Maybe some kind of exoskeleton."

"Armor-plated power-suits are common on Earth, aren't they?"

"So they are aliens?" Shana said, staring at Bradley.

"No. I mean, I don't think so. I don't know."

"You know, I heard that Neil Armstrong actually saw aliens on the moon back in '69. Maybe we'll find out. Then you can ask one of those things if it's from Jupiter or New Jersey."

"All I know is that the thing could speak. It had awful breath, and it didn't like the look of me."

Bradley opened his bag and lifted out the broken drone, being careful to check that the blinds of the carriage compartment were still shut. He turned to Shana.

"Can you look up stuff on, I don't know, 'flying insect drones' or something? Whatever's happening, the graphene is being made right here on Earth. We've got to speak to this scientist in Vegas – presumably a human – about light technology. And this robot thing was made somewhere, but where?"

Shana nodded, her gaze returning to the screen.

Bradley shoved the drone into the bag and leaned back against the window, trying to calm himself, prepare himself. He'd need to be alert for Vegas and their visit with Doctor Jerry Pullins, especially if the Feds were there to meet them.

Chapter 10

Hawk watched the sun disappearing behind the buildings from the back seat of his car, noting the orange haze in the sky caused by the cocktail of hydrocarbons and carcinogenic particulates that the human race seemed so intent on dispersing to the four corners of the globe.

He felt the familiar anger grow at the thought of all this wanton damage, most of which could easily be corrected if it wasn't for the moneyed interests of those who viewed any form of regulation as somehow detrimental to business. What with China and the other emerging economies cutting ever-greater corners, US business prospects were only going to get worse as they attempted in vain to try and keep up.

They turned onto a dirt road, and Hawk thought back to Vietnam – a paradise that had fallen victim to a blend of politics and greed. The jungles and fields had teamed with life and beauty, even as it was invaded by the hell of warfare – a mechanized abattoir that could only have been conceived by the collective mind of Man.

He'd accepted it at the time. War was inevitable, no matter how virtuous a society. There would always be evil, and the Communists had to be stopped. But he'd soon realized that evil was far more subtle. It lived in the heart of every man and manifested itself in unexpected ways.

Now, after decades of relative stability, the sad truth was that the planet was losing a war waged upon it by the very people who thought themselves so wise and capable. The environment was treated as a resource to rape, wildlife was seen as a mere commodity, and now that the Far East had picked up the mantle, Hawk knew the end was in sight. The Earth would be ravaged and that would be that.

The car slowed as they reached the barrier. An armed soldier lifted the long arm of metal, waving them past.

There were thirty prisoners on the site, all of them high-security, and half of them considered dead by the world at large. Hawk wasn't a fan of such places, though he knew they had to exist given the injustice and hypocrisy endemic within the modern democratic system. Today, though, he was excited, because the prisoner in question was Terrance Sullivan, and if anyone deserved what he got, it was that corrupt son-of-a-bitch.

The car stopped outside what appeared to be an abandoned building, the driver opened the door. Hawk got out and stretched, watching as a man in a blue suit walked across the concrete to meet him, flanked by two marines.

"Get yourself a cup of coffee, Bill," Hawk said to the driver. "I'll be an hour at most."

Bill thanked him and headed off as the man in the blue suit arrived.

"Mr Hawk," he said, reaching out to shake his hand. "Jack Colbern. Can I get you some refreshments, sir? Tea? A sandwich?"

Hawk declined – traitors like Sullivan always made him lose his appetite. "I would like to see the prisoner immediately," he said. "And I need strict privacy. This is the matter of the highest security."

"He's already been transferred in preparation for your arrival," Colbern said. "The guard present has clearance."

"Not good enough, I'm afraid," Hawk said. "This is beyond classified."

172

The man frowned. Even here, in the domestic equivalent of Guantanamo Bay, protocol was usually followed.

"Very well, sir," he said. "I'll see that you're alone."

They walked across the concrete to an old gray building with peeling paint and broken windows. Inside, the floor was covered in dust. Hawk followed Colbern into the back, flanked by the two marines. Steps led down into the cellar, and the short corridor ended in an elevator that would take them down to the cell-block.

Colbern pulled the door firmly across before they descended upon the whirr of a motor.

"The prisoner was quite a handful, Mr Hawk," he said. "But he understands the gravity of his situation now."

"What has he told you?"

"That he's innocent," Colbern said. "That he's a loyal patriot. You know, the usual."

"If only it was true," Hawk said. "People like him will say anything."

"He also claims he was abducted by some kind of alien force."

"The mind is such a fragile thing," Hawk said, contriving a concerned frown. "But some of the intel coming out of Russia and other hotspots around the globe is also troubling. It's possible the prisoner is associating that with the military operation we carried out to get him."

Colbern frowned in return. "Does the intel concern aliens, sir?"

Hawk opened his mouth, paused, then said, "I can't really speak on the matter, Mr Colbern. Things should become clearer in the next few days, I'm sure."

Colbern looked agitated and Hawk turned away, his face stern. Internally, he was just about containing his amusement. If "aliens" did indeed land on Earth, people most certainly would believe it, he was sure of that.

The elevator reached the bottom of the shaft, stopping with a heavy jolt. One of the marines pulled the door open. They walked along the dusty corridor, past thick metal doors and panels of one-way glass, until they reached the very end.

Hawk looked through the glass and saw Sullivan pacing the room, his jaw coated in stubble and his eyes wide and bloodshot.

"He hasn't slept since he was brought in," Colbern said.

"Good," Hawk said. "More likely he'll slip up."

The marines unlocked the door and Colbern opened it. "There's an alarm in the wall, just in case," he said. "Are you sure you don't need any assistance?"

"I'll call you when I'm done."

Hawk waited until the three of them were gone, then walked into the room. The lights activated as he entered, and he saw Sullivan on the other side of the screen.

The prisoner's eyes grew even wider when he saw Hawk.

"Secretary Sullivan," he said. "I believe you could use a shave."

Sullivan walked up to the glass. "Hawk," he said. "What… what is this?"

Hawk pulled a chair over to the glass. "I thought I'd made it clear that things were going to change."

Sullivan wiped his mouth with a shaking hand. "That was you, wasn't it? Those things!" he said. "All those people killed?"

"I think both of us are content with some collateral damage," Hawk said. "But our agendas are quite different. I'm saving the world, Terrance, while you want only to line your greedy pockets whenever you can."

"The market governs our every action, Hawk!" Sullivan spat. "You think you're above the fucking law?"

Hawk chuckled. He loved it when people tried to argue for the legitimacy of the free market. "You and Leary are playing Monopoly," he said, his smile fading. "But I don't play games, Terrance."

Sullivan swallowed. "I was just following Leary—"

"I couldn't really give a shit about your pathetic schemes to get rich," Hawk interrupted. "There are a million people like you out there, and you will all learn the error of your ways."

"So what am I doing in here?" Sullivan snapped. "I demand that I talk to the President! I'm a citizen of the United States, God-dammit!"

"Shut the fuck up!" Hawk said, letting his rage take hold for a second. "You aren't fit to breathe American air, let alone dictate policy! You've done nothing but enrich yourself at the expense of others, and you dare claim to be a patriot of our country?"

Hawk realized he was standing, and quickly seated himself again. Sullivan was pale and silent.

"The reason you are here and not already dead in a ditch somewhere is because you know something," Hawk said, this time controlling himself. "Something that can assist me."

"What?" Sullivan said, eagerly.

Hawk sneered. The man was a rat abandoning ship. Well, what had he expected? "Leary had Sheen tailed back in DC," he said. "And my people discovered federal agents operating on his orders in Detroit. I want to know what he's looking for."

"What guarantees do I have you'll let me go?"

"The only guarantee you'll get from me if you talk is that I won't have bamboo shoved under your nails," Hawk said, leaning forward. "Something I learned in Vietnam. Believe me, your associate Mr Leary will get no such courtesy."

Sullivan didn't say anything, but Hawk could see his brain working. The man was a spineless opportunist, following Leary's every lead. Now that he'd been backed into a corner, there'd be little problem extracting the information he needed.

"Leary was onto you, Hawk," Sullivan said, finally. "You aren't as smart as you think you are."

"I want details, Sullivan, and I want them now."

Sullivan walked up to the glass. "Tunguska," he said.

Hawk felt his pulse quicken. *The meteor?* "What about it?" he said, feeling cold.

"You found something, right? Something way out there from outer space?"

"Care to enlighten me on what I'm supposed to have found, Terrance?" Hawk said, keeping his voice calm. "And make it quick. My patience is already stretched damn thin."

"It's common knowledge that you have shares in cutting-edge algorithmics," Sullivan said. "I've seen how much money you've been funnelling into your little pet projects, and all of your research leads back to that meteor fragment you acquired two decades ago."

176

Hawk starred at Sullivan, unblinking. The algorithm was the key to the Maneuver, granting his scientists the ability to build the intricate equipment and transmitters necessary for the operation of the space elevator and the orbital fighters, and now with the new meteor fragment he'd just relieved from the Russians, even greater applications would soon be in his hands. If such information got out, if they learned what those apparent lumps of rock really were, what they contained, Hawk would lose his greatest advantage.

But Leary and Sullivan didn't know – not really.

"I fail to see how a lump of extra-terrestrial rock is supposed to help my programmers," he said, looking Sullivan in the eye.

"Well, that depends on where the lump of rock came from, doesn't it?" Sullivan said. "I haven't seen any of the research, but Leary thinks it's more than a rock – in fact, he managed to trace a leak from one of your labs." Sullivan was smiling now, clearly enjoying Hawk's apparent discomfort. "Someone got hold of your research, Hawk, and Leary wants that intel, too."

"Who?" Hawk snapped.

Sullivan leaned back in his chair. "Someone who doesn't trust you," he said. "Someone who's never trusted you."

"Who?" Hawk said again, gritting his teeth.

Sullivan laughed, but he managed to pull himself together. "What am I getting out of this, Ronald?"

"It would be very helpful to you if you told me," Hawk replied.

A long pause followed. "Christine Sheen," Sullivan said, finally. "She was nosing around your business and Leary found out."

Hawk's mind raced. So Leary had been tailing her? *This is nonsense,* he thought to himself.

"Why did Sheen have people working off stolen blueprints?" Sullivan said. "And why did she meet secretly with a reporter in DC? Leary had the stolen research traced to her. He thinks Sheen has duplicated your work, and obviously it's worth a lot of money."

Hawk took a deep breath. He'd suspected Leary of some knowledge, but he'd no idea it would be linked to Sheen and that reporter Wilcox. If she'd somehow managed to replicate his technology and if Wilcox realized what he'd gotten his hands on, who knew what complications could arise. And there'd already been that incident at the graphene factory.

He may have underestimated her, but the fact that Sheen and Leary were both still coming to work showed they'd failed to recognize how much danger they'd just put themselves in.

Hawk stood. "Thank you, Mr Sullivan. You've been most forthcoming."

"Well?" Sullivan said. "What about me?"

"I'll have someone come get you," Hawk said. "Once I've had a chance to speak with

Mr Leary, naturally."

"Just tell me one thing, Hawk," Sullivan said. "Those things, those aliens. They're your doing, right? It's all a part of this Maneuver thing?"

Hawk looked him in the eye for a second. "Such an imagination, Terrance. It's a shame you had to become a politician."

He left the room, ignoring Sullivan's shouts and the banging on the glass, and followed the corridor back to the elevator where Colbern was waiting with the two marines.

"The prisoner was very cooperative," Hawk said.

178

"Do you want him kept on site, sir?" Colbern asked.

Hawk shook his head. "Clear the facility and utilise the standard disposal protocol." Nothing more needed to be said.

They took the elevator back up to the surface. Hawk met his driver, his mind now focused on what needed to be done. Sheen had crossed the line. Leary had proven himself to be an unacceptable risk. Perhaps the entire Cabinet had outlived their usefulness, too.

"Back to the White House, Bill," he said, settling himself in the back. "I have work to do."

***

Carrington scanned the lines of code, capturing each number with his eye and linking them simultaneously into the incredibly complex algorithms that were developed by his team of programmers – not forgetting the additional resources from his own brilliant mind, of course.

He finished the last one and turned to look the monitor which displayed his team. Each programmer was working fast and efficiently, punching data quicker than any lab Carrington had ever previously worked in. Every man and woman utterly engrossed in their work, stopping only for essential food and sleep, apparently caring for nothing else.

His watch beeped and he realized it was past 2 AM. He'd been up for eighteen hours and had worked at his present station for the last nine, and yet he still felt wide awake.

He got up and rubbed his eyes, knowing he would be unable to sleep, so he decided to check the 3D printers situated on the lower level. The first consignment of his newly-designed IQ modules had come up from Tombside, and what with the next generation of Droniks coming off the production line, he might as well oversee the installation procedure.

Carrington passed the usual guards and technicians on his way to the elevator – all of them so rigid and doggedly intent on doing their jobs, even with the incredible view spread out below them.

He paused to watch the horizon where the east coast glowed against the darkness, an electrically powered cobweb with an entire species caught within it. There was no way out – with only an exponentially increasing need to go faster, work harder.

Carrington knew he was a product of that wacky world, but even he, a genius when it came to technological systems, sometimes doubted the wisdom of such an artificially-inflated "bubble." What would happen when humanity could no longer sustain the system? Would it come crashing down with a sudden bang, or would it be a more gradual slide into darkness?

He snorted in amusement. Christ, he'd been listening to Hawk far too much. But there was no going back, whatever the dangers. Now, at least, there were people like him, with the clarity, the vision, to recognize such risk – people like him, like Hawk.

He entered a nearby elevator and felt it rapidly drop, then exited seconds later onto the factory floor. One of the techs was down there overseeing the systems. Carrington couldn't remember his name – maybe he'd never even introduced himself. The task at hand was the only thing that mattered now.

"Mr Carrington," the technician said. "Have you come to inspect the first of the new models?"

Carrington didn't reply. His eyes had already been drawn to the massive Dronik on the construction pad.

It bore little resemblance to the tiny models he'd initially used, with only the cluster of eyes and sensors at the front reminiscent of the primitive insectoid machines he'd devised back at MIT. However, this was the size of an F-15, or about half the size of an OIV, and it weighed twice as much as any jet with the newly-installed MAG fusion engine. Two weapon pods bulged beneath the anti-gravity system, but it was behind the weapons, and sensor clusters, that the real product of his genius was installed.

"The IQ modules arrived an hour ago," the technician said, passing Carrington a tablet. "We've installed the first one as ordered and have run all the computer models. It's running perfectly."

Carrington looked over the specs. Everything was there and seemingly correct. Given the incompetence he found at every level in both government and corporate firms, it was refreshing to have people he could rely upon. Hawk had assembled a team of the best, no doubt about that.

"How long until it can launch?" he asked.

"It's prepped," the technician replied. "I thought you'd want it ready sooner rather than later."

"Make sure it's recording," Carrington said. "And see if you can get Hawk on the comm. I want him to see what the new weapons are capable of."

The man immediately began the process of firing up the countdown program together with the activation sequence. Carrington took the steps down to the factory floor and approached the Dronik, marvelling at its seamless construction.

The holo-graphene plate shimmered in the light as the computers ran through every configuration, and it became momentarily translucent as it bent the light around itself. Carrington knew that armor-plated maniacs like Colonel Forge and his men would always be necessary, but with these new machines, Hawk would have a weapon that had never been seen before – fast, undetectable, practically invulnerable, and devoid of emotion.

He walked past it to the observation platform and looked down at the 3D printers where a dozen more Dronik chassis were being constructed. He smiled. Very occasionally, he impressed even himself.

Carrington heard a clunk and saw the prepped Dronik being lifted onto the launch rail. It connected with a sharp click and there was a sudden low hum as the thrusters engaged on low power.

He heard the technician call him and walked over to the terminal where Hawk's face filled the screen.

"Good morning, Ronald," Carrington said. "I thought you might be up."

"*I'm always available, Oswald,*" Hawk said, his eyes bright and alert. "*You've received the first batch of modules?*"

"The first one's already been installed," Carrington said. "And they're working exactly as predicted in the development sequence. We're ready to launch."

Hawk shifted in his seat, and Carrington realized he was in a car. The guy just didn't stop.

The technician moved aside to let Carrington access the controls. The Dronik slid along the rail and into the launch bay where heavy steel shutters slammed closed, locking it off from the space station proper.

"The algorithms will take over once the firing sequence has begun," Carrington said, his hands moving swiftly over the keys.

"*Could this code ever be exploited?*" Hawk asked.

"Not unless someone has access to all the algorithms," Carrington replied. "And given its mathematical complexity, I think that it is safe to say that our Droniks are way beyond the capabilities of other sovereign states."

"*Begin the test,*" Hawk said. "*I'll look over the technical aspects later.*"

Carrington mumbled an affirmative and began the launch protocols. The countdown began, and he watched the energy levels rise as the drive warmed up.

"Channelling power to defensive systems," the technician said.

Carrington watched the flowchart on screen. Everything was functioning correctly, but the key moment would be when the IQ module was started.

"Monitor ground agencies," he said. "We want a response, but not until the Dronik has safely cleared our space."

The energy spiked. Now was the time. "Launch."

The glass window flashed, there was a mild tremor, and when Carrington looked again the Dronik was gone.

"Camouflage is active," the technician said.

Carrington's finger hovered over the screen. Once the IQ module was activated, there'd be no going back for any of them.

He tapped the screen and felt a flutter of satisfaction as it started. The Dronik was already over Canada, its holo-graphene armor functioning perfectly. Once it revealed itself, the Canadians wouldn't wait around.

"The Dronik is following its programmed instructions," Carrington said. "Dropping camouflage… now."

"The Canadians will scramble fighters," the technician said.

"Yeah, and so will our side," Carrington replied. "Uncle Sam's not exactly immune to the alien threat – the event in San Francisco proved that," he affirmed, watching eagerly as multiple blips appeared on the screen. "Got any popcorn?"

He smiled at the technician's look of surprise.

"Don't worry. It's heading north, our guys won't be able to catch it."

He switched the monitor to the Dronik's internal display and saw the planet speeding past beneath them.

"Time to sit back and relax," he said. "Our baby will take care of things."

***

Captain Tim Benton had flown thousands of hours in his CF-18 Hornet, including missions over Iraq, Serbia, and Libya. But now, with the news of recent alien attacks, he felt rather more nervous than he had during his first flight in a single-prop Beechcraft back in his teens.

His men called out over the radio, each giving their positions and coordinating their advance.

The bogie had been spotted by Peterson air force base in Colorado, the home of North American Air Force Command, traveling over Ontario and moving fast – much too fast to be a plane. Benton had been sceptical of what he'd heard from the higher-ups, but the damn thing was maneuvering at speeds that no human could possibly survive. Could it really be an extra-terrestrial threat?

"I've never seen anything fly that fast. It's gotta be doing fucking Mach 50."

"Shut it, Hunter," he said. "Stay spread out. We need to cover its approach vector."

Lieutenant Lenitz's voice came over the radio.

"It keeps changing direction, sir. Where's it headed?"

"Just focus on the intel, Lenitz," he said, "and watch each other's backs. We'll lock on when it's in range. It's fast, but it's got a heat signature. If it thinks it's getting through without a fight, it's going to be disappointed."

The other pilots signalled their understanding as they converged on the UFO's position. US planes were coming from other directions. One way or another, that thing was going to learn it couldn't invade Canadian airspace with impunity.

Ground control was a constant murmur in his ear, advising and assisting. The enemy really was flying unpredictably, but it was aiming straight for them, almost like it wanted a fight.

"It's coming in from the southwest," he said. "Hunter, can you get a lock?"

"It's too fast! It keeps disappearing! I think it's… what the f—"

Hunter's line went dead. Benton wished it were a malfunction but he knew it wasn't.

"Close in on its position," he said, trying to keep his voice calm.

Lenitz called out over the radio, then Turner, but each line in turn went silent.

Hunter checked his radar, but the screen was a blur of static, then his radio crackled so loudly he thought his head was going to split. He pulled the jack free with a curse and checked the back-up systems, but there was nothing.

Hunter's eyes strayed to the photograph on the dash of his wife and daughter. He realized he wasn't going to see them ever again.

He saw a flash of metal far off. Time slowed as he pulled back on the control stick, sending him into a spin as proximity alerts began shrieking loudly.

The flash surprised him, then a sudden heat wrenched his breath from him, and the last thing he saw was brilliantly white metal and multiple red eyes.

***

Carrington turned to Hawk on the monitor.

"How'd you like that, Ronald?" he asked. "Those maneuvers weren't programmed by us. It thinks autonomously, and will learn every nanosecond it's in the air – at the equivalent of 100 hours for a human pilot."

"*Most impressive and very effective, Oswald,*" Hawk said, grinning. "*Get the rest up and running. We'll deploy them immediately.*"

"I can't wait to see what the media thinks of these," Carrington said. "And I have a few modifications in mind which should make them a little more creative."

186

"Try to get some rest," Hawk said. *"We're ahead of schedule and I don't want you to wear yourself out."*

"Okay, sure," Carrington said, but there was no way he was going to sleep now.

He signalled to the technicians to prepare for the Dronik's return, and made sure all the relevant data had been recorded and sent to Hawk. Then he went back to work on the algorithm. No time like the present.

***

Most of the train passengers were asleep, but Bradley had heard a few discussing issues with their phones when he had gone to get a drink at the buffet car.

They were also talking about what had happened in Russia with a certain air of nervousness beginning to unfold, but for the moment there was enough doubt in place to stop a full-blown panic from occurring. Bradley just hoped that they wouldn't encounter any further problems once they'd gotten to Vegas, which he estimated would be about three hours after the train finally stopped at Flagstaff.

He yawned and tried to get comfortable. They'd been on this damn train for hours now and he'd been dozing most of the way.

"Bored?" Shana asked.

"Yeah. This train ride seems to be going on forever. God knows what's happening out there."

"We could have taken a plane."

"We already discussed that."

"Try this," Shana said, taking the jacket off and passing it to him. "It's still plugged into the algorithm."

Bradley put the jacket on, and thumbed the interface on its cuff, immediately seeing the search engine appear.

"I'll see if I can find any news," he said.

"Last I checked it was all watered down. Typical fake media."

Bradley typed in "alien attacks" and a large volume of news came up. There had been a few personal accounts of the Moscow incident, showing only amateur video footage that covered most of the channels. He browsed several sites referring to a similar attack on San Francisco, but they all came back with only the barest details being given.

"Everything's being suppressed," Shana said. "I can't get my phone network up anymore, and I bet you anything they've been taken down to stop further panic spreading."

Bradley cursed. The internet was supposed to be the ultimate information source, with immediate access to anything anywhere, but whatever people claimed, it was still very much owned by governments and corporations. The moment it became a problem was the moment accessibility ended.

Fortunately for them, they had the drive.

Bradley clicked on the History icon and saw the information on Jerry Pullins immediately display. Shana had found his website and his organization, Photonix Inc. He scanned the text and looked over the company's various products and services: photovoltaic panels, LED illumination, light-measurement technology, UV technology, but nothing about bending light.

"You think this guy will be there when we arrive?" Shana asked, looking over his shoulder at the screen.

"If he isn't, we're hitting the casinos," Bradley said. "But there is a definite connection between him and Sheen, so there must be something there – there has to be."

"You know, I'm glad I bumped into you, Brad," Shana said, a serious expression on her face. "I hate to think how much trouble you'd have gotten into without me."

"Yeah, well, trouble and I go way back. In fact, we're on first-name terms."

"For sure, I can certainly agree with that," Shana replied.

"I forgot to ask if you had found anything on that drone thing," Bradley said, removing the jacket and passing it back to Shana. "Any leads?"

"As you'd expect, there are a lot of companies working on drone technology, if that's what this thing is," Shana said, pulling the jacket back on and zipping it up. "I narrowed it down to a couple of companies in Japan and one in Germany, but they don't have anything like this. There was a young guy in MIT a few years back working on something similar, but I can't imagine him having the resources. He still lives with his parents."

Bradley felt the hair on his neck prick up.

"What's his name?" he asked.

"Oswald Carrington," Shana said. "Apparently a very bright young guy by all accounts, but he keeps a low profile and he's hardly a global player."

"We need to check him out," Bradley insisted.

Shana typed the name on the jacket keypad and multiple images appeared. "I'll try MIT," she said. A picture of a young man in glasses emerged, a bored expression on his face.

Bradley opened a link to his work at MIT and immediately found further photographs of his work.

"Have you seen these designs?" he asked, scrolling down the page with mounting certainty.

"No, I assumed we'd be looking for a company," she said, frowning.

Bradley shook his head. "No, I think we're looking for a genius, someone who thinks abstractly, someone who has new ideas." He froze. "Holy shit."

Shana leaned closer and Bradley clicked the link: *House Invasion Leads to Manhunt.*

"He's fucking vanished?"

"The roof was torn off," Bradley said, feeling cold. "Neighbors reported an explosion and strange lights in the sky, but the authorities have found nothing. Apparently he isn't the most stable of individuals. They're claiming an experiment must have somehow gone wrong or something like that and now he's gone on the run." He looked at Shana. "That's him, it has to be. Hawk must have him somewhere and I wouldn't mind betting that he's behind the appearance of these things, willingly or not."

Shana swore quietly. "You could be on to something."

"Hawk doesn't think like a journalist," Bradley smiled. "If we can stay one step ahead, we may have a fighting chance."

"That's assuming this Photonix guy can give us something."

"Something this big can't be kept entirely under wraps," Bradley said, "even by someone as powerful as Hawk."

Bradley looked out of the window and realized they were slowing down. He craned his neck to see what was going on and swore under his breath.

A black car was traveling alongside the train, and looking further ahead, to where the track curved, he could see two more cars parked on the tracks. A man in sunglasses was frantically waving and jabbing his finger for them to stop.

Bradley jumped up and made his way to the front of the carriage.

"It looks like the Feds have caught up with us," he said to Shana as the train came to a grinding stop.

"If they get on board, we're done for," Shana said, getting up.

Bradley gritted his teeth. He thought about contacting Sheen, but there was no guarantee she'd answer or indeed that she'd be able to do anything. If Hawk had sent these men, a shallow grave would most certainly be waiting in the desert.

"Get your things," he said.

"What's going on?"

"We're going to get arrested, unless you have a better idea?"

She reached into her bag and took out the damaged drone. "Desperate times call for desperate measures."

Shana stood and walked up to the front of the carriage, ignoring his questioning glance. What the hell was she up to? Bradley slung his pack over his shoulder and followed her, smiling at the other passengers, who were looking at them with suspicion.

"Return to your seat, ma'am," the conductor said. "We'll be on our way again soon."

Shana held the drone up to him. "Open the doors and tell everyone to get out now," she said. "Unless you want me to detonate this fucking bomb."

The conductor looked startled. Shana glared at Bradley and mouthed the word "gun." He looked at her in disbelief. This wasn't how he'd envisaged their journey going!

"Now, lady," the conductor said calmly, "I'm sure we can clear this up."

"I told you to get out now!" Shana screamed. She reached into Bradley's bag, pulled out the automatic and levelled it at the conductor.

A mad frenzy broke loose, with all passengers making a panicked clamber for the doors, while Shana gave the conductor a helping kick off the train.

The men in black suits were heading straight for their coach, and Bradley ducked down, pulling Shana with him.

"I hope your plan goes further than just compounding our crimes!" he yelled at her. "They're gonna think we're fucking terrorists now!"

"We need to get the train moving again!" she yelled back, shrugging off his hand and jumping through the carriage door opposite to the incoming Feds. "Hurry, will you?"

Bradley followed her on through, jumping down onto the trackside and almost tripping over someone's discarded suitcase which had been thrown from the carriage.

The other passengers were running away from the train in all directions, looking around in confusion, but Bradley and Shana ran straight down the track, making it to the front locomotive without any confrontation.

Shana climbed up onto the huge engine, tapping on the window with the barrel of the gun, and shouting to the startled engineer to open the door. He opened it with a yank, then stumbled back with his hands in the air.

"Get this fucking thing moving!" Shana shouted as she climbed aboard the engine.

Bradley jumped up after her, watching as the engineer hesitantly sat back in his seat while simultaneously slowly pushing the drive handle forward. Then he heard the familiar sound of gunshots. Bradley realized he was laughing, but all he felt was cold fear – fear, and a desperate need to escape.

"I can't see them!" Shana cried, looking out the window. "What if they're already aboard?"

"Speed up, man!" Bradley shouted to the engineer.

"This thing weighs a ton," the engineer replied in a shaky voice. "I could detach the carriages if you want."

"Yes!" Bradley yelled. "Do it now!"

The engineer moved towards a handle at the rear, pulled it up, and then cranked it. There was a clunk as the carriages slowly disconnected from the locomotive, and the engine started to gain precious speed.

"Now keep this thing running," Bradley said. "And keep your eyes on the track. She'll let that gun loose on you if you try anything."

The engineer nodded and returned to his seat, flinching as he passed Shana.

Bradley rolled down the window on the other side of the engine. The Feds were jumping down from the slowing carriages and making for their cars. Bradley laughed even louder.

"Viva Las Vegas!" he roared, before a bullet ricocheted off the metal door, making him sidestep rapidly backwards.

"We won't make it to Vegas if we can't stop them," Shana said.

Bradley heard the window smash and felt a bullet zip past him. He peeped through the remains of the glass pane and saw two cars keeping pace with them, and another stopped dead further back in a cloud of red dust, apparently having strayed too close to the track.

At least the odds had gotten slightly better, but they were still in serious shit. They'd stolen property, made a bomb threat, and now they were having an armed exchange with federal agents. And that was ignoring the fact that one of the most powerful men in America wanted them dead.

"We're almost at Flagstaff," he said. "What are they doing?"

"They're keeping their distance now," Shana said. "But they're still with us and they've probably radioed for help. What if they try to block the track or something?"

"Can you short out their engines again?"

"Maybe," she said. "Take this." She passed the gun to him and began examining the drone in her hands. "This drone thing still has plenty of juice in it. Maybe I can get it started."

One of the cars pulled up alongside the cab, keeping level on the road running parallel to the track. Then the sound of sirens cut through the roar of the loco's engine, and Bradley saw lights further off and gaining.

"The police have also joined us," he said. "I think we're gonna have to stop this. I'm going to throw the gun out the fucking window. We're outnumbered and if anything happens to you... well, that would be my fault. I brought you into this and—"

He heard a high-pitched whine and spun around, then almost choked when he saw the drone in Shana's hand light up.

"What the fuck are you doing?" the engineer screamed.

"You just keep the train going," she said, as the drone ascended above them with another whine. "They won't know what hit them."

***

Carrington was deep in his work when the alarm algorithm initiated. He frowned and opened the file, looking for whatever Dronik had activated.

He watched the trace pass through the network, leaping from satellite to satellite until Arizona appeared on the screen.

The serial number scrolled down as his eyes strayed to the two damaged Droniks sitting on the desk next to him – their memory cores were fried, though the basic functions were just about working, but more worrying was the one that had gone missing. And now there it was, five miles outside of Flagstaff and moving.

Carrington took the phone from the cradle and dialled Hawk's private line. The woman he knew only as Barb answered.

"Hey," he said. "Get Hawk. He's going to want to hear this, believe me."

When he saw the flash, Bradley thought there were more police cars on their tail, but Shana's cry of surprise sounded more like triumph than fear.

He glanced over his shoulder and saw the car traveling alongside them, the driver's cold stare and the man in the passenger seat leaning through the window, his pistol aimed directly at them. There was a silver blur, a crackle of blue energy, and the car's rear tire burst into flame, sending it skidding onto its side and crashing into a shrub, while also raising a thick cloud of red dust.

"Got him!" Shana cried.

"*What* got him?" Bradley shouted.

"The drone has pre-programmed routines," Shana said, gripping the rail beside him and pulling herself closer. "Once I'd removed the shutdown on its motor, the drive linked straight to it and set the vehicles as targets. This shit is incredible!"

Bradley shook his head. Was she completely unhinged?

He saw another car coming up fast, then a flash erupted under its hood, cracking the windshield and causing an eruption of steam and coolant that blinded the driver, forcing him to a stop.

There was another blur of metal and one of the locomotive's remaining side windows suddenly exploded as the insect-like machine entered the cab and clung to the control console. Bradley recoiled in his seat, letting out a string of expletives as it turned its glowing white sensors on him.

"Calm down, Brad," Shana said, thumbing the sleeve of her jacket. The drone's eyes dilated, then gradually dimmed as she picked it up. "It's switched off now."

"We're not out of this yet," Bradley said, still looking back at it. "The police are waiting and I doubt they'll show much restraint after this."

"We could jump."

"At this speed?" Bradley could see more lights coming up from behind them and he imagined there'd be helicopters overhead soon, if not already. Should they just stop, lie down and surrender? The authorities might believe them what with all this shit on the news. But what would happen when Hawk got to them? Would they be locked up, killed?

"I shouldn't have let you come," he said.

"Oh, will you please shut it?" she said. "We're not finished yet."

Brave words, but Bradley could spot bullshit a mile away. There was a fleet of cars trailing them and they seemed to be gaining. He turned to the dumbfounded engineer.

"Can't this thing go any faster?"

**

Hawk was being driven back to the White House when Carrington's call came through. He listened to the scientist's urgent words, feeling the heat building with each sentence.

So the reporter had surfaced with the missing Dronik and was almost at Flagstaff. The Photonix building, Las Vegas – that must be where he was heading. It was Sheen's doing, it had to be.

Hawk opened his tablet and punched in the security clearance, checking the police frequencies and the local media. Cops were converging on a speeding train and shots had already been fired.

He had no doubt that the police would take care of the journalist, but if they found that Dronik, they might find a link to the algorithm, and if someone identified any of its components, the Maneuver could be put in jeopardy.

"Can you trigger the Dronik's detonation mechanism?" Hawk asked, already knowing the answer was no. That would have been the first thing Carrington did – the man was one of the few people Hawk had faith in.

Hawk thought furiously. His orbital fighters were currently engaged over Eastern Europe and Asia. There were a couple in South America, but it would take some time to get them to Arizona.

"Listen to me carefully, Oswald," he said. "It's time to use your new-model Droniks. I know it's early, but a baptism of fire is in order. I need the security risk disposed of and I want those people dead. We'll level Flagstaff and Vegas if we have to."

Carrington mumbled an affirmative.

Hawk hung up, then dialled Barb.

"Tell the President I need to meet with him and the Cabinet. Tell him it's urgent, a matter of the highest priority. Yes. Yes, Barb, I'm sure he'll agree to it."

He hung up again and told the driver to step on it. This was a tight spot, but handled carefully, Hawk's position could be made even more secure. Whatever happened, Leary, Sheen, and Wilcox would pay dearly for their interference.

***

Bradley Wilcox gritted his teeth as a police car accelerated right up beside them. "Keep your head down," he said, just as the nearest window exploded in a hail of gunfire.

He was running on adrenaline, and praying that the engine wouldn't give out. The big locomotive had taken a few shots but it was still running.

Shana was next to him, hanging on for dear life, her usual chirpy voice silent. Bradley could see the low residential areas around them. Soon they'd be in Flagstaff, and then what?

"You should've stayed in DC," he said.

"You worry too much, Wilcox," she replied. "There's no point talking about how we got here."

"I think I love you."

"You could've waited to tell me that."

"The track ends soon," the engineer said, looking almost apologetically at both of them. "I thought I shouldn't wait any longer to tell you that."

They thundered under a bridge as the train entered the Flagstaff railroad depot, with the wailing sirens of cop cars still resounding in their ears.

"The Photonix building is on the other side of Vegas ," Bradley said, "but we're not going to get there like this. Engineer – what's your name?"

"Bob," the man said, staring straight ahead as if his life depended on it, which was what he probably did think, given what he had just experienced.

"Calm down, Bob. Just pull the brakes."

Bob sighed in relief and slowly pulled a lever.

Shana screamed, and Bradley barely managed to hold on as he felt his stomach rising in his throat, but when the front of the locomotive finally slid to a grinding halt just short of the buffers, they were, incredibly, still alive.

Bright lights were trained on them from all sides and a voice came over a megaphone, warning them that snipers had them in their sights. Bradley saw a dozen cops with automatic rifles levelled at him and knew this was the end of the line. He caught sight of a man in a long, black leather coat.

"I'll tell them I kidnapped you," he mumbled to Shana. "We'll claim magic mushroom syndrome or something."

"Not sure they'd buy that," she said, her face white as a sheet.

Bradley stood up, his hands in the air. "Me neither."

"*Come out and lie face down on the ground,*" the megaphone announced. "*Any sudden movements will be taken as an act of aggression and you will be shot. This will be your one and only warning.*"

"Come on," Bradley murmured. "I'm sorry."

"You're quite a guy, Brad," Shana said, following him onto the platform. Her voice shook a little. "We did our best. I just want you to know I think it was worth it. Maybe the world will learn about us someday."

"Yeah, someday," Bradley said, taking a deep breath as armored SWAT troops approached at a jog. "Just do what they say and claim ignorance."

He placed his palms on the ground, feeling the rough concrete under his palms and wondering whether he'd spend the rest of his life in prison.

The SWAT troops were shouting at him to stay down, but he felt disconnected, almost as though he was playing a part in some movie. He heard the dreadful hum and felt the hairs on his neck rise and the world came sharply back into focus.

Oh, no. Oh, fuck, no.

The first SWAT trooper disintegrated into a cloud of dust as a loud burst of energy vaporized him. The others didn't even have time to turn around.

Bradley raised his eyes, not wanting to, but was unable to look away. The sky was rapidly growing dark as brooding storm clouds blew in from the east, but the crackle of lightning and the smell of ozone wasn't being caused by the weather.

He watched in horror as the clouds rippled and folded apart, and then smooth metal and bright lights were floating where nothing had been only a second before. It descended with a groan of thrusters, a cascade of what looked like pure plasma blasting aside the cars and men that blocked its way.

Bradley was on his feet, hauling Shana with him and making for the nearest alleyway. Shana momentarily pulled back and he roared at her to come with him. She snatched her bag with her free hand and they were running.

He could hear her sobbing, but they kept going until they reached the next road.

"We need a car!" he shouted. "That fucking thing's here for us!"

Shana fumbled in her bag. Bradley saw the glinting handle of a gun and grabbed it, not sure whether there were any bullets left or whether they'd be of any use anyway.

The strange, unworldly whine of engines sounded and suddenly the massive machine appeared before them, burning its way through the building. Chunks of masonry were flying through the air, hurtled away from the craft as if some energy field surrounded it, manipulating gravity itself.

Bradley fired the pistol at the glass front of a nearby Starbucks, shattering it. He and Shana made it through just as a wave of energy tore the road apart, scattering cars and debris in every direction. Bradley led the way, kicking a door through to a corridor. He sprinted to the far end and opened the fire exit, barely aware of the screech of the alarm in his ears as they exited onto a back street.

It was empty, and he realized this part of the city must be on lockdown, almost certainly due to the previous attacks.

Shana's hand was in his as they ran. He could hear the crump of falling masonry, then a deafening rumble and they were knocked off their feet. Bradley got up, spitting sand and grit, and felt Shana pulling him away from the massive cloud that engulfed them.

When his senses returned he saw they were behind a dumpster truck. He sucked in clean air between coughs.

"What… the fuck…" he stammered.

"The whole building just came down," Shana said, working furiously at the hologram screen that projected away from her jacket. "That thing is hunting us, isn't it? But I doubt the police give two fucks about us anymore."

She was right, but those federal agents may not give up so easily.

202

"We still need to get to the Photonix building," he said.

A car revved up close by. "I've got us another ride," Shana said. "We'll be sitting ducks if that thing finds us, but we can't walk all the way there."

Bradley peeked over the dumpster and saw a Mustang, its engine humming and its lights on. The locks popped open and Shana pushed past him.

"You want to drive?" she asked.

"You navigate," he said, popping the clip from his pistol and seeing it was half full. He snapped it back into place and shoved the gun inside his waistband. "That thing's close. I can hear it."

"If it finds us, we're totally screwed."

"Whatever it is, it's not going away." He opened the door and slid behind the wheel. It was much more comfortable than the locomotive. "Let's go."

Shana got in beside him and pulled the drone out of her bag. "I'll see what I can do with this," she said. "In the meantime, we need to head for Vegas. If we can get across town you can take Route 589 all the way to the Photonix building. Do you think this Pullins guy will even be there?"

Bradley shrugged. They'd been lucky so far, but how long would that hold?

He gunned the accelerator and they took off just as military helicopters appeared overhead. They wouldn't stand a chance against that thing. He just prayed the government had decided not to nuke its own soil as well.

*Memorandum for the Secretary of Defense
and Joint Chiefs of Staff*

<u>*Subject: Global Extra-Terrestrial Attacks*</u>

1. Attacks on Moscow, Shanghai, Tehran, and Indian Navy Ship Kalkata, followed by the sinking of the aircraft carrier USS Wright in San Francisco, has caused panic and troop build-ups on all continents. International banks are reporting viral penetration on all networks, leading to shockwaves hitting the global financial markets. This has led us to conclude that the entire planet is now under threat by an unknown and very hostile technologically superior force.

2. India and Pakistan have both claimed that their nuclear technology has been rendered inoperable, with both sides blaming the other. The real cause has yet to be determined, though a computer virus, coupled with industrial sabotage, has not been ruled out. Confirmation has been difficult due to poor relations between the respective governments and the U.S. But given the current tensions between the two neighboring powers, a decreased nuclear capacity could be a positive thing.

3. Nations in Southeast Asia have reported lights in the sky and sporadic radar contact. Our fleet in the Pacific is on standby for possible further aggression. More intel to follow.

— C. J. McCormick

Chapter 11

The security guard at the gate waved the car through, but Hawk barely noticed. His thoughts were on the coming meeting with the President.

Everything the Brotherhood was doing was for the long-term good of the planet – its creatures, its essential ecosystems, and, ultimately the majority of the human race – but with the interference from the likes of Sheen and Leary, it was obvious he could take no more chances. Nor could he trust others in power to understand the overall vision of the Brotherhood.

It was a shame. Christine Sheen meant well – he knew that. But the road to hell was paved with good intentions, as they say, and if she'd somehow got a copy of the algorithm, she would soon find out about the Counterweight Masterplan.

Leary, on the other hand, represented the twisted self-centered mind Hawk had vowed to do away with. That son of a bitch would pay dearly for his interference.

Hawk's phone beeped and he held it to his ear. "General," he said. "Are all systems go?"

"*Ready and waiting, sir,*" Morgan said. "*Each man is fully apprised of the situation and prepared to do their duty.*"

Hawk nodded grimly. At least some people understood the evil they were fighting.

"*Carrington's already begun the tech assault, not that they'll know anything about it until we pull the trigger,*" Morgan continued. "*There will be minimum resistance. Should be a piece of cake.*"

"I have the highest confidence in your men, General," Hawk said. "This operation will speed things up considerably."

He hung up as they pulled into the underground lot.

Hawk got out, not waiting for his driver to get the door. He was met by security and walked with them to the elevator that would take them up to the ground level. The suited guards said nothing, but the guard nearest to Hawk was one of his own.

The operation was delicate, but Hawk knew he had the right men and the right tools. It was a shame that President Moore would have to pay the ultimate price; however, some healthy cells had to be sacrificed when a cancer was removed.

The United States needed a new leader, and when the dust had settled, that leader would be Hawk.

The elevator opened and they walked out onto the carpeted floor, passing portraits of former Presidents and representatives of Congress, all posing back at the onlooker with a broad smile at how successful they'd been in their own time at the dual game of politics and economics.

Hawk passed the human drones tapping away at their computers, burning up energy while propagating a system they'd been raised and educated to work for, each one oblivious to the fact that as they built their homes and lifestyles, they were assisting the banking system in printing money at the expense of the very planet that sustained them. The fools.

They reached the security checkpoint and passed into the Presidential rooms. He saw some aides milling around, probably discussing why this meeting had been called and wondering whether there was any chance the situation could be used to their advantage.

He saw his own aide and waved him away. He didn't need any additional DC insiders getting involved.

Vice President Taggart approached him.

"Ronald," he said, his brow furrowed. "This is quite unconventional. President Moore is extremely agitated. Could you fill me in on why we're all here? There has been an attack on our navy, and —"

"The whole planet is under attack," Hawk said, walking past him. "I got tired of waiting for the President to address the matter, so I thought I'd force the issue."

"The President is preparing an address as we speak," Taggart snapped, falling into step beside Hawk. "We've lost an aircraft carrier, apparently to a terrorist attack. San Francisco is on fire, and panic is spreading. You make far too many assumptions for someone of your station, and I'm going to see to it that President Moore recognizes that."

Hawk stopped and fixed Taggart with a cold stare.

"Taggart, we're at fucking war," he said. "Your useless games are utterly meaningless."

"I'm wondering how much of this is your doing, Hawk," Taggart muttered. "Or is it just a coincidence that this madness coincides with the initiation of this Counterweight thing of yours?"

"You tell me," Hawk said. "I'm just an advisor, not the Vice President of the United States."

He continued on his way, ignoring the looks as he walked into the Cabinet Room. The President was already there, surrounded by politicians. Leary was there, too. He glared at Hawk. The stupid prick had no idea how serious things were about to get. He thought he was untouchable. Well, soon he would be.

President Moore broke off from the group and approached Hawk. He was pale, his shoulders slumped. "Ronald," he said. "What the hell is going on?"

"New intel, Mr President," Hawk said. "The whole world is in great danger and further steps must be taken."

"We could have spoken first." Moore was almost whispering. "I value your contribution, but protocol—"

"We don't have time to jump through the usual bureaucratic hoops," Hawk interrupted. "You'll understand once you hear what I've got to say."

The room was filling up. Each Cabinet member sat in their chairs, all watching Hawk while they sipped their Perrier. Some, like Taggart, must be suspecting the "alien" invasion was his doing by now, but they couldn't be sure.

Hawk walked over to the mainframe and linked his tablet to the large screen computer.

The world was burning, governments were closing their borders and imposing martial law, but the United States with its docile population and corporately controlled media still labored under the impression that it was terrorism. The population largely felt safe behind their military and vast network of spies. Now it was time that the fools leading them learned the truth, if only so they could die with the knowledge of their own idiotic folly.

He set up the screen, ignoring the conversation, much of which was about him and deliberately spoken loud enough for all of them to hear.

210

The screen went blue and he stepped back to observe the room. Leary was here, though Sullivan wasn't, of course. But where was Sheen? She must have guessed something was about to happen.

No matter; that wouldn't be enough save her, especially after he'd finished with the Cabinet.

The discussion abated and Hawk took his seat near the President. Moore took a nervous sip from his glass, then cleared his throat. He looked at Hawk for a moment, then sighed.

"Ronald, can you please explain why are we here?" he asked.

Hawk almost laughed out loud. The President couldn't even pretend he knew what was going on any more.

"Some of you might be aware the planet is under attack," Hawk said, tapping his tablet's screen.

Right now, in the shadows, men selected by him were locking down parts of the White House and dealing with security. When he acted, the poor fools would have no one to protect them.

"Some of you," he continued, "may even believe that these attacks are of my doing."

The silence vanished. Everyone was talking at once, some standing, some banging their hands on the tables in an attempt to be heard. For a brief second Hawk was struck by how they resembled a crowd of chimpanzees – though he had the greatest respect for primates, which was more than he could say about this bunch of morons. He looked at the President, raising an eyebrow as if to say, *Are you going to calm the class down, or should I?*

Moore waved his hands and called for silence. He was completely white now, but too fearful to stop Hawk. Leary looked furious.

211

"You'll have a chance to speak soon, my fellow Americans," Hawk said, smiling. "But for now, I'd greatly appreciate if you remembered where you are."

"We know what we represent," Leary said. "It's you who seems to have forgotten where you are. You're just an advisor."

"And yet my advice has been followed to the letter," Hawk said, narrowing his eyes. "Every person in this room, and some who aren't here—" all eyes strayed to Sheen and Sullivan's empty seats "—agreed that action had to be taken to ensure US dominance. The Counterweight Maneuver was that action."

Jonathan Haseltine, Secretary of Education, leaned forward in his seat. "These extra-terrestrial attacks," he said. "I was under the impression that we'd be engaging in covert action, but are you saying these... *aliens*... are ours?"

Hawk shrugged. "We have the technology. I thought it prudent that we use it."

"I said this before!" Leary said, standing angrily. "This isn't about American dominance! This is about bringing down the free market and imposing a dictatorship on our great country! Well, I won't stand for it any longer!" He looked at President Moore. "I'm sorry, Mr President, but the American people must hear about this. No, the world must hear about it!"

"Mr Leary, shut the fuck up," Hawk said, tapping his computer and starting the video on the screen behind him. "There's something I want you to see. Once it's done, you are by all means free to leave."

Leary looked at Hawk with disgust, but the move had got his attention. "I'll watch your little B-movie, Hawk," he said, sitting, "but don't think it will change anything."

"On the contrary," Hawk said, sitting back. "Everything will change."

The video began with polluted oceans, the rape of the seas, and then showed elephants, apes, and the big cats all being executed and hacked up into parts destined for Eastern markets. It showed vast rainforests being cut down and burned. Pipes gushing florescent chemicals into scum-coated rivers, black smoke saturating the skies, and human beings crammed into cubicles, processing parts and livestock as mechanically as the robot arms that moved automatically in the background.

"If this is intended to move us—" Leary began.

"Leary, I have told you before that you're a sociopath," Hawk said, not taking his eyes from the screen. "I doubt very much that anything would upset you short of a fall in the stock market, but please be quiet while the film is on."

The footage changed to Moscow. A fearsome alien-looking creature was holding up a stone object; then the picture changed to lights over Tokyo, Mumbai, Jakarta, Beijing. Massive explosions and people running and screaming.

Carrington had managed to hack into the relevant computers and had found video footage from fighter pilots, flying over cities chasing unseen shadows that inexplicably materialized into a shape. Hot scorching plasma was seen burning everything in sight with focused energy beams.

Hawk watched the looks of fear on each person's face as hideous-looking monsters tore through military and civilians, decimating security forces and razing entire buildings. Moore looked like he was about to cry. Well, he'd okayed part of this – he should take some responsibility.

The film ended with a massive bomb blast over Shanghai, and then the faces of various world leaders, talking calmly before the cameras, each one pretending that everything was fine, that the perpetrators would be caught.

The film finished and Hawk looked over the audience. They were silent, even Leary.

"It's quite upsetting, isn't it?" Hawk said, standing. "Billions of people devouring a world so they can live in decadence, stealing the future from unborn children while innocent creatures and the rainforests of our world are slaughtered and abused without a hint of compassion."

"It's terrible, Hawk, but life's a matter of survival." It was Vice President Taggart. "You think what you're doing is ethical? Because if we're really guilty of these attacks, I would say we're far, far worse."

"You think that destroying our planet for the sake of profit is survival?" Hawk said, glaring at him. "Our society isn't interested in survival anymore. That is why it is going to change. And it will change. We are going to start all over again, with or without your blessing."

Leary clapped slowly, then took his briefcase and stood. "Hawk, you're going to be fucking arrested and you will stand trial for treason," he said. "You're a fucking twisted monster."

214

Others also got up, some looking at Hawk with anger, others with pity, but all with fear. Hawk looked at the President, but Moore wouldn't make eye contact.

Leary walked to the door but it didn't open. "What's this?" he said, immediately turning to Hawk.

Hawk sent the signal on his phone and sat back. "Vice President Taggart," he said, smiling. "I may have spoken hastily. You were actually quite right when you said this is about survival. Survival of the planet, its species, and the survival of society. That is all I've ever valued and we will do whatever is necessary to save humanity from itself."

"What is the meaning of this?" Leary snarled, slamming his hand against the glass. "Open the fucking door!" He pressed his face to the glass, looking for the security that wasn't there.

"Ronald, please." President Moore was slumped in his chair, defeated. "We have to stop this."

"I agree, Robert," Hawk said. "That's what I'm in the process of doing."

An explosion sounded far off, then the room shook.

Hawk pressed his hands over his ears and closed his eyes, so that he was prepared when the far wall melted in a flash of heat and sound. He opened his eyes as emergency lighting flicked on, watching the flashes of energy and the movement of his troops as they stalked into the room.

Those nearest to the wall were already crumpled and burning on the floor; the remainder were barely capable of controlling their bowels, let alone their legs. One by one, the worthless fools were silenced, until only he, Leary and the President were left.

Hawk took his old Colt revolver from his briefcase and stood, walking past the towering "creatures," past the shaking ball on the floor that was the President, to where Leary knelt, his face bleeding, his hands raised, his mouth moving silently.

Looking at the snivelling coward, Hawk could barely contain his disgust. Leary had been so assured in his little world, playing his little games, safe behind privilege and money. But now he had nothing.

"I'm quite annoyed with you, Mr Leary," Hawk said.

Leary's mouth was moving like a fish, but finally he managed to speak. "This… this is madness!"

"I have a question for you," Hawk said, "and I want it answered. If you do not satisfy my request, I will have you cut into fucking shreds, starting with your fingers and toes. You will not die easily, and you will suffer for the rest of your life. Do you understand?"

Leary's face was a picture of terror. That was the great thing about sociopaths. They cared about only one thing: themselves.

"You've had your men trailing a pair of fugitives," Hawk said. "I know that you're aware of my algorithm, and I want to know how you found out about it and what knowledge you have. Speak quickly and clearly and, above all, you had better be honest."

There was another tremor from the far end of the building where the second attack was taking place. Carrington's cyber-hacking would have effectively shut down the city, and with Hawk's knowledge and the algorithm, there was no way a coordinated defense could be mounted.

Leary was staring at one of the aliens, and Hawk kicked him hard in the gut.

216

"Focus, Mr Secretary," he snarled.

"Sheen!" Leary gasped, through sobs. "She told me you were dangerous, that you had an agenda!"

"That's hardly a surprise, is it?"

Leary sucked in a breath, his eyes squeezed shut. "She told me about your research," he mumbled. "That you were working on a surveillance code, one that could work the markets."

Ah. Of course; this cockroach was motivated by money.

"Then why tail a couple of fugitives?" Hawk said. "Why not hack my files?"

"We tried!" Leary said, gritting his teeth in pain. "But then I thought Sheen knew more than she was telling me! So I got into her computers and I found it!"

"Found what?" Hawk said, feeling cold.

"The algorithm!" Leary said, pulling himself up with the aid of the wall. "But it didn't make any sense! Then I saw that she'd made a copy! I had my men follow her—"

"And you found Wilcox." Hawk sighed.

So Sheen had gotten the algorithm somehow and now the reporter had it, as he'd suspected. No wonder he'd been able to disable those Droniks and evade capture for so long. And if the journalist understood its true potential... well, surely that couldn't happen.

"How did Sheen get it?"

"I don't know," Leary said. "I don't even know why she told me. We hardly see eye to eye."

Hawk knew why. Sheen had known he was watching her, so she used Leary as a distraction, a greater threat requiring Hawk's attention. She may not have counted on Leary pursuing her own agents, but the woman was smarter than she appeared, and Hawk had let her go.

Hawk cursed and turned to the nearest alien creature, knowing that behind the ghastly face, Colonel Forge would be waiting for his orders.

"Finish it," he said. "Level the whole place. I want it looking like Shanghai when you're done."

Leary was crying now and begging for mercy. Hawk looked back and raised his Colt, then lowered it again. It was his father's gun, and he wasn't going to cheapen his name by using it on vermin.

"Thank you. Mr Leary. And now, you're going to hell."

He nodded at Forge and walked over to the President, hearing Leary's choked cry end with the satisfying snap of his vertebrae.

"Mr President," Hawk said, speaking quietly.

Moore whimpered, then shook as another explosion rocked the foundation. He opened his eyes and looked at Hawk.

"Ronald?"

"I've helped you for a long time, Robert," Hawk said. "But now I'm afraid history has caught up with both of us. It's time for you to depart this worldly stage. Now, up on your feet."

Moore looked confused, barely registering the barrel of the Colt pressed against this forehead.

"Goodbye, Robert." Hawk pulled the trigger and watched the President's eyes glaze over. He deserved a good death, even if he was incompetent. In another age, in a post more befitting his inferior intellect, President Moore would have been a decent man.

Vietnam flickered in Hawk's memory. Those days were gone, but they'd laid the platform for the future. Moore had taught him much, even if it was overwhelmingly by negative-example.

"We'll make sure history judges him well," Hawk said, standing.

"*We have a suit for you, sir,*" Forge said, his scrambler deactivated. "*Once we're clear, the entire area will be sterilized.*"

Hawk nodded. "Colonel Forge, are you sure that all of your contacts in the military have been suitably reined in? I don't want some renegade atomic weapon going off once they find out that half of Congress is dead."

"Everything has been taken care of and the appropriate safeguards have been put in place."

Hawk walked through the hole in the wall and let Forge carry him up to the ship hovering above. It was time to visit Carrington. Once the situation was settled, he'd return to claim the Presidency as the sole surviving member of the United States Government – well, the sole survivor once Sheen had been duly eliminated.

***

The Mustang was doing 120 and Bradley was almost enjoying himself. They had made it to the city limits but he'd never seen Vegas so bereft of traffic, both vehicle and pedestrian.

Apart from the occasional fire burning in the back alleyways where the homeless tried to keep warm, there was hardly anyone in sight – but now they were only a couple of miles from the strip.

He looked in the mirror and saw in the distance the orange glow of an inferno, where that giant robot thing was engaged in battle with the US military. It reminded him that this place could get crowded very quickly.

Shana was strapped in beside him, the radiance of the projected screen illuminating her face. His eyes lingered on her for the briefest of moments, and he thought of how beautiful she was, how capable. He wasn't sure if he'd even been able to survive had she not insisted on coming along, but then he probably would have given up long before now.

"The police frequencies are crazy," she said, over the roar of the Ford's engine. "That thing is taking the city apart."

"There could be more, and if they know where we're going…" Bradley didn't bother finishing the sentence. If Hawk knew they were here, he was bound to take measures to protect his assets, no matter how miniscule the threat might appear to him. "Can you get hold of Sheen?"

"Still nothing," Shana said. "I left a message, like she said."

A voicemail wouldn't help them now. Bradley braked hard as he took the corner, accelerating immediately into the bend.

Flashing lights sped past in the opposite direction, narrowly missing them. Well, the authorities really did have something far greater to worry about now.

"We could be driving into a trap," Shana said, lowering the phone. "I'm beginning to think this isn't a good idea."

"The Photonix building holds the next clue," Bradley said. "If we can't find it, everything will have been for nothing."

"Sheen could get back to us."

220

"Unless Hawk's got to her, in which case there won't be anywhere we can hide. He'll ensure we just simply disappear."

Shana was silent for a second, then she let out a sigh. "I might be able to use this drone to find out where the algorithm is being broadcast from. Maybe I could get into that big machine thing, too."

Bradley swerved to avoid an abandoned car. "The last time you did that, it found us immediately. If that scientist, Carrington, is behind this technology, he'll be waiting for you to try something, and I don't think even you can match him with this shit."

"Well, then let's take a room in the Bellagio," she said, throwing up her hands in frustration. "At least we'll have some time to ourselves."

For one long, beautiful moment, Bradley pictured her on a king-sized bed, her clothes on the floor, and the whole of Vegas visible through a window.

Then the dream ended in a flash as he saw the flames in his rearview mirror and heard the unmistakable groan of alien machines in the distance. "If we get out of this, Shana, I want to take you to Mexico, or somewhere quiet on the coast where nobody speaks English and the only person I can talk to is you."

"This is quiet for Vegas."

"Yeah, but it isn't calm, and I don't like gambling," Bradley said, flinching as helicopters buzzed overhead so low that he could see soldiers manning the machine guns. "Maybe we'll go swimming, or take a boat out."

"I hate the water," she said. "But I hated journalists until I met you."

He felt her hand on his as he tightly held the steering wheel.

The moment was cut short as they passed an intersection, heavily lit and crowded with troops. Bradley saw the huge shape of a tank and put his foot down.

"That was our exit," he said.

He slowed at the next intersection and saw another roadblock, then the noise of horns filtered through and he suddenly realized where everyone was. "The entire city's trying to leave," he said, catching sight of the first cars beginning to slow down. "We're on the wrong side of a city-wide lockdown."

"It will be hard getting to the Photonix," Shana said. "Even if we could get through that mess. You know Hawk will have people waiting. Hell, this Dr Pullins has probably already gone, and I doubt he'll have left any evidence."

She was probably right.

Bradley drove to the next street and saw cars filling it as far as he could see. In between them and the slowing traffic, police cars with flashing sirens and armed police appeared to be everywhere. Then, without warning, the wing mirror suddenly exploded and the right headlight went out.

"God, they're shooting at us," Shana said, her voice calm, but he was already accelerating down a side street. His foot pressed hard to the floor, the speedometer declared they were going 100 as he passed a rollercoaster that loomed directly overhead.

The car screeched to a halt. They'd finally reached the strip. The last time he'd been here, he'd been on a mission to get paralytic, stopping at each hotel along the way. Bradley remembered how he'd just made it back to Margaritaville before he blacked out. But now the street lights were off and the roads were empty. God knows how much money these places were losing. He wanted to laugh. Even at a time like this, he was still thinking about the greenback.

He saw blue lights blazing behind them. So, the cops still had time to go after them – unless it wasn't the police. Shana swore.

"Can you get that drone thing working?" he said. "We need to shake them off and trace Pullins. Can you come up with something?"

***

Oswald Carrington had all monitors switched to the official channels, but his personal terminal was hooked up to the two Super-Droniks currently operating in Nevada.

Hawk had already contacted him regarding the Photonix building, and now a second Super-Dronik had been dispatched to ensure this Wilcox character didn't make it. Carrington had to admire such persistence in the face of overwhelming force. Like ants trying to resist the burning lens of a magnifying glass. Not that Hawk would approve of such an analogy.

His personal line beeped and he answered. He was expecting Hawk but instead heard General Morgan's gruff voice.

"*Carrington,*" Morgan said. "*Your deranged machine is decimating our fucking troops. Focus on your target and try to minimize the casualties, for God's sake.*"

"The Super-Dronik is operating on a search and destroy function, General," Carrington replied, sipping water from a bottle. "Keep your men out of the way and you'll see fewer die."

He winced as a shard of pain cut through his thoughts, and automatically popped a pill from the silver tin. Man, the headaches were getting worse, and his dreams were crazy. Sometimes he thought he was dreaming, only to discover he was most certainly wide awake, and he'd gotten some damn weird looks from the personnel who'd witnessed such events.

"I've ordered them to pull back and focus on keeping the civilians in line," Morgan said, his words cool but infused with anger. *"They have a job to do. And the Maneuver isn't common knowledge, so take care at your end. You don't want me coming up there, do you?"*

Carrington stifled a laugh. Maniacs like General Morgan were a dime a dozen, but he'd like to see them find another Oswald Carrington.

"You could always deal with Wilcox yourself, General," he said. "Once he's dead, all Droniks will be recalled and we can focus on other parts of the globe which really need their asses kicked."

"Do your job and I'll do mine, Carrington," Morgan said. *"Just remember what we're trying to achieve here."*

The line went dead and Carrington burst out laughing. He knew what they were trying to achieve. A controlled firestorm designed to burn away a large mass of humanity, while bringing the United States back to the forefront and establishing the new world order. That was what Hawk wanted. But with Carrington's Droniks maintaining the peace, did the General really think his old-fashioned primitive military would have anything more than a visual presence? Did he really think that soft flesh and organic minds, encased though they were in armed exoskeletons, could ever match Carrington's superfast machines?

The algorithm flittered on screen as different signals twisted and broke from the web of code that flowed through Carrington's computer. So the idiot journalist was trying to mess with his machines again? Very foolish.

Carrington took deep breaths, until the urge to laugh subsided. The first Super-Dronik was already on its way, and he fed the next line of code into the algorithm, watching the second respond. It was pure mathematics, but Carrington could see each "thought," each "idea," forming within its electronic brain, as it lifted itself from the top of the Photonix building where it had been perched.

He could almost sense its joy at being unleashed – a bird of prey searching for small quarry.

***

Bradley passed the Bellagio – its ever-present fountains now a placid pool beside the road – and turned into a side street. Shana had the drone in her lap. She was struggling with the hologram, which was projecting into thin air from her jacket.

"Do you know where we're going?" she cried, flinging her hand out to grip the dash as he narrowly missed a wall.

He didn't answer. He was far too busy.

The lights of the pursuing cars appeared to be closer in his wing mirror, but then they were out onto another street, the sound of car horns and people just audible over the sirens. He turned left, away from the traffic, and headed back the way they came, the casinos and hotels still looming over them.

"They're blocking us off!"

"Is that thing ready?" Bradley said, spotting the cop cars at the far end of the street.

"It's on," she said, "but its battery's damaged and it's slowing down. I have to make sure its route is programmed correctly, otherwise the damned thing won't buy us the time we need."

The cops had pulled their cars across the street and gotten out, shotguns in hand. Bradley's mind strayed to the pistol, knowing he could never win this gunfight – and he wasn't even sure he could really shoot at people just doing their jobs, even if the world was on the brink of war.

"I'm running out of ideas!" he snapped, slowing down. He looked for an exit, but there weren't any.

"Almost got it," Shana said. "It's much easier to work on this when we're going under 100."

Bradley slammed on the brakes, and Shana swore.

He watched the police sheltering behind their cars, then more cars appeared on the street behind them.

"Time to get out," he said tersely. "We'll have to take our chances on foot."

The robot on Shana's lap twitched. "I think it's ready," she said.

"We have to go!" Bradley said, opening his door. The window exploded into fragments of glass, and he heard the report of a shotgun. "Fuck!"

There was a hum and the drone was in the air, buzzing past him at lightning speed.

226

Before he could even register what had happened, another shot rang out, taking out the car's remaining headlight, but then something far more terrifying happened.

A screech of electronic distortion was the only warning the police had before the gigantic robot descended from the sky like some mythological creature, flattening the cars and sending cracks through the tarmac. Red sensors turned in their direction, and a pulse of energy burned through the air, blasting the police cars behind them into ash and leaving the stench of ozone in the atmosphere.

Bradley's hands were on the wheel, but he couldn't move. His eyes were locked on the creature as it rose up on armored legs.

He saw a helicopter crest the battlements of the Excalibur, before a jagged ray of light shot from a compartment, catching the helicopter and blasting the top floors of the hotel to rubble, sending seething hot debris strewing across the street.

Shana was screaming at him, but he couldn't hear her, then a sharp sting brought his senses back and he realized she'd just slapped him.

"Drive, for fuck's sake!" she shrieked.

He put his foot down automatically and drove straight at the machine, sure that it would focus on them at any moment and that everything would go dark. The machine lifted itself on articulated limbs, a glow of energy flashed, but then it was over them, its thrusters hot against his face, and it was gone.

"It's after the drone!" Shana said, eyes wide. "I have Dr Pullins' address. Let's go before it figures out what it's chasing!"

Bradley mumbled something about not knowing how to get there, but Shana read directions from the hologram map beaming out from her jacket. He flinched as a fireball rose in the distance, but they sped on.

They had to find the next link to Hawk, but what if this was happening everywhere? He wasn't sure what good they could do.

"This is crazy," he said, surprised at hearing his own voice.

"Crazy? I thought we were dead!" Shana said. "You think this is happening all over the planet?"

Bradley nodded.

"Well," Shana said. "So much for what happens in Vegas staying in Vegas."

***

Hawk let the woman pin the microphone to his lapel and sat back while the cameras were set up. His face was sombre, his words to the executives measured.

The United States Government had just been annihilated by the alien menace, and now it was the time to reassure the American people that, in Hawk, they had a man capable of reacting to such a threat.

"We'll be going live in five," the woman with the clipboard said.

Hawk thanked her and checked his tablet.

Most of the networks were down or had been co-opted by the majority of foreign states. But he was still receiving updates from Barb and everything was going to plan.

China and Japan had partially collapsed. India and the Philippines were in utter chaos. Western Europe had been spared the worst of it – at present, at least – but Russia and the old Soviet

228

nations were now under martial law, as was the United States, for obvious reasons.

But out of this mess, Hawk's new world order would rise, and the American people would soon see a completely new horizon, one filled with hope and possibility, rather than the ecological and economic destructiveness of the old order which people like Leary had actively pursued.

Hawk would nationalize the energy sector, as well as seizing the assets of various banks, mining companies, and technology-based industries. And when this was done, any dissenting voices would be quickly silenced. The global economy would be redirected towards fixing the environment and instilling new values in the minds of its people.

But there was still one problem.

Hawk's phone rang and he answered it. "General?"

"Have you seen what's happening in Vegas?"

"I'm aware of it. Awful business."

"Carrington's machines have created carnage, wiping out our military! We've lost a dozen helicopters, ten tanks, hundreds of men—"

"I'll call you back, General," Hawk said, holding his hand over the microphone and keeping his voice steady. "I understand the situation is dire, but this is hardly the most appropriate time to discuss classified material."

"Yes, of course, sir," Morgan said. *"Just be aware that your academic cuckoo might not be playing from the same hymn sheet as we are. San Francisco and DC were planned, but this..."*

Hawk hung up and accepted a glass of water from the woman with the clipboard.

He turned back to his tablet and quickly checked the Vegas situation. A massive military presence was building up, but the new Droniks were impervious to their weaponry. Vegas had been locked down and people were in panic.

But Las Vegas was in many ways the physical manifestation of the greed that had brought them to this moment, and now no one should cast doubt that the US was in as much danger as the rest of the world. Morgan was understandably annoyed, but once the new military order was created, Hawk was sure he would fall back in line, especially after his Ospreys and F-15s were proven to be obsolete.

It wasn't an ideal situation, but with Wilcox still on the loose and Sheen yet to be found, a high price had to be paid.

He dialled Barb.

"Move on Carrington," he said, before hanging up. No point taking any further risks.

***

The teleprompter was positioned before him as he drained his glass of water, straightening up in his chair and placing clenched fists on the desk. The camera was adjusted directly at him and his face was viewed on a dozen monitors.

Then the woman with the clipboard held up her hands, signalling five, four, three, two, one.

"My fellow Americans," Hawk began. "It is with the most sombre regret that I have to inform you that our planet is now at war."

Chapter 12

With the city echoing to the sound of explosions and gunfire, Bradley and Shana had somehow managed to find a way through the chaos to the apartment of Dr Jerry Pullins.

They parked on the next street, and walked the rest of the way to the apartment complex. It was an eight-storey block, and Bradley motioned for Shana to stay back while he looked around for any Feds that might be covering the area.

"Coast is clear," he said. "But there's no telling whether Hawk has his people on their way."

"I'm surprised that robot thing hasn't arrived," Shana said.

"It must still be chasing that drone," Bradley replied. He didn't want to think what would happen when it figured out their ruse. "It doesn't mean those men in suits aren't still after us."

"They won't get very far if they're using cars," Shana said. "I don't even know how we're going to get out of here."

Bradley sighed. "Let's cross that bridge when we come to it."

He walked as casually as he could to the front door, then stepped back as a family piled out, suitcases in hand. He waited for them to pass, noting the terror in their eyes, then flinched as an explosion erupted into the sky from the south. He waved Shana over and they entered into the foyer.

People were milling around, some trying to get signals on their phones, others sitting on the floor, perhaps waiting for family or friends to make it back.

"Which floor is he on?"

"Apartment 3C on third," Shana said.

They took the stairs, Bradley making sure the pistol was easily accessible in his waistband. He didn't want to use it, but just the mere sight of a firearm could have a positive effect.

They reached the third floor, passing numerous people. A couple begged for a lift, others asked if they had a working phone.

"This sucks," Shana said. "The whole planet appears to be under attack. I wonder what it's like elsewhere."

They arrived at the door of 3C. Bradley looked up the hall, but no one was in sight.

"Should we knock?" Shana asked.

Bradley shrugged. He could shoot the lock off, he supposed, but they might as well try the door first.

"Stand here," he said, moving Shana in front of the peephole. "He's more likely to answer if he sees a beautiful woman."

"Now that was a compliment," Shana said, smiling.

Bradley shrugged again, then pushed the doorbell. He realized he was feeling nervous, though after all that had happened, a little anxiety was better than pure fear.

There was no reply and he was about to push it again when he heard movement and the sound of the lock being drawn. The door opened a crack, while the rattle of metal suggested it was on a chain.

"Yes?" a voice said.

"Hello," Shana said, smiling. "I'm from upstairs and... I was wondering if you had a working phone."

"I'm afraid not," the voice said. "Everything's down, from the look of things."

The man's voice was calm, but Bradley could hear the apprehension in his tone. Well, everyone was on red alert.

"It's crazy what's happening," Shana said. "Do you have any idea what's going on?"

"No idea."

"I'm rather frightened, to be honest," she said. "But I've seen you around a couple of times. Another explosion has just sounded in the distance…" Shana feigned a look of terror. Bradley also noticed that she'd unbuttoned her shirt a little. He felt a pang of jealousy even as he commended her for her ingenuity. "I'm feeling down. Would you mind a bit of company?"

There was a moment of silence, the door closed, and Bradley thought he was going to have to do this the hard way, but then he heard the rattle of the chain, and the door opened again.

Bradley immediately barged in, the pistol tightly clenched in his hand, and saw a slim man in his fifties with red hair and spectacles. "Sorry to intrude like this, Dr Pullins."

Pullins swore under his breath, but he didn't seem too concerned. He turned and walked to the sofa a little unsteadily, and Bradley realized the man had been drinking. "I was expecting someone," Pullins said. "But I didn't think you'd bother knocking first. Would you both like a drink?"

Shana nodded. Bradley almost refused, but then he realized a drink would go down well. "Why not," he said.

Pullins frowned. "You're not professionals. So who sent you?"

"Who were you expecting?"

Pullins stared at him, then walked over to a liquor cabinet. "Grunts, special agents. God knows."

He took a bottle of whiskey and poured three glasses, then knelt to open a cupboard. Bradley raised his gun.

"Slowly, Doctor."

Pullins took out a bucket of ice. "Freezer," he said. "Can't stand warm liquor."

Shana took two of the glasses and passed one to Bradley.

"We aren't here to hurt you," she said. "We just need answers."

"I assume you're after my chameleon research," he replied. "I'm afraid I don't have anything to offer. It was all confiscated sometime back. I was put on paid leave and notified that my work was classified." He swirled the liquid in his glass, then sipped it. "Fucking government contracts. I should have known better."

"What else can you tell us?" Shana asked.

"I was working on flexible materials with the ability to bend light," he said. "It was at a very advanced stage and was showing real promise."

Bradley held out the strip of graphene they'd taken from the factory in Detroit. "Graphene?" he asked.

"Of course," Pullins replied, looking at the material with a quick glance. "What else has the strength and versatility?"

"So why'd you get put on leave?"

"The military took over," he said. "I was offered a large payment, of course, but no one appreciates the theft of their life's research." He finished his drink. "Now, who sent you? Is it a foreign government after my work, or is it to do with these so-called alien attacks that the planet is experiencing?"

"You know about the aliens?" Bradley said.

Pullins sighed and picked up a TV remote. "With your permission?" he said, pointing at the television.

The screen flashed, revealing Hawk, his chiselled features frozen on the HD TV. "This was just broadcast," Pullins said. "I recorded it. It appears there's some weird, serious shit going on."

Bradley watched Hawk talking, feeling his anger growing inside even as fear clutched at his chest. The White House half destroyed, the entire Cabinet dead – was Hawk behind it or was he actually trying to stop it?

Bradley still had the gun in his hand, but Pullins seemed relatively harmless. Then again, he did say he was expecting a visit. "Have you had any dealings with someone called Christine Sheen?" he asked, taking a drink.

"Yes."

"And yours truly on the television screen?"

Pullins put his glass on the table. "Why?"

"We think he might have something to do with this, and that Photonix is also involved," Bradley said. "I've seen machines materialize out of thin air. Does this sound like a connection to your work?"

"Sounds like science fiction to me," Pullins said. "What exactly is it you're trying to get at?"

Pullins wouldn't meet Bradley's eyes and his words smacked of evasion. Was he hiding something?

Bradley raised his gun. "I want to know where your research was taken," he said. "And I'd much prefer if you told me yourself."

Pullins snorted. "I haven't got a clue."

Bradley looked at Shana. "Find his laptop, his phone. Anything that might have some information."

Pullins refilled his glass and slumped onto the sofa. "You don't have the slightest idea what you're getting into, do you?"

"You'll be surprised what we get into, Doctor," Bradley said, keeping the gun trained on the scientist while Shana looked through the room. She returned with a laptop and two phones.

"Look," Pullins said. "You're welcome to search through my files, but there's nothing on them that isn't public knowledge."

Shana opened the laptop and connected it to her jacket. "I can copy everything," she said, looking at Bradley. "I think we should hurry, especially if the Doctor is expecting company"

"Oh yes, I did say that, didn't I?" Pullins said. "Damn. I'm a bit drunk."

"And why are you expecting someone if your research isn't connected to any of this?"

Pullins' calm expression vanished and Bradley saw fear in his eyes. "A phone call," he said, taking another drink. "Now, get what you want and go."

Bradley glanced at Shana. "I've got it," she said. "The drive just burrows through everything. We could hack into the damned Pentagon with this thing."

"Hear that, Doctor?" Bradley said. "If there's anything on your computer, we have it."

Pullins leaned forward on the sofa. "If you have what you want, you should leave."

"Aren't you worried that the people coming for you might think that you helped us?" Shana said. "You let us in and you gave us your laptop. Thank you very much, by the way."

"You really have no idea who you are up against," Pullins hissed.

"Doctor, the planet is under attack," Bradley said. "How could things get any worse?"

Bradley heard the tinkle of glass. He looked around wildly, then felt a draught and saw the hole in the window. When he glanced back at Pullins, the doctor was looking down at an expanding red stain on the front of his shirt.

Shana stifled a scream, but Bradley had already hurled himself at her, knocking her to the floor before the next shot took out a vase in the middle of the room. He crawled over to where Pullins had slid onto the carpet and instantly knew it was too late for him. "Doctor, you're about to die," he said, quietly. "If you want to get even with these bastards then tell me what you know."

Pullins looked up at him. "Arizona," he said, eyelids fluttering. "I was dealing with a scientist… in Kingman, Arizona." His eyes glazed over.

"Bradley!" Shana yelled from the hall.

Bradley crawled across the carpet, keeping out of sight until he'd cleared the window, then jumped up and ran after Shana for the stairs. They knew where they were going now, but first they had to get out of here alive.

***

Sheen unplugged the drive from the jack on the side of her laptop and grabbed her bag from under the desk. She placed the drive in the hidden compartment before grabbing what clothes she could find from her drawer.

She'd gotten Shana's message and done what she could, sending a code to the few remaining men that she could still trust. She prayed they could get there in time – everything hinged on the algorithm, and if that was lost…

Her PA, Tom, appeared at the door.

"The car's been brought round," he said.

Sheen took her gun, sliding it into the concealed holster under her jacket. They couldn't risk the car, not now that Shana Grey and the journalist were being tracked. Her algorithm was separate to Hawk's, so he couldn't trace it, not unless it was used to infiltrate his systems. But if the Blackhawk she'd now sent to pick them up was shot down, there was a chance he'd retrieve the drive, and if that happened it would only be a matter of time before they found her.

"We'll take the subterranean route," she said, closing the bag. "Tell Sam to take exit Beta. I'll contact him at the established time."

Tom hurriedly left. Sheen set the explosive under the desk near the gas line, and took the steps down to the cellar, to the hidden tunnel that she'd had constructed a year earlier, when she had first suspected Hawk might be preparing to use his algorithm.

Of course, she'd underestimated his ambition – and his total madness. With that ingenious program of his, he now had the means to carry out something truly awful, and with his connections, his power, she knew her life and that of many others would be forfeited if she revealed her findings to him. And now it would seem that the journalist, Bradley Wilcox, would be paying the ultimate price. After all this time, all this planning, had it finally come to this?

She reached the bottom of the stairs and passed through the old room and into the tunnel. She heard Tom behind her and waited for him to join her.

"Sam's gone," he said. "You think he'll make it?"

"He'll make it," Sheen said, continuing along the tunnel to where it opened into the basement of a house three doors along. "He knows the risks. He'll find some way to get through."

"And if he doesn't? Hawk's men are getting closer every time we move," Tom said. "The guy's like a bloodhound. If Sam talks…"

Sheen didn't reply. Hawk was cunning, but so was she. Hopefully she could stay one step ahead of him for a while. Sam knew better than to be taken alive. And if he somehow was caught? Well, even the number he'd been given was a dead end. Sam wasn't a part of her initiative anymore – he was on his own.

The next building was abandoned like the first – most of Mexico City had been evacuated after the first wave of aliens had descended on South America. Sheen knew Hawk was behind it, but no one would believe her, and what with the Mexican government now gone and military rule established, Hawk was essentially controlling the entire continent.

They couldn't trust the authorities anymore, not with Hawk providing the intel. It was time for Sheen to leave, but with surveillance everywhere, she could only coordinate with her people using the algorithm.

She took the short flight of steps up to the ground floor where three of her most trusted men were waiting in plainclothes.

"Taking a bus with the last remaining evacuees," Tom said, frowning. "It's risky."

240

"Yes, but Hawk won't think of it," Sheen said, catching sight of herself in the cracked mirror hanging askew on the wall. She was dirty, her hair dishevelled. But at least she'd fit in. "Once we're out of the city, I'll contact my people in Arizona. If they're still alive, we continue with the next stage."

"And if they aren't?"

"Then we're freedom fighters," she said. "All the rules change."

Tom scratched at a day's worth of stubble. "I'll see what progress I can make here."

Sheen placed her hand on his arm, then turned and left. She walked onto the street closely followed by her men, a shawl pulled over her head, and filed in slowly with the men, women, and children all making their way to the pickup point.

With thousands still leaving the city, most of whom didn't have IDs, her identity should be safe until they reached the camps. But despite all the damage and the removal of the government, Sheen knew that the country was essentially intact, and once Hawk had achieved his aims, it would quickly fall back in line with the rest of the Western powers, installing themselves once more as the planet's undisputed custodians with Hawk presiding over them as the ultimate lord protector.

She heard a scuffle behind her, but her men kept close, their hands on their concealed weapons. Sheen kept moving, seeing the coaches up ahead and the armed soldiers separating the mass of people into different lines. She filtered into one line and waited patiently for her turn to board the coach. Eventually, a bellowing soldier in green fatigues gave the order and she climbed aboard, seating herself near the back, close to her men.

As the bus started on its journey, she glimpsed waves of jets flying overhead, leaving contoured trails in the sky. She quietly whispered to herself, "Hawk, you bastard. What have you done?"

From: *Yachi Okabe*
To: *Yoshihito Kodama*
Date: *2/16/2025*
Re: *Nuclear Failure in Ikata Power Plant*

Dear Yoshihito,

I hope the season finds you well. The terrible events unfolding around us have pushed our resources to breaking point, but after the Fukushima disaster and considering the high threat level, we obviously aren't taking any chances.

The JSF have allocated troops and anti-aircraft guns in response to the waves of attacks hitting our cities, the reactor was taken offline, and we have so far weathered the storm. As the attacks have migrated to the north, we sought to bring the reactor back online, but at a lower output in order to accommodate the energy needs of the nearby JSF base.

· Unfortunately, the control rods were unresponsive and upon closer examination were found to be utterly depleted. Our scientists have no explanation, and I am currently seeking information from other power stations. We fear the enemy may have somehow nullified our energy source, which will cause severe impacts across Japan, particularly with industry and the residential sector. That is assuming, of course, that we are not crushed beneath the extra-terrestrials heel.

I pray that I hear from you soon,
Yachi

Chapter 13

Shana made it to the other side of the street before the shouting started. Bradley, sprinting after her, glanced back to see a Blackhawk helicopter hanging menacingly in the air, depositing armed men with body armor onto the ground by rope.

They'd killed Pullins and now they were coming for them. Hawk was going to finish them, and everything they'd learned would come to nothing.

Shana hissed at him from behind a low wall in the yard opposite. Bradley jumped the wall and crouched down behind it, wiping the sweat from his brow.

The soldiers would be wearing thermal goggles, they were highly trained, and with the city on lockdown, he had no idea how they were going to escape.

Shana gestured for him to follow her, and he did, but then very nearly stumbled after losing his footing. The pistol, however, was firmly in his hand. Should they go out fighting?

Shana was focused, like she knew what to do, but maybe she hadn't figured out they were quite possibly already finished. Sometimes hope could cloud the mind. And God knows the USA had been relying on clouded optimism for long enough.

They reached the street, and he glimpsed soldiers in night-camo jogging in their direction. He made it behind the wall just as a hail of bullets ricocheted off the old brickwork.

"Come on," Shana said, her voice shaking. "We can't give up."

Bradley couldn't say anything. He was totally exhausted. He hadn't asked for this – he'd just been doing his job, looking for the answers. But in this age of lies and corporate semantics, truth was almost a dirty word, and now it looked as though he'd never be able to reveal what he'd learned, that he'd never get to the bottom of this fucking conspiracy.

How he dearly wished he could see Hawk just once, face to face, so he could tell him what an asshole he was, how totally disconnected he'd obviously become. But now Hawk would have the final word and it would probably end with a bullet to his temple.

Bradley forced himself to stand and ran with Shana across the street, hearing the screams of nearby civilians as the pursuing troops rounded the corner.

A few shots rang out, but apparently the soldiers retained enough professionalism to avoid mowing down innocent bystanders. They'd made it to the next street, and Bradley was looking around for some cover, when he felt a searing pain in his shoulder and found himself lying face down on the sidewalk.

Shana was shouting and he tried to lift himself up, but the agony tore the breath away from him in a scream. She pulled him up, and he saw blood pooling on the ground beneath him.

"Go!" he roared, shoving Shana away with all his strength. "Get the fuck away from here! Please!"

She was still trying to lift him up, tears streaking her cheeks and her hair blowing wildly in the wind, when he saw the dark shape of the helicopter against the starlit sky.

Bradley's shoulder felt like it was on fire as Shana pulled him to his feet, the sound of the helicopter growing louder and louder.

He heard automatic fire and resigned himself to death. Any second now. Any second.

246

But then, somehow, he found himself beside Shana as the wind grew stronger, and the crescendo of churning rotors became truly deafening.

He looked up and saw the helicopter – another Blackhawk, like the one from before – and more men descending, clad in fatigues and body-armor similar in appearance to the others. But they weren't shooting at him or Shana.

A burst of gunfire momentarily blinded him. Bradley looked away, staring back at the pursuing troops, but watched in amazement as they were cut down where they stood.

He heard the crump of an explosion and a bright flash lit up the night sky as the other Blackhawk became a rotating fireball of metal and flame, falling to the ground. And then, from nowhere, he saw a man standing over him, a rocket launcher held in his arms, his face obscured by a mask.

Bradley was hauled up into the helicopter and dropped into a seat. Someone in goggles strapped him in, and he saw Shana across the compartment, similarly seated. His stomach dropped as the Blackhawk lifted.

The soldier sat across from him was speaking urgently into his headset, and another was pulling back Bradley's shirt, inspecting the wound even as the helicopter bobbed and lurched in the wind. Then the doors were pulled shut and the noise subsided.

Bradley felt the sharp jab of a needle in his shoulder, but he barely noticed. His eyes were locked on Shana's.

She looked back with guilt in her eyes, and he knew she'd been playing him all along.

"You're a lucky guy! The bullet passed straight through!" the soldier beside him shouted into his ear. "I've given you a shot for infection, but you need stitches!"

Bradley nodded dumbly. There were six soldiers seated around them. He heard the pilot shout something, then the helicopter's engine slowed significantly, the noise decreased further, and the ride became smoother.

The soldier had a needle and thread in his hand and was stitching up his shoulder, but the discomfort Bradley felt was nothing compared to the pain he'd experienced previously. The real pain was in his heart.

Shana Grey, so beautiful, so strong – had she only come with him because she'd been ordered to? He'd thought that something good had happened in the midst of all this mayhem, but now he knew she'd just been using him. He was just another disposable asset for investigating Hawk.

The soldier cut the thread and covered his wound with a sterile dressing.

Shana looked at him across the compartment, then she said something to the soldier next to him, and they got up, switching seats. Shana belted herself in beside Bradley and looked him in the eyes.

"I told you before you were lucky to have me along," she said, "but luck had nothing to do with it."

"Obviously."

"We're forty minutes out!" a soldier shouted to Shana. "Things will get rocky soon! Be ready in case we have to ditch!"

"You're working for Sheen," Bradley said.

248

"Yeah," she said. "My orders were to keep you on track and make sure you didn't do anything stupid. Much harder than it sounds, actually."

"Why use me at all? Why didn't Sheen just use the military?"

"This chopper has been adapted for stealth, but you already fly under the radar, Brad. Sheen had long suspected something was going on, and when you got dragged in she saw it as a golden opportunity. You can think quickly, you're honest, and you had a motive to stop Hawk. But we had to move rapidly once the scheme was set in motion." Shana shrugged. "These guys were on standby to pick us up once we'd found out where Hawk has his base. I sent the code just before we left the apartment complex."

"You knew the helicopter was on its way?"

"Yes. I spoke with Sheen yesterday to let her know we were close," Shana said. "I couldn't let you know anything in case we were caught. Your analytical skills are superb, but you aren't a combatant and I doubt you'd hold out well under torture."

Bradley snorted, then hissed in pain as he jerked his shoulder. Having to withstand torment clearly wasn't his forte.

"My instincts weren't good enough to see through you," he muttered.

"You almost figured it out," Shana said. "To be honest, I don't think you wanted to know."

She was right. He'd wanted to believe she cared for him, loved him. Christ, the more he thought about it, the more he hated it.

"Sheen could have told me," he said. "You could have told me."

"Like I said, I had to keep my role secret in case you were caught," Shana said. "And the true importance of the algorithm had to remain as vague as possible. I know it's paranoid, but there was just too much at stake."

"So, am I even needed anymore?"

"We couldn't have gotten here without you, Brad," she said. "But now it's time to let the professionals do their job. Unfortunately, you and I aren't out of this yet."

Bradley looked around the helicopter and couldn't help but think half a dozen men would do little good against the resources Hawk had at his disposal, no matter how well trained they were.

"Just drop me off at the next town," he said.

"That wouldn't be a good idea," Shana said. "Look, I'll make sure Sheen gives you the exclusive – assuming we succeed, that is."

His career – that was why he'd traveled to DC in the first place. Would he have agreed to any of this if he'd known the true danger he was heading into? Would he have endured if he'd known Shana was just simply sent along to watch him?

"Drop me off and come find me later. Shouldn't be too hard to find me. I'll be in a bar, if that helps."

"Listen, Wilcox. I'm still planning on us going to Mexico," she said. "I know you probably don't believe this, but I meant what I said about you."

Bradley flinched at the memory. He wanted to believe her, but the thought of being fooled again was painful. "What's your name? Your real name, I mean."

"It's Shana. My surname's classified."

"Well, thank you, Miss Classified. We obviously don't know enough about each other to be on full name terms."

She looked away, but then a shrill beeping sound cut through the drone of the rotors overhead.

"Your pride will have to wait," she said, undoing the clasp of her belt and pulling herself up. She stumbled up to the cockpit, helped by one of the soldiers.

Bradley swore. The wound in his shoulder didn't matter anymore. He moved his arm, welcoming the burning pain. It helped.

The soldier in the seat beside him looked at him, his goggles pulled back, revealing eyes open in a questioning stare.

Bradley stared back at him. "What?"

The soldier passed him a submachine gun. Bradley recognized it from the movies, but he'd never used anything bigger than a pistol before.

"Safety here, point and pull the trigger," the soldier said. "Take the recoil with your good arm. You don't want your stitches popping open." He passed it over together with a strap and two extra magazines. "You know how to ride a motorcycle?"

"Yeah, why?" Bradley replied.

"This chopper has a motorcycle on board. You'll need it when we drop off."

Shana returned from the cockpit, a glum look on her face. "Sheen's coordinating our flight from a secure location," she said, sitting back down beside Bradley. "She's located a sizeable piece of private land in Arizona not far from Oatman that's apparently linked to the US military. There's no further information about the site, but sometimes things are less conspicuous by their absence. We were due be there in less than fifteen minutes, but Sheen's using the algorithm to monitor military communications and—"

"Let me guess," Bradley interrupted. "Fighters are being scrambled to intercept us?"

Shana shook her head. "They're taking no action. All conventional forces are being used for crowd control and defense against the alien threat."

"So, what then... aliens?"

"Whatever's coming for us isn't going to give any warning. If it's an extra-terrestrial creature or one of those robot machines, we won't know until it's too late."

"So we're going to be shot out of the sky? Is that what you're saying?"

Shana leaned closer to him, her eyes clear, not angry, but sad. "This is the end of the world, Brad," she said. "But I love you."

He wanted to shout at her, to tell her he wasn't a government drone, that he didn't appreciate being lied to, being used. He wanted to tear the dressing off his arm, where he'd taken a God-damn bullet for the fucking world, but when the shouting came it wasn't his voice, and a moment later the Blackhawk was dropping.

Bradley craned his neck to see through the windshield, but in the darkness all he could see was the outline of rock and sand flying past and beneath them. They accelerated, and he felt Shana's hand tighten in his. When he looked at her, he saw the fear and the guilt, but this time he knew it was genuine.

He looked back toward the pilot and co-pilot, who were talking urgently. The co-pilot pointed at the sky and that's when he knew it had found them. He yelled at them to land, but then Shana was screaming, and all he could see were lights streaming in his eyes.

The side of the helicopter was torn clear, and Bradley felt the awful spin pulling his body harder and harder against the belt across his chest. Somewhere, the screech of metal and the groan of engines cut through the terror, and then everything went silent.

***

As he watched the Dronik descend upon the Blackhawk helicopter, Carrington felt a moment of separation, as if his mind and body were in two different places. Time ruptured, and he was back in his parents' home, watching *Animal Planet* on their TV.

The Super-Dronik, a metallic bird of prey, ingeniously crafted to look as though it had come from another planet by the mind of Oswald Carrington, the engineer, the creator – God. The Blackhawk attempted to escape, but its primitive design was destined for extinction, its blueprint mere fodder for the next species.

As the Dronik cut through its rotors, Carrington felt a shudder of pleasure. He rose to his feet as it clasped the helicopter with its powerful talons and then climbed effortlessly through the sky on hydrogen powered thrusters, making a ninety degree-turn with the barest movement.

It sped back towards the surface. The Blackhawk was crumbling under its powerful grip, and then the helicopter hit the ground hard, scattering into fragmented pieces, finally skidding to a stop on the slope of a sand dune, flaming fuel marking the groove it had scoured in the dirt.

"Kill them. Kill them all, Dronik, and make sure it's a very slow death," he said, grinning.

Something clicked in Carrington's head and he found himself back in the present. He noticed the technician on the other side of the room looking at him aghast. Carrington screamed at him to leave, suddenly furious – furious that a simple worker drone would dare to look directly at the supreme creator.

The man left hurriedly, along with the half-dozen other technicians in the room, with Carrington swiftly following them to the door. He locked it, pulled the electrical cable from the wall camera, and returned to his seat, shaking his head. Such people were bound to be scared, he supposed. Competition was not something the weak appreciated.

On the screen, the Blackhawk burned on its side. Bodies lay on the ground, growing cold within the Dronik's thermal eye. Carrington felt the same awe he always felt when nature revealed itself so ruthlessly.

There was a rapping on the door and muffled voices.

Carrington sneered and turned to the nearest workstation. He punched in his personal code and locked down the entire level, then sent commands to the Droniks ensconced in their container-pods on the lower floor.

Hawk had been right about the need for change, the need for balance. But he hadn't fully understood that everything he had been working for had been just another strand in the great evolution of thought.

Carrington's brain was the key. It was his mind that would bring about the next stage in this great evolution: his superior brainpower, his will, would encompass a higher salvation.

"You're a primitive predator, Ronald," he said, opening the container-pods with a tap of a key. "Top of the food chain. But the circle of life doesn't allow for such things. Even the strong are devoured eventually."

He watched the Droniks activate, then sat back to study the corpse of the helicopter on the screen. Nature was truly fascinating.

Chapter 14

When the Blackhawk's engines had cut out, the sudden quiet had chilled Bradley more than the shrill whine of the attacking robot. He'd looked into Shana's eyes and thought about saying something, but then they'd hit the ground.

The rear of the helicopter had vanished in a cloud of dust, and the inertia had pulled him in every direction, while a thousand particles sandblasted his face.

The soldier beside him had vanished as his seat was flung clear of the wreckage, but before Bradley could take in anything else, the front of the helicopter exploded into glass fragments. The floor shook, resonating hard, and he smelt a combination of acrid oil and burning electrics.

It took Bradley a good minute before he trusted himself to open his eyes.

The Blackhawk was torn open like a tin can. Its front was a crumpled burning mess, and he felt sick when he spotted the limp arm hanging from within the cockpit's crushed interior. His seat was still half-attached, hanging over scorched sand where the side of the vehicle should have been.

Shana was beside him, unconscious. He reached for her with his bad arm, gripping her wrist, oblivious to his own pain.

Her pulse was strong and steady, but a cut to her forehead suggested that she'd been struck by something. He prayed it was only a superficial injury.

The smell of aviation fuel was strong as he unclasped his belt and got up, a little unsteady but miraculously okay. He saw the corpses littering the ground, heard a moan, and saw the soldier who had swapped seats with Shana earlier slumped in a shrub close by.

Bradley unbuckled Shana's belt and, favoring his good arm, climbed from the craft's remains, dragging her over to where the sandy ground formed a natural cushion. He gently laid her down in the shadow of a rocky outcrop, then ran over to the injured man as the eerie, other-worldly engines sounded in the sky above.

When Bradley reached the soldier, he saw a pool of dark liquid around his body. It was blood.

"Take… the pack," the soldier said, gesturing towards a satchel. "Map. I've marked where…" His voice faltered, then his eyes slowly glazed over.

Bradley stared, horrified, before a groan from Shana roused him. She was moving her head. He slung the satchel over his good shoulder, and when he got to her, her eyes were open.

"Brad?" she said.

"That thing is still up there," Bradley said, helping her up. "Can you walk?"

She nodded, grimacing. "Is everyone dead?"

Bradley looked around, but nothing moved. "We will be soon if we don't get out of here." *And it might already be too late,* he thought.

"We're going southwest," Shana said. "That way."

The unearthly groan of weird, humming engines broke the quiet. Bradley instinctively threw himself on top of Shana, knocking her down as a tremendous gust of wind hit. Then the remains of the helicopter exploded in a hail of plasma. He felt the heat singe the back of his neck, and when the blast had finally faded, the flames were burning high into the night sky. He could see the outline of the flying machine against the backdrop of stars.

"What the hell are we supposed to do now?" he said, not scared, just bewildered.

"We need to find a hiding place. It might not have seen us," Shana said, getting up.

They made for the next dune, running as fast as they could on the soft sand. Bradley wasn't sure whether it would work, but he wouldn't give Hawk the satisfaction of seeing him give up.

They made it to a ridge and he looked down over the arid terrain. He didn't know where they were headed exactly, but there was no way they could avoid that thing out in the open, and even if they did make it, Hawk would know they were coming.

"Damn," he muttered.

"What?"

"I was just thinking that I'm going to die in Arizona, but I never liked this State. Way too hot for me, and they tax their beer."

Shana grabbed his arm and he hissed in pain, then her lips were on his, hot and desperate. He returned the kiss, pulling her against him.

"I didn't mean to use you, Brad," Shana said, drawing back slowly. "I never thought it would be like this. I know that's not an excuse. But we've been through such a lot together, and I just wanted you to know that I really do care about you."

Bradley pushed her hair back from her forehead. It had been so long since he'd felt this way.

After his parents' problems and then his career stuttering out, he'd worked and drank and worked some more. It was funny that

258

only now, when the world was on fire and he was almost certainly going to die, he'd find someone, someone special, an undercover agent using him, lying to him... and perhaps loving him.

He held her and looked up at the sky. Out here, away from the lights of civilization, he could see so many stars, the beautiful glow of the Milky Way. Some said the vastness of the cosmos was proof that the individual was insignificant, but he didn't think so. All that space meant little to him compared to life down here: the fighting, the surviving, the love and the hate. The big things didn't make the little things pointless.

"We should go," he said. "Now that you've given me a reason for living, I wouldn't mind stretching it out a bit longer, even if it's only a minute or two."

The awful groan of the engines returned and Bradley looked around for where it was coming from. Deep down, he hoped he wouldn't have a clue when it happened.

"What's that? Where'd you get it?" Shana asked.

Bradley realized she was looking at the satchel.

"One of the pilots gave it to me," he said. "Maps and supplies. A bit late for that, though."

Shana pulled it from his arm. "Not if Sheen's left me what I think she's left me."

Bradley heard the excitement in her voice and felt the beginnings of hope despite their desperate situation. She took his hand and jumped down the slope, sliding on her feet as she dragged him with her. Shana half-pulled him down against the sand, and tugged open the straps.

Bradley looked up as the giant machine buzzed overhead. It was moving slowly, a blue glow where its thrusters kept it aloft, and then it turned lazily to focus on them. All the heat drained from his face as he reached for Shana's hand, but she batted it away as she tinkered with something in the bag.

The machine stared at him, almost like it was examining him. Was it sentient? An artificial intelligence? Or was it a drone controlled by a human being? It was watching them, and taking its time as it did so. Did it want them alive?

Then he saw metal slats open from the front of its hull and he knew they were about to die.

He reached for Shana and this time she took his hand, squeezing hard. At least they wouldn't die alone.

***

Carrington saw their faces through the video feed. He savored their horror, watching intently in the knowledge that they were going to die, the fear blossoming in their eyes.

He'd suspended the Super-Dronik's kill function in order to witness the terror his creation inspired first-hand, and now he saw the two of them, lying before him, their primitive technological defenses strewn across the dirt behind them, and nothing but skin and cloth and a pathetic firearm clutched in hand to protect them.

Agony pierced his mind and he reeled back in his seat, screaming. He reached out a shaking hand for the tin and threw two more pills into his mouth, dry-swallowing them and feeling the relief immediately. His thoughts shook in his head like pebbles in a can, but then clarity returned and he could think again.

Carrington heard more banging at the door and checked his monitor, seeing his Droniks moving through the hangar. Soon they'd reach Orbit Station's Gallery and then the fun would begin. He would have to check their functions were correctly allocated, but he had time.

First, the two survivors from the helicopter must be dealt with. He returned his attention to the main screen and froze. His thoughts moved so quickly he knew what was about to happen a second before the Super-Dronik did.

Unfortunately, that wasn't quick enough.

***

The machine looked down at them, swaying gently in the air. Bradley wanted to close his eyes but he couldn't move. The only thing he could hear was the awful sound of its fucking engines.

He blinked. They were still alive.

He heard Shana saying something and jerked his head around to see some kind of antenna in her hand. She moved her hand over the hologram projecting from her jacket. Her teeth were clenched, sweat was running over her face, then she jabbed at a button on the antenna's handle.

Bradley heard a strange noise, like static, and realized it was coming from the machine. The glow of its thrusters suddenly failed and its eyes dimmed, then it fell to the ground with a mighty crash, sending sand and dust in all directions.

"What the hell did you do?" he asked.

"I really don't know," she said. "But I think it temporarily disrupts the algorithm, or rather, it disrupts the flow of energy the algorithm relies upon. Sheen told me that she had acquired a prototype and that she'd have one for us if we ever got close to Hawk's base, but I didn't know if it would actually work!"

Bradley let out a breath, feeling something close to relief. He wanted to sit down, but Shana was already on her feet.

"They'll be coming back for this," she said, looking at the massive machine embedded in the sand. It was very still, its eyes cold and dark. "There's no way Hawk will let this thing fall into the hands of anyone outside his circle."

"Come over here and sit down," Bradley urged her.

"But they know where we're headed," Shana said, still watching the deactivated machine. "You know that thing could come back online at any time."

"I need you now, Shana," Bradley said, earnestly. "I really fucking need you."

She looked at him. "What do you mean?" she asked. "Do you mean... No, surely you don't mean that you want to fuck me out here in the desert."

"Yes," he replied. "I want to fuck you. I *need* to fuck you, urgently, right now!"

"You can't be serious," Shana said, looking deep into his eyes. Bradley said nothing. But he'd never been more serious in his entire life. "You are one hell of a strange guy."

He kissed her gently on the lips as they both lay down, urgently touching and caressing each other. "We might not get another chance," he whispered.

***

After what seemed like an incredibly beautiful age, but in essence must have been minutes, they returned to their senses, the fear from earlier replaced by a feeling of total serenity.

"We should leave," Shana said, doing up her shirt. "I mean, we have to."

"Yeah, I know," Bradley said, sitting up. "Thank you."

"The pleasure was all mine," she said. "You were right, we may never get another chance if Hawk wins." She pulled the jacket back on.

Bradley gently caressed her face. "Where do we go now?"

"We'll go as far as we can, then I'll see if I can reach Sheen. Maybe we can get to Hawk's lair another way. Maybe we can hit his base with a missile or something. I don't know if Sheen still has the capacity to order a strike, but there could be other options."

Bradley checked the map and saw the mark where Sheen believed the entrance to Hawk's base was. It was too far by foot.

"I wonder if the motorcycle is still intact," he said.

"What motorcycle?" Shana asked.

"One of the soldiers told me the Blackhawk was carrying a motorcycle," Bradley said. "If it's still intact, we could ride out of here."

"You look over there," Shana said, jumping to her feet. "I'll check over here."

With the debris scattered far and wide, there were many pieces to go through. Raging fires were making it even more hazardous. Bradley felt about giving up when Shana gave a shout. He ran over to her.

"There's something big in this sand dune," she said. "Give me a hand to pull it out."

The motorcycle had been stored in a crash-proof shell. Bradley couldn't suppress a laugh when they opened it.

"Bingo," he said. "It's in one piece!"

"But you aren't driving it with your arm in that condition," Shana said. "Fortunately, my dad had a Triumph Bonneville and taught me how to ride."

"You think you can handle this thing?" Bradley asked. "I'm okay to—"

"Of course I can handle it," she snapped. "I've rode Harleys, BSAs, anything you could name!"

"Okay, okay," Bradley said, raising his good hand in supplication. "First, let's see where we're going and check whether this thing is still working."

With the algorithm, they had access to GPS, and Bradley could see that they were forty miles away from their destination – not too far, but if another one of those things arrived, it might as well be a thousand.

He stood the bike up and climbed on, then anxiously turned the key. The engine fired up first time. He gestured to Shana to get on.

"Come on then, if you insist on driving."

264

"One second, Brad," Shana said, relieving two dead soldiers of their night vision goggles, as well as a pistol, ammunition and a couple of ration packs. "We're going to need supplies."

Bradley adjusted the motorcycle's controls and scooted back onto the rear seat to let her on. A smooth click to the gearbox with positive throttle control ensured she knew exactly how to ride the thing as they revved away from the crash site. The stunning Milky Way stretched out far and wide before them.

"Hey, how about playing some music?"

Shana turned up the audio volume and the music of Bob Seger's "Roll Me Away" began to play loudly in their earpieces as they drove into the desert night.

Bradley reassuringly clutched a machine gun he'd found holstered to the side of the bike. They rode on beneath the stars, through the pristine wilderness, listening to the awesome song as they headed west.

If it hadn't been for the incapacitated drone and the dead men behind them, it might almost have been romantic.

***

Hawk had finished his conference with the world's leaders and was now seated on Air Force One, sipping an espresso and speaking to Barb on his phone about the coming schedule.

The meeting had gone perfectly – no, better than perfectly. The entire planet was shaking with fear, its populations rioting and rebelling against each other, its armed forces almost paralyzed and

265

shooting at shadows. Greece and Turkey had already begun fighting each other, and the India-Pakistan situation was as tense as ever.

Hawk was pleased that the algorithm had infiltrated and neutralized the world's atomic option – clearing up a radioactive hell would have been difficult to say the least, while the Brotherhood's mandate was such that serious damage to the planet's ecosystem should be avoided at all costs, no matter how many human lives had to be taken out of the equation.

The whole world cried out for leadership; Hawk had provided it with his cool head, proactive stance, and knowledge of military tactics. Even the ambassador in Beijing had agreed enthusiastically with Hawk's plan to coordinate worldwide defense and alter the Capitalist infrastructure, changing the fragmented nations and parasitic corporations into one compliant planet, now totally focused on protecting itself, with all business geared towards a common goal.

A change was most definitely going to come, and it would come, by God.

The tone in his ear meant General Morgan was trying to get through. Hawk dismissed Barb, and switched the line over.

"General?"

"Your Brainiac scientist has crossed the line, Mr Hawk! But I did warn you about this! Now that little shit has gone off the deep end, and Christ knows how much damage he could cause!"

"What's happened?" Hawk said, placing the espresso down.

"Carrington's secured himself in the operations room and cut all controls to the Dronik control algorithms!" the General snapped. *"My men are trying to cut through and the technicians are doing*

their best to reroute the power, but he keeps adjusting it! There are more Droniks attacking on the lower levels, and I'm losing men faster than I can send up. But that's not the worst of it!"

"What else, General?"

Hawk was trying to remain calm, but becoming more and more agitated. They were at a delicate stage. If Carrington ruined it now, there would be severe consequences for all of them.

Morgan sighed. *"One of the Super-Droniks has gone down near Kingman. Don't ask me why."*

"Seal Tombside and set up the defenses. We need to get that thing concealed," Hawk said, signalling to his aide to come over. "I'm altering course and will land at the Phoenix facility."

Hawk's aide nodded in comprehension and ran off to inform the pilot of the change in destination.

"I'll deal with it personally, General, but in the meantime, inform Tombside to be especially vigilant," Hawk instructed. "And for God's sake make sure those Super-Droniks are deactivated. If Carrington gains access to them, we'll have a serious problem on our hands."

"Already done, sir," Morgan grunted. *"Tombside's on heightened alert, though this crap with Carrington is stretching our security to breaking point. I don't suppose you want to hear about the progress we've made tracing Sheen?"*

"I know she fled to Mexico. But If you find her, kill her," Hawk said. "Otherwise, I'm not interested. Just keep the elevator secure."

Morgan signed out.

Hawk sat staring at the espresso as it cooled. The nootropics – the pills Carrington had been put on – were essential to the entire

Maneuver, but now they were its biggest threat, and there was nothing Hawk could do until he reached the elevator. Until then, he had to rely upon his men.

He breathed deeply and felt his heart rate slow. If Carrington had fucked this up, that eccentric son-of-a-bitch would pay a heavy price indeed.

Hawk's plane soon landed at the Phoenix installation. He waved at his aide to get the door open the moment the plane stopped. His people were there on the tarmac waiting for him, and he quickly walked to meet them.

Colonel Forge was standing at the front, his usual military apparel exchanged for a black suit.

"Good to see you, Colonel," Hawk said, striding with Forge toward the limo parked nearby. "Anything new on the situation?"

"I just got in from the East Coast, Mr President," Forge said. "All the men are now fully prepared, and the Maneuver is looking good. However, General Morgan thought that I could perhaps be of more assistance up top with you."

Hawk agreed. The OIVs would continue their attacks under Morgan's direction, the planet would continue to come together under Hawk's banner, and the deadly tide of unfettered capitalism would quickly recede.

But Hawk could not unveil his ultimate strategy until Carrington had been properly dealt with. Only then could the next stage of the Maneuver begin.

Hawk got into the back of the limo, Forge sat beside him and it pulled away.

"Carrington is a genius," Hawk said, stroking his jaw in deep thought. "Far too smart for his own good."

"He's closed our backdoor into the system, and that shouldn't have been possible," Forge said. "And what with his new Droniks performing more efficiently than the earlier models, our technicians haven't been able to keep up with the safeguards. The only good thing is that he can't access the OIVs or the Super-Droniks."

"Yes," Hawk muttered, "but he has everything else he needs up there. We're gonna need to put a bullet in his head. That's the only way to stop him."

"I'll make sure he's taken care of," Forge said. "But first we have to get to him."

"If you want that cherished promotion, Colonel," Hawk said, "then Carrington has got to be stopped, even if extreme measures have to be taken."

They continued along the dirt strip to the perimeter of the property. A wire fence with a small gate manned by two heavily armed marines were the only signs that they'd reached it, but the real security was on the inside.

They were let through and continued across rocky terrain, broken only by shrubs and cacti. At the site's epicenter, a dark smudge could be seen. From the air, it looked like a small innocuous lake fed from an underground aquifer, with a simple boathouse built on its bank, but in reality it was a massive underground base with a concealed entrance to the building.

In normal circumstances, Hawk would never have risked driving directly to it, but with all remaining satellites now under his control there was no risk of him being tracked. Still, as he scanned the horizon, he felt uneasy.

What if Wilcox had indeed survived and what if Sheen was helping him? Could he actually make it to here? No, the man was a fool, and not even having access to the master algorithm would give him the skills to stop things now. But he wasn't working alone.

"Colonel, I want men on the ground. The usual defenses may not be enough given Carrington's interference."

"It will be tricky, sir," Forge said. "Most of our troops have ascended to Orbit Station."

"Double the guard," Hawk ordered. "There is a chance that the algorithm may have been compromised – nothing that can't be resolved, but it could present a problem nonetheless."

Forge frowned, then shrugged. "As you will, Mr President. We can always lock down the monorail. Tombside can't be accessed without that."

Hawk agreed, but there was no guarantee the rail couldn't be restarted, especially if the algorithm was being used skilfully.

Christ, if he hadn't been distracted by Sheen, this Carrington mess would never have occurred, not with his critical eye overseeing the whole thing.

They entered the boathouse and got out, waiting for the limo to leave before descending on the concealed elevator. Soon, he'd look Carrington straight in the eye, and then that mad bastard would definitely know he'd made a huge mistake.

Genius or no genius, all men bled the same.

London, 20th February, 2025

I don't normally keep a diary, but after the events at Parliament this morning, I now feel that I have to. I'm just an ordinary backbencher (as anyone who keeps abreast of politics should know) and I tend to keep to the local arena. I play squash and a spot of golf to keep my blood pressure down, and yes, I also like reading. But after witnessing those things and what they did in London today, I'm having a very hard time…

Had to take a moment there, but the brandy has helped a little. Anyway, those things, those fucking alien things, they have killed nearly everyone. The Prime Minister's dead, everyone's dead. But I made it out onto the street and my God, the sights that I have seen. The city is on fire, thousands of bodies lying dead on the roads, lights in the sky, and those awful things stalking through the streets, their terrible eyes, their teeth aglow, the strange chattering voices.

I managed to bribe a cabbie and yes, it cost me a fortune, but I eventually made it home, and so here I am writing in order that one day my experience can be related. But first, my goodness, I need another brandy.

— Michael Moriarty Burns (MP)

271

Chapter 15

At this elevation, it was cooler than one would expect in Arizona. Shana drove them carefully over the rutted ground, navigating through the cacti and rolling brush that littered the sand.

It was surreal riding through the night with everything rendered in green and yellow by the night vision goggles, but even stranger was the fact they were being hunted by robotic machines.

Bradley paused to look around while Shana examined the map. "There'll be a fence, right?" he said. It should be coming up very soon. Surely they wouldn't miss it.

Shana lowered the map and looked at him through the elongated lenses. "It will be monitored," she said. "I'd rather not give them any idea we're coming."

Bradley stretched his neck and back, feeling the pain in his shoulder. The adrenaline from the crash had made him numb to it, but now it was aching terribly.

He heard a noise in the brush and raised his gun.

"Just a roadrunner, I think," Shana said.

Bradley lowered the gun and went to wipe the sweat from his forehead with his left arm, lowering it again with a hiss of pain.

"Are the stitches holding?"

"Yeah," Bradley said. He wasn't sweating because of the pain, though – it was the gun in his hand. He'd have to use it at some point and when that happened, he'd better shoot straight because their enemy most certainly would. At least the fear was a distraction from the throbbing ache in his shoulder.

"We're getting close," Shana said. "Come on."

They crested another hill and switched off the engine when they saw the glint of razor wire in the distance. Shana motioned for him to drop and they stared out across the sand at the fence stretching into the night. Atop each post, Bradley could see small bulbs that he imagined must be sensors or cameras. Shana already had the antenna aimed at the fence and was messing with the sleeve of her jacket.

Bradley looked back to the fence and saw the glow of distant headlights. He nudged Shana and pointed as a small buggy fitted with a heavy machine gun drove around the perimeter, driven by a security guard. They ducked down and waited for it to pass.

"The algorithm won't work on those guys," Shana said, putting the device back in her jacket pocket. "Let's move before another one turns up."

He followed her at a jog down the slope to the fence, and crouched beside her while she looked through the bag for the wire cutters.

"The sensors are down, at least," she said. "The algorithm is doing its job."

Bradley didn't answer, silently willing her to hurry. There was a lot of area in the compound, but there could be an equally large quantity of men patrolling it. He suppressed his nerves. They'd come this far with a combination of Sheen's assistance, Shana's technical skill, his nose for a story, and, naturally, a large amount of luck. Hopefully, their good fortune would hold out.

Shana cut through the wire while Bradley acted as sentry. It seemed to take an eternity, but she finally made a hole large enough for them to crawl through. Bradley followed after her.

They pushed the wire back into place, holding it down with a rock. Shana still had the antenna out – without that, he was sure a hundred soldiers would be descending upon them – but it was nerve-racking. He wished they had some of that graphene material to disguise themselves from the naked eye.

Shana's voice drew him from his thoughts and he looked to where she was pointing. There was a small structure before them, maybe a quarter of a mile away. Bradley watched as headlights blazed forth – security leaving on another search.

"That has to be it," he said.

"We'll be invisible to their sensors," Shana said. "But if Hawk is as sharp as Sheen says, he'll know that we're coming. It's possible that he's also aware we have access to the algorithm. Once they notice the problems with the cameras and whatever other security they have, we could be in deep shit."

"So what do you think we should do?"

She snorted. "I really don't know. It looks like we're fucked, actually."

Bradley swore. There had to be some way to even the odds. He heard the roar of an engine and saw the lights coming back their way. *Shit. Shit, shit.* "Lie down," he said.

"They'll see us," Shana replied, her voice drained of emotion.

"Just lie down. I have a plan, and if it works, you'll be buying the drinks in Mexico."

She lay down, confusion on her face, but hope, too. Bradley stepped back and made sure his goggles were on properly. His only hope was that in the dark and in his fatigues, they might mistake him as one of their own, and if the algorithm was doing its job, and the security guards couldn't radio for help, there was a chance that his bluff might just work.

Bradley levelled his gun at Shana and waved at the armored buggy. As it approached, he saw two men on board – one driving, the other holding a gun and speaking urgently into a radio. His legs felt weak.

The buggy skidded to a halt and the passenger jumped out, pistol in hand. "Drop your weapon and identify yourself!" he shouted.

"I followed this woman from the crash site," Bradley replied with as much authority as he could muster. "I shot her, but I think she's still alive. Hawk will want her for interrogation."

"I said identif—"

Bradley sprayed the man with a burst of fire, watching him fall to the ground like a shaking ragdoll. The driver had been trying to get his radio to work and couldn't bring his gun up in time. When Bradley eventually lowered his automatic weapon, two corpses lay dead on the sand. He stared at them, the memory of the dead security guard from the graphene factory still fresh in his mind. But these two were dead by his hand.

He realized this would happen, that he'd been gearing up for this ever since Detroit, psychologically preparing himself for what he knew must inevitably occur. He felt Shana's hand on his arm but it took him a while before he could look at her.

"Come on," she said, speaking softly. "We can take the buggy. Someone might have heard the shots."

276

They walked to the vehicle. His whole body felt numb, wondering if the two men had families, whether they had even known the details of what they were supposed to be protecting.

He swiftly shook the thoughts away. This wasn't the time nor the place. Now they had to stop Hawk so that millions more people didn't end up the same as these two slain souls that were rapidly cooling into the particles of desert sand.

Shana got behind the wheel, but Bradley stopped to pull the ID badges from the two dead men before getting in beside her. He passed her one of the badges. They appeared to be of standard issue, with a photo of the respective wearer and a metallic hologram fitted underneath. Maybe they'd help, maybe they wouldn't.

"Let's check out that building," Shana said, putting the buggy into gear and accelerating over the bumpy ground. "Maybe it's the entrance to whatever Hawk's trying to hide."

"You think they heard the shots?" Bradley asked, feeling slightly nauseous. There was a spray of blood over the back of the vehicle.

"Yeah, maybe," she said, glancing at him. "You had to do it. I know you aren't trained for this kind of thing, but this is war. They would have tortured you, maybe even killed us both. They'd have done whatever they had to do to find out what we know and how far our resistance goes."

Bradley glimpsed movement by the building and saw a guard standing by the entrance to what looked like a small hangar at the edge of a calm lake. A boathouse?

"Heads up," he said. "It's the welcome committee."

277

Hawk and Forge were in the space elevator, clad in silver pressure suits and holo-graphene armor plating, accompanied by half a dozen marines. Hawk had a prototype E-8 pistol at his hip, while the others carried laser rifles and algorithmic disruptors, but even with these highly-trained men and the cutting-edge equipment that they carried, he was concerned.

Carrington was far more dangerous than he'd ever imagined. A lot of good men had been sacrificed just clearing a path to his lab. Hawk had by now evacuated Orbit Station of all secondary programmers and non-essential personnel, and had also recalled the majority of the OIVs, leaving only those essential to the Maneuver to carry on targeting key areas of the planet. But now he focused his mind and listened to Forge as he briefed the men.

"The main objective has control of the launch bays and the workshops," Forge said, his voice gruff and as no-nonsense as always. "He's directing advanced Droniks from the control room, which is sheltered by blast shields, and he's taken down all connections to the Orbit Station CPU, so we can't disconnect his machines or cut life support without damaging the station. Because of this, you've been issued with the new disrupters. They aren't field-tested as yet and their radius is unpredictable, so make sure your helmets are connected before we arrive – you'll need them if the hull is breached or if we lose atmosphere."

Hawk felt another surge of anger. He hadn't intended on deploying the disrupters anytime soon. They were limited in many ways, and in the wrong hands they could become a serious threat to his algorithm. But the alternative was far worse: a tactical strike on the elevator wouldn't only damage billions of dollars of equipment, it would also alert the world to its presence, and that would be catastrophic.

Hawk shrugged off Colonel Forge's helpful assistance and pulled his helmet on, watching various icons appear in his visor. They were wearing streamlined versions of the exo-suits – all the strength and durability, but without the extra-terrestrial accessories – and he'd logged over a hundred hours in them, both on the ground and in zero-G.

The elevator started to slow as a female voice signalled that they were nearing Orbit Station. The marines checked their guns and environmental systems. This was it.

The lights flickered and died. Hawk looked around, then felt gravity shift slightly. It was pitch-black and he switched to thermal, seeing the others doing the same.

Forge's voice came over his headset. "All power to the elevator has vanished."

"Open the damn door," Hawk snapped at the nearest marine.

He watched as the man tried to open the maintenance hatch in the wall, then pulled the switch to manually open the doors. The power outage was Carrington's doing, and Hawk was damned if that was going to stop him.

The door was pulled open just enough for them to pass through. Hawk went first, his weapon in hand. He missed the weight of the Colt, but this new age had no place for nostalgic sentiment.

"Get the power back on," he said, stepping onto the walkway. "We need all systems up and running."

Forge directed one of the men to the power terminal beside the door. A scorched body lay on the ground next to a burned-out Dronik, and when they reached the edge of the main chamber, the true horror of Oswald Carrington's betrayal became apparent.

Emergency lights were flashing silently. Bodies were strewn across the floor, together with the charred remains of various Droniks and other debris from the surrounding rooms. Hawk saw other men in exo-skeletons coming their way.

"Any developments?" Forge asked, hurrying to meet them.

"We've gotten into the programming suites," one of them said. He was limping, his armor pierced and blistered from where a Dronik energy pulse must have hit him. "The Dronik problem has been brought under control for now, but the target has moved to the edge of the level. EMPs are obviously out of the question, we can't risk explosives, and the doors have been designed to withstand a great deal of punishment. It will take an hour to cut our way in."

"Can you access environmental controls?" Hawk asked.

"No, sir. The algorithm alters every time we attempt to hack into it. It's like trying to break into a mainframe that teleports to a different country with every failed attempt."

So it was doing exactly what it was designed to do. Well, at least with the disrupters Carrington would be vulnerable.

"Lead the way, Sergeant," Forge said.

Hawk holstered his weapon and followed them to the sub-elevator that would take them to the programming level. He glanced down at Earth, which was visible through the Gallery's massive windows. When dawn came, Carrington would be dead, and the

280

Maneuver would accelerate once more. If anyone else tried their hand against him now, they would also pay the ultimate price.

***

Bradley had taken out the first guard with the butt of his gun, but the second had required sterner measures.

When the report from Shana's pistol had died, another corpse lay dead on the ground. She didn't seem too concerned, but then she'd had military training. Maybe she had killed before. Bradley felt uneasy when he thought of her past, of what he didn't know about her, of the lies she'd told, the lies she was still telling.

"Brad." Shana pointed in the direction of a cargo elevator.

They entered the elevator and inspected its controls – a simple device with only a couple of buttons visible. Shana stood next to him as Bradley pushed a button. Nothing happened.

"Maybe it's voice activated," she said. "Look, there's the mic."

"Down," Bradley said, feeling awkward as he leaned close to it.

The door rapidly slid shut, then the elevator let out a dull motorized hum and began its quick descent. Bradley looked at a camera in the ceiling and prayed it wasn't working. God help them if they were walking into a trap.

"We're going very deep," Shana said, breaking the near-silence of the elevator hum.

Bradley agreed. They were certainly moving down fast, and getting much deeper every passing second.

When the elevator finally ground to a noisy halt, they stepped out onto a long platform. Bradley looked around cautiously, but the place appeared to be deserted. Looking further up the platform, he could see a tunnel carved neatly into the rock, rigidly supported by metallic beams. A narrow rail hung down from the central section, while fluorescent tubing illuminated the semi-circular structure as it stretched ad infinitum into the distance.

"How far do you think this tunnel goes?" Shana asked.

"I really don't know," Bradley said. "But I suppose another walk won't hurt."

They entered the tunnel and followed it for what seemed like an eternity, glancing frequently at the metallic track hanging above their heads and wondering what kind of weird machine ran through this thing.

"I've been thinking," Shana said, echoing his own thoughts. "What if a train or something comes through this tunnel? What are we going to do?"

Bradley had been quietly pondering the same thought. "Don't even go there!" he said. "I've been trying not to think about it… but I've noticed that there are escape culverts in the side walls every so often. So keep your eyes peeled for them, just in case?"

They'd been walking for hours when Shana suddenly stopped.

"What is it?" Bradley asked, wincing as the pain flared up in his shoulder.

"Can you feel that?" Shana said, looking back down the tunnel in the direction from where they came. "Like I felt a slight wind."

"You must be imagining things," Bradley said, growing impatient.

"No, I definitely felt something."

282

"I can't feel—" Bradley paused. It was warm down here, but he realized there was a cool breeze just beginning to strengthen against his forehead. "Wait a minute…" He stood motionless, straining his ears.

"There it is again. Brad, can you feel it?"

Flakes of light powdery dust appeared to float down from the tunnel roof. A distant metallic noise had now broken the eerie silence.

"I think the track has started to vibrate," Shana said, her voice raised a higher pitch. "Something big and fast is coming this way and we're directly in its path. Are you thinking what I'm thinking?"

"Yeah, I think we had better run for it."

They began to run as fast as they could, every now and again quickly turning their heads to glimpse back along the tunnel and see if they could see anything in the distance. By now there was a pronounced high-pitched noise that filled the air and the wind had grown much stronger.

"I've got a real bad feeling about this," Bradley panted.

"No kidding," Shana snapped. "Hurry up!"

"I'm—" Bradley broke off as he spotted a faint red light in the distance. "Shit."

"Brad! We can't hang around!"

"I think it's too late for running," he shouted. The wind and sound pressure had increased to a mind-blowing intensity.

"This way!"

He spun around and saw Shana by the edge of the tunnel. "I think I see one of those culverts!" she shouted, "Yes! Over there, on the right side, about fifty feet! Follow me!"

Bradley could feel his heart pounding as he sprinted after her. His legs felt as though he was carrying lead weights. He risked another look back and saw the distant red light had become a brilliant crimson circle, flashing menacingly as it came screeching toward them at the speed of a bullet.

He concentrated all his efforts on running, trying to ignore the threatening turbulence. Their shadows were cast long before them and the incessant red glow now illuminated the entire tunnel. He saw Shana's face, her eyes wide open in terror. In one split second, he grabbed her with his good arm and dived headlong from the tunnel into the darkness of the culvert.

No more than a second later, the combined force of noise and the rush of wind was so insanely loud and so awful that Bradley could barely hold on to consciousness. The machine raced past them at incredible speed, missing them by inches, then it disappeared in a pulsating whine that lowered in pitch until it finally vanished down the tube. For a second or two they just sat there looking at each other, shocked that they were still alive.

"That was so fucking close," Shana whispered.

"Never a dull moment," Brad responded, laughing.

They sat there in the safety of the culvert for a minute, not really wanting to move, just looking into each other's eyes, trying to gauge where this crazy adventure was going to lead them. Bradley caressed Shana's face and kissed her gently.

"Let's go," he said, smiling. "We've got work to do."

They continued down the tunnel, looking back at the slightest sound, but nothing else came their way. Bradley was beginning to worry that they may end up walking all night when he saw

284

something far off down the track. He signalled to Shana to stop and strained his eyes as he peered into the distance.

"What is it?"

"A platform, I think," he said. "Cross your fingers, this might be what we are looking for."

"Do you think somebody could be waiting for us?" Shana asked, anxiously.

"Let's tread carefully."

They continued, walking slowly so as not to make any loud noises, until they finally reached a seemingly deserted platform. At the far end of the platform was a heavy door, which was wide open, and beyond it, a reflective silver tunnel. It was like something straight out of a sci-fi movie.

"It doesn't look like anyone is here," Shana said.

"No," Brad replied. "But this place is gigantic." He kept his finger on the trigger of his gun as they made their way. He certainly wasn't going to get complacent now.

Shortly, they reached a closed door with a security scanner and placed their stolen IDs over it. The door silently slid open and the sound of a muffled siren grew louder.

"What if they're working on something dangerous down here?" Shana said, following Bradley across the threshold. "What if something's gotten loose?"

"Something dangerous? Like a virus?"

"Or something really weird, like an alien," Shana said. "What if those fucking things are down here and are on the loose?"

Bradley shrugged. He wasn't sure what difference it made. The world was under attack by an enemy using technology far superior to anything any nation on Earth could deploy. Human or alien, the result was the same.

They cautiously followed the corridor without meeting another soul, but nearing a junction, Bradley heard voices. He motioned for Shana to hang back, then peered around the corner. Two men in silver armor with strange-looking weapons hanging from their shoulders were standing at a large steel door, talking in urgent tones.

Bradley ducked back, breathing fast. "Two big grunts around that corner," he whispered. "I don't think these guns will cut it."

Shana risked a look. "At least they're human," she said.

"But that armor will stop anything," Bradley replied. "How are we supposed to get past them?"

"Their heads aren't protected," Shana said.

"Yeah, but if we miss—"

Before Bradley could finish his sentence, Shana had stepped around the corner, her pistol levelled at the two men.

She fired two shots and looked back at him. "Come on. We can take their weapons."

Bradley followed her, stunned at what had just happened. The two soldiers were slumped against the door, a neat hole in each of their heads. By the time he reached them, Shana had already started removing the armor from the nearest soldier.

"I've been shooting since I was a kid," she said, undoing a clasp on the man's chest. "But I'm not in the habit of murdering people, before you ask."

"I wasn't going to say anything," Bradley responded.

"But you were thinking it," she said. "Yes, I have killed before, I won't deny that. But this is not the time to talk about it." She turned

286

the man over and inspected the mechanism on the spine of his armor. She jabbed at a button and pulled a slim handle. The whole assembly loosened. "Put this on," she said. "It won't fit me, but it may help you to blend in, and maybe give you some protection."

With Shana's help, Bradley got into the armor, feeling it automatically tighten around his back and shoulders. He felt much lighter, much stronger.

"It's an advanced exoskeleton," Shana said. "I've seen prototypes, but nothing like this." She lifted one of the rifles with both hands and passed it to him. "God, this weighs a ton."

With the armor, it weighed practically nothing. Bradley took a few steps, surprised at how easy and agile he felt .

"You think that's what those alien things were wearing?" Shana asked.

"Hard to say, but they were real ugly fuckers."

"At least we have an advantage now," Shana said, pushing a button on the panel beside the door. "Something's definitely going down. Those guys were highly trained, but they looked seriously nervous about something – and whatever that something is, it isn't us."

The door opened, revealing another elevator. "Looks like we're about to go deeper," Bradley said, following her inside. With the armor firmly strapped around his shoulders, he felt a little more reassured about having infiltrated this bizarre cavern. "Stay close to me."

"I'm not leaving your side, Wilcox. Don't you worry about that."

He hoped she wasn't lying.

The last Remote died and the signal ended. Carrington was finishing the next algorithmic spike, but had a lump in his throat at the thought of his dead Droniks. They'd certainly bought him the time he'd so badly needed, and he could always produce others at a later date, but it had been a great sacrifice.

"Your loss will be avenged my loyal friends," he pledged aloud. "I will make thousands more, a million more like you – and then the Counterweight Maneuver will be mine, all mine."

Hawk had possessed the vision, but even with his formidable will and intellect, the ultimate step was way beyond his means. No, this was his call now! The destructive, useless, parasitic tide of humanity must be culled if the planet was ever to be saved. Now it was up to him, Oswald Carrington, to finally finish it.

Carrington's headset beeped and he saw the colored blips appear on the lens above his left eye. So another batch of Hawk's dogs had entered the elevator? He finished the code and injected it into the algorithm with a final keystroke, then stood and made his way to the ventilation duct, watching as the panel slid apart. He'd have clear access to the assembly hall, and those pursuing him would have no idea where he was until it was far too late.

A muffled murmuring at the door declared the soldiers had reached his lab. They'd be chomping at the bit to get to him, to inflict a painful revenge for the dozens of men left dead at the hand of his Droniks. He slipped quickly through the hole and resealed the panel, then dropped down to where the shaft curved. Let them waste time cutting through. By the time they achieved that, they'd soon learn how powerful Oswald Carrington's intellect really was.

***

The disrupter burned through the defenses Carrington had built around the algorithm, cutting out his defense codes and reinstating power back to all machinery.

Hawk let out a long breath borne of both concern and relief. The disrupters worked and had given him an edge over Carrington, but with such a powerful tool, the effectiveness of the algorithm was compromised.

Assuming this situation was resolved, he'd have to get his scientists to research further solutions for repairing this Achilles' heel. Technological innovation was as ruthless as natural selection, and Hawk had no intention of becoming obsolete just as his plan was being put into effect.

"I'm opening the door," one of the marines shouted.

Forge and his men were crouched, rifles levelled. Hawk drew his weapon and moved to stand beside them. A part of him doubted Carrington was in there. Surely it couldn't be this easy. The door whispered open with barely a sound and the men moved in, covering every angle of the room with their guns.

"It's empty, sir."

Of course it was.

"Find his exit," Hawk said, walking over to the terminal. The screen was blank, but the disruptor would have caused a reboot in most of the systems. "Check the ventilation shafts."

"The panel's locked down," Forge said. "Get the schematic up. We'll cover the exits."

Hawk knew Carrington would never attempt a blind escape route. He couldn't take the space elevator down – that would be tantamount to suicide – and even a genius would have severe difficulties piloting an OIV without the appropriate training.

A heavily armed soldier arrived at the door. "Sir. I've been informed that the elevator's running again. I've contacted Tombside and they're locking it down at their end. It will be ready when we need it."

"Monitor the escape capsules," Forge said. "If he tries to escape that way, we'll blow him clean out of the sky."

Hawk brought up OIV status on his headset and noted that twenty-three of the thirty currently active machines were nearing the space elevator, having now made the high-speed transit around the moon in order to maintain the illusion of an alien base on the dark side.

"Prepare the docking bay for the returning OIVs," he said to the Colonel. "Carrington's looking for a way out. I really can't see him piloting one of those things out of here, but he could have something up his sleeve."

"I'll send a warning code," Forge said. "The crews will be ready when they get here. If Carrington tries to board one, he'll be taken out immediately."

Hawk felt a pang of regret at the loss of such a brilliant mind, but Carrington was never expected to come through this once they'd started him on the course of nootropics.

"When he's been dealt with, the programmers and techs can be brought back up," Forge continued. "There's a helluva lot of damage to fix, and there's no telling what booby-traps Carrington may have left for us."

"Are all the Droniks accounted for?"

"The two Super-Droniks back on Earth have been secured. One is seriously damaged, and we disconnected the other the moment Carrington began his assault on the algorithm. The three in Bay Gamma are similarly locked down."

They'd better be, Hawk thought.

***

Carrington dropped to the metal floor and crawled across it, using a stack of fuel cells for cover.

They'd broken his code much quicker than he'd expected, which meant they must have utilized some kind of tool or device that he hadn't been aware of. Well, it made sense that Hawk would keep something in reserve – any intelligent person would.

Carrington heard the access door to the launch bay opening, then muffled voices entering the chamber. He quickly made for the coolant line of the nearest Super-Dronik. The soldiers would be using a variety of imaging measures, but with the freezing coolant and the radio magnetic interference from the nearby transmitters, he should be safe... for now.

"Sweep the room," one of the soldiers barked. "We'll have OIVs returning in five. The target could be anywhere on this level."

Carrington took out the explosive he'd improvised from a Dronik battery. Once this went off, he'd have a very limited time to act, but when he did, Hawk would finally realize who the real Oswald Carrington was – the young guy who was about to prove he wasn't just your standard crackpot. Carrington didn't know whether it was the pills he'd been taking or just the stress of his situation, but he'd been pushing the envelope since day one, making plans in case he ever became superfluous to Hawk's requirement. But rather than him becoming redundant, it was Hawk who was no longer necessary.

He heard footsteps as a soldier rounded the corner, clad in special armor and impervious to conventional weaponry. Carrington had already activated the explosive and was on his feet by the time the device went off.

He ran, his eyes focused on the massive Super-Dronik parked before him. It would be locked down, of course, and now they had the algorithm running there was little he could do to modulate it. Carrington had known this would happen; in fact, he'd already prepared for it when he'd developed the improved Dronik designs. But now he was underneath the machine as the first tugs of the vacuum caught his hair. The compartment in its underbelly opened and he hurled himself in.

He caught his breath in the dark interior, blinking as the lights activated. The chair and control mechanism filled most of the space, but it was fully programmed, and wasn't running on the same algorithm as Hawk's. It was new, it was separate, and the micro-Dronik he'd ensconced within this thing was entirely under his control.

Carrington hauled himself up into the chair as the flight console illuminated. The camera turned from the suffocating soldier on the ground to the others running back towards the bay door. He smiled in amusement as the group of soldiers shot wildly in his direction. They didn't know he was in there, but the Super-Dronik's holographene armor had been designed to repulse the E-7 rifles, and even if they'd managed to inflict superficial damage, the micro-Dronik inside was perfectly safe.

Carrington whistled a tune while he waited. Soon he'd act.

Very soon.

Chapter 16

Bradley paused while Shana leaned against the wall, breathing heavily.

"Thanks. I need a break."

"We need to get moving as soon as you can," he said, looking around. "I feel okay, to be honest."

"You're wearing an exo-suit," Shana said, glaring back at him. "You were panting like a bitch back when we were running from that monorail."

Bradley had totally forgotten he was wearing the armor, it was so comfortable. "Well, we can't stay here much longer," he said. "It's only a matter of time before we run into someone."

"What do you think they're hiding down here?" Shana asked.

Bradley shrugged. "We'll find out soon enough." He hoped.

"I guess if you're going to hide a massive base, then deep underground is the place to put it," Shana said, getting back up. She sighed. "Would you mind going first? I really don't want to get shot."

They continued along the silver tunnel. After a while, Bradley noticed there were doors on each side, and windows at regular intervals.

"Looks like this area may be inhabited," he said.

"Just act cool and casual," Shana said. "With you in uniform, we might just get overlooked."

Yeah, especially if something else is distracting them, Bradley was about to reply, but deep down he thought they'd just as easily get shot on sight.

"You have any family, Brad?" Shana asked.

"My parents died last year."

"Oh, I'm sorry."

"Don't mention it," Bradley said. "I thought you might have done a check on me. Isn't that what governments do when they're using civilians?"

"Sheen needed you urgently," Shana said. "All I knew was that you were a disgruntled journalist with a high-profile story. And maybe a couple of other things."

They got to a junction. A man and a woman in silver lab coats were walking hurriedly in their direction. Bradley half-raised his gun, but Shana hissed at him to lower it. The two people – *scientists?* – passed them without a word, their eyes transfixed on the tablets held in their hands. They practically looked like zombies.

"They don't look too good," Shana whispered, once they'd passed.

"We'll be lucky if everyone else is so… erm, vacant," Bradley replied, searching for the right word. "Come on."

They kept going, occasionally passing people dressed in the same uniform. At one point, they passed a room of computers with technicians intently hunched over their screens.

"They gotta be drugged," Shana said. "Something very strange is going on."

They reached a sign with arrows pointing to various parts of the complex: Residential Units, Programming Suites, Medical Center, Cafeteria, Main Elevator.

"Main Elevator? This thing goes deeper?" Bradley said.

"Or it could be an exit to the surface," Shana mused. "I don't like this. I mean, what is this place? Do you think it's being evacuated? Have we come all this way for nothing?"

"We've made it this far," he said. "But we really have to get to the bottom of this."

They continued past glass-fronted rooms with people hard at work. They saw the occasional marine and one even nodded at them, but they weren't stopped. Something was keeping them too busy.

Finally, Shana stopped a man in a lab coat. "Any word on the situation?" she asked, casually.

The man sighed. "The main elevator's still closed to everyone but the military," he said, rubbing his temple as if in pain. "You really should return to your work station, technician. The project doesn't stop for anything, you know that."

He continued on his way, turning into one of the computer rooms. "These guys are sure dedicated," Bradley said, watching the door slide shut behind him.

"They obviously don't work directly for the government," Shana said, frowning. "Nobody on a government project would be so driven."

They continued until they reached a T-junction that broadened into a wider hall than the corridors they'd just navigated through.

"Please tell me the algorithm's still broadcasting," Bradley said, quietly.

Shana nodded.

They took a right, following the sign to the elevator. Bradley immediately saw armed soldiers at the end of the corridor. There were four of them, all standing by a complicated-looking, heavy door made of synthetic metal and glass. It looked very different to the rest of the compound.

"That must be the elevator," he said.

"It looks damn sophisticated for an elevator," Shana remarked. "But the rest of the place is hardly primitive."

One of the soldiers was speaking into his headset, while the others stood toting their guns. They looked focused and ready for anything. "Maybe we should make tracks outta here," Bradley mumbled.

"Corporal!" the nearest soldier shouted at him. "We've just had word from Control that the sensors topside have been compromised! What's the status in the South Warren?"

Bradley thought about faking it, but he knew nothing about the military save what he'd seen on TV. The moment he opened his mouth, those soldiers would know he wasn't one of them. A glimmer of perplexed suspicion crossed the soldier's face, but suddenly Shana ran forwards.

"We've just heard intruders have entered!" she shouted. "Multiple units converging on the programming suites!"

Three of the soldiers immediately started running down the hall, leaving one at the door. Shana pushed a button on her wrist and Bradley had to move aside quickly as heavy blast shutters suddenly dropped from the ceiling, separating them from the three soldiers. The remaining one looked over in alarm, but Bradley reacted first, burning a hole through his chest and dropping him like a fallen marionette.

"I noticed those things throughout the compound," Shana said, heading for the elevator. "Blast doors or something."

Bradley looked at the heavy shutter, noting a red glow at its center. He thought he could hear banging on the other side.

"They're using their energy weapons to cut through," he said, catching up to Shana.

"It'll take a while." She examined the code panel on the elevator door, while looking at the complicated mechanism. The hologram keyboard instantly materialized from her jacket. "This thing's locked, all right. Not sure if I can crack it, even if I use the algorithm. It's changing constantly."

Bradley glanced where the soldiers were attempting to cut through, and noticed that the blast shutters had come down in the opposite direction.

"Is there another way out?" he asked.

Shana shook her head. "I can open the shutters, but then they'll be in and it's mission over."

Bradley hefted the gun and covered the door. He hadn't planned on seeing his mom and dad again quite so soon.

***

Hawk shoved past the soldiers, taking the steps down to the lower level three at a time. The door opened the moment he entered his personal code, and he strode into the main chamber, weapon in hand.

The access door was closed and he ran up to the glass, pressing his face hard against it to peer into Bay Gamma. A white-faced soldier floated past the screen.

"He's used an explosive to depressurise the bay," Forge said, appearing at his side. "Logan got caught in the blast and died when his suit got ripped."

Hawk scanned the interior, but apart from the dead soldier, there was no sign of Carrington. "Did he get out?"

Forge shook his head. "Not unless he was blown out of the bay because of the explosion."

Hawk gritted his teeth. There was no way Carrington would kill himself, no matter how far those drugs had pushed him. If his body wasn't in there, he was somewhere else.

Then his eyes alighted on the Super-Dronik at the back. Had he seen something move? A light or the glint of metal?

"We need to double check everything," he said. "Make sure that Dronik isn't powered up."

"It shouldn't be. The disrupters have nullified the algorithm," Forge said. But still, he ordered one of the marines to perform an authentication of the now moribund equipment.

Hawk stared at the massive killing machine. It was indeed switched off, the algorithm blasted out of the system by the disrupters' high-powered signal. Not even Carrington could make Hawk's algorithm function differently – it was too unique, far too *alien*. But could he have discovered some other way?

"All power is off, sir," the marine said. "But there is something…"

"What?" Hawk snarled, turning on the man. "What the hell is *something*? Be specific, soldier!"

"A faint heat signature," the marine said, quickly. "Warmer than a body, but nowhere near that generated by machinery."

"Coming from where?"

The marine checked the screen again, then looked at Hawk with fear in his eyes. "Inside that thing, sir."

"How long until the OIVs get back?" Hawk asked, the blood draining from his face.

"ETA is three minutes, sir."

"Get reinforcements up here, Colonel," Hawk said.

"Looks like we've found Carrington, sir," Forge's voice buzzed in his ear. But he was wrong. Carrington had found them.

***

A thick metallic section of the shutter fell, glowing red, to the floor.

"Any luck?" Bradley hurriedly asked, while looking anxiously at Shana, who was frantically working on the elevator codes.

She mumbled a negative, then asked him to hush up so she could concentrate. Bradley swore under his breath.

Hawk possessed the algorithm – he could have created the damned thing for all they knew – and if he wanted that elevator door locked, there was nothing they could do about it. It was infuriating to have come this far only to be thwarted by the very thing they had depended so much upon.

And to come this close to Hawk's secret! What was he up to here? Why the extraordinary levels of security, the incredible technology, the zombie-like scientists? And what the fuck did it have to do with aliens terrorizing the planet?

Another section of the shutter crumbled and voices sounded. They'd be through any second.

"What the… Wait! It's on!" Shana stood back as the doors opened.

"You did it?" Bradley exclaimed.

Shana didn't answer, but stepped into the elevator to examine the control panel inside.

Bradley followed and the door shut tight. "Come on, they'll be on us any second."

Shana punched a button, but there was no movement.

"Try saying Up or Down," Bradley frantically shouted at her.

"My God, we're moving," she said, smiling. "We're going up."

"I hope they aren't waiting for us at the other end," he said, as the elevator quickly gathered speed. "That soldier said something about equipment failures. They're bound to be waiting for us."

"Well, I think we have a while," Shana said.

Bradley suddenly noticed she looked pale and frightened. "A while?" he repeated.

"The next stop is 22,369 miles up."

He did a few quick calculations in his head. *Around 22,400 miles?* He felt faint and shook his head to clear the fear from his mind. "That means we're going beyond normal satellite orbit?"

"This could explain where those alien ships are coming from," she said. "Do you think Hawk has a base up there? My God, and I thought his algorithm was impressive. That clever bastard's constructed a space elevator that's invisible to the rest of the planet!"

"This thing was shut down for a specific reason," Bradley said. "All that commotion back there – I wonder what caused it?"

"Let me see if I can get something… on… the…" Shana's eyes grew wide, and Bradley turned to see the view through the glass: a dark patch of ground, the light of a city in the distance, and the stars spreading out across the sky, then a vast stretch of cloud floated beneath them. Now they were lifting faster and faster.

"We're going into space, Brad," Shana said, her voice getting higher.

Bradley found his throat getting tighter as the light of the stars grew more distinct than he'd ever seen them before. The heavens were so awe-inspiring, so sublime, and this small planet that they lived upon so unique and so precious. And yet this beautiful paradise was a constantly evolving warzone, in a seemingly eternal state of flux. Eden was a commodity now, a thing to be taken before it was used up. Maybe humanity didn't deserve any of this.

"It's truly amazing," he said, feeling anguish welling up inside him. "But will this thing prove to have an ulterior motive? It certainly wasn't designed as an amusement ride."

"I know," Shana said, still watching the view. "But if we don't get to Mexico, at least we got a few minutes to ourselves somewhere incredibly enchanting."

Bradley turned and kissed her gently on the lips. "You are so beautiful," he whispered to her.

Shana sighed. "I love you so much, Brad."

Their eyes met for several seconds, before the moment was interrupted by a chiming sound coming from the elevator panel.

"The climb indicator says we have another seven minutes until we reach the next level – Orbit Station, it's called."

"Very appropriate."

Shana frowned and ran her finger over the screen. A compartment in the wall popped open and she took out what looked

302

like breathing apparatus. "Here, put this on," she said, taking one for herself. "If there was an accident up here – well, I'd rather not think about it."

She pulled the mask over her face. Bradley put his own mask on, and felt it connect to the collar of his suit. He'd be okay, possibly even in a vacuum if the suit was as effective as he imagined it to be, but Shana was only wearing a mask. It wouldn't be enough. He thought suddenly that she might die the instant the exterior door opened, and in that moment, he realized that they were both pawns. She might have played him, but only because she'd been ordered to, and regardless of her duplicity, she was, in a sense, more of a victim than he was – a puppet, conditioned by the system to protect it at all costs.

He touched her cheek with a gauntleted hand and felt a connection – a connection he'd never felt before. Sure, they'd faced death together, killed together, even made love together, and now they stood thousands of miles above the Earth, heading into danger and almost certain death on a journey that had begun way back in a sushi restaurant. She looked at him, her eyes conveying something… fear, thanks… love?

"I meant what I just said to you, Brad."

He embraced her, looking through their masks into her eyes, cut off by technology yet closer than they'd ever been, but now departing from their home planet so far beneath them.

***

Hawk felt the structure shudder under his feet and engaged the gravity mechanism on his boots. The space station was very strong and flexible enough to handle the heaviest of impacts, even a direct hit from a small meteorite, but he hadn't expected this.

"Orders, sir?"

Forge's voice was calm, precise. Hawk appreciated a good soldier and Forge was clearly that – strong, fast, aggressive, cool – but in this instance he needed a superior head to give orders. Hawk watched as Carrington's single-man pod rose from the open doors of the Super-Dronik, having cleverly been disguised from within. It resembled the Super-Dronik, but was smaller, with longer limbs and lighter armor, designed with agility in mind.

It scuttled backwards, raising its forelimbs to protect itself and unfolding dual-pulse guns from its rear. Carrington was inside, no doubt about that, and now, using his creative genius, he had somehow also managed to corrupt the algorithm to his advantage.

The fire of Vulcan was about to let loose, but Hawk still had the upper hand.

He checked the status of his men – most were either dead or cut off from this level. He could see that the space elevator was almost at Orbit Station, but the additional troops he had called for wouldn't be of much use against this beast. His only chance now was to allow the scientist a route out of here. The last thing Hawk wanted was a cornered rat – there was no telling what damage he might inflict if his exit was cut off.

"Open the access from the launch bay to this level," Hawk said. "Have the OIVs remain cloaked, and secure the immediate space around the station. Carrington wants off, and when he jettisons into space, they can blow him to smithereens."

Forge grunted commands into his headset while Hawk withdrew further behind the damaged wall. What was Carrington about to do now? What was he thinking? In a few careful moves, the scientist had virtually decimated Hawk's platoons, shut down most of the Orbit Station, and secured an escape route. Yes, he was mad; however, mad people rarely pursued a logical agenda. Would he try to destroy the entire platform, including himself?

Well, there was little Hawk could do in that event. The only thing remaining would be that the Brotherhood could somehow pick up the pieces and pursue the Maneuver to its final conclusion: if that never materialized, then planet Earth was most certainly doomed to a slow death.

"Ronald? Ronald, are you there?"

Hawk exchanged a surprised look with Forge. It was clear that the Colonel could hear Carrington, too.

"Oswald," Hawk said. "Would you care to inform me what you hope to gain by doing all this?"

"Well, you got me thinking, Ronald, about saving the world."

Hawk gritted his teeth. "That's what we were supposed to be doing. But now you've put everything that we strived so hard to achieve at risk. Why?"

"My precious machines, Ronald." Carrington's voice crackled over the speakers. *"They were my conception and they are all mine... and then I realized something. I realized that this world isn't commensurate or ready for my superior mind – this world needs to be enlightened to something new! Something you and I have both*

created together, Hawk! A merger of mind and machine, science and nature! Don't you see? My Droniks are the future! I will rule this world with an iron fist with the backing of my machines!"

Hawk felt numb inside. The man had well and truly fucking lost it. He glanced over at Forge, who was shaking his head in utter disbelief. Behind him, two more soldiers were making their way along the corridor towards them, magnetic locks engaged, E-9 weapons hooked up to packs on their backs. Hawk gestured for them to hang back.

"Your Droniks are the future, Oswald. But now you've forced my hand. You need to get off my station. Our partnership has formally terminated."

"Leave?" Carrington laughed. *"So that the ships you have waiting in orbit can blow me out of the sky?"*

There was no point lying to him, of course. "You're a dead man walking, so what do you plan on doing about it, Oswald?"

There was silence for a moment, and then Carrington's words came over the headset, crisp and clear and lucid.

"Ronald, my dearest friend, Ronald. I'm going to take the algorithm, and then I will sow its consciousness throughout the planet."

***

When the elevator door finally opened, Bradley half-expected to face the vacuum of space, but instead the corridor was pressurized and Earth gravity was present.

The corridor was deserted. He stepped out cautiously, levelling the rifle down the hallway, then noticed a light flashing in the corner of his mask. The moment he focused on it, a crackle of audio sounded in his ear.

"Dronik incident in Bay Gamma. Immediate backup required, soldier."

Bradley mumbled an affirmative and the light blinked out.

"I heard that," Shana said, pushing her mask back. "You should head there."

"Where?"

"Bay Gamma." She walked over to a monitor on the wall. It activated on her approach, showing a three-dimensional image of the elevator, from the huge subterranean complex at its base to the wide brim of Orbit Station at its tip. "Look. We're at the edge of a massive chamber – the Gallery, it's called. We can take the hallway elevator up to the bay level and then... well, we'll see."

"That voice said there was a... Dronik?"

"Must be one of those drone things we've been dealing with," Shana said. "It sounds like Hawk's technology has turned nasty."

Given the scale of Hawk's plan, Bradley didn't like the sound of that. "We can't just head up there without any idea of what's going on," he said. "You heard that guy earlier, the space elevator's off limits to everyone but military. And, in case you've forgotten, we need to get back to Earth somehow."

"I wonder if there's another way off this thing," Shana mumbled, deep in thought. "Escape pods or a ship or something."

"A ship?" Bradley said, frowning. "Even if we found one, how the hell would we fly it?"

Shana looked back at the diagram. "I'm going to the programming suite. I need to find proof, just in case we ever get a chance to present it. You go deal with the Dronik problem."

"I'm not a grunt," Bradley protested.

"You're in an exo-suit with a weapon you clearly know how to use." She leaned closer. "Your armor must be connected to the network, so they know you're here and they know precisely where you are, but for the moment they still think you're one of them. This Dronik thing could give you the distraction we need. This is your one and only chance to destroy Hawk's operation."

Bradley felt short of breath. He was close to the end, but Christ, did he have a story if he ever got out of this. "Promise me you'll find evidence," he said. "Files, photographs... whatever you can. In case I don't make it."

Shana loosened her oxygen mask until it hung from her neck, then examined his collar with her fingers until he felt the material give a little, and his helmet released with a hiss. She pushed it back and put her lips against his, warm and full.

He returned the kiss, wondering if they were the first two people to ever do this at the fringe of deep space. When she drew back, he didn't know whether to be happy or sad.

"Don't get yourself killed, Wilcox," she said. "I'd hate to appear on the front page by myself."

Incoming Transmission. Delta Code Initiated.

I don't know if you're getting this, Sheen, but I'm still working within Hawk's intelligence unit, though little has changed.

This place is a hive of activity, with pretty much everywhere on the planet being monitored. The alien threat is real, no doubt about that. I've seen communications signed by President Hawk and, if anything, he's more proactive against the invasion than Moore ever was. But now the attack on the White House has occurred, he'll be seeking further control.

I'm going to have to dig deeper to find something. The good news is that my intelligence work has been noticed and I'm being promoted. I have a meeting with Barb – that's the only name I have?

I don't think our cloning of the algorithm has been noticed yet. Hopefully I'll have more news on the Counterweight Maneuver soon.

Got to go now. Someone's at the door.

Chapter 17

Like the algorithmic disrupters, Hawk hadn't intended to deploy the E-9 weapons so soon. Carrington's betrayal had, however, changed all of that.

The moment the scientist's Dronik had lifted itself from the hangar floor, Colonel Forge signalled for the attack. Hawk had moved behind cover before the first high-intensity energy beams carved through the air towards Carrington's silver machine.

Forge roared and threw himself at Hawk, knocking him back before the Dronik's response blew the partition wall clean apart. Hawk got to his feet clumsily, thanking the Colonel. The soldiers carrying the E-9s weren't so lucky: a barrage of energy fire vaporized them where they stood. Hawk cursed. With his weapons appearing ineffective, and his supply of marines rapidly decreasing, it was obvious he wouldn't be able to stop Carrington by conventional means.

"The E-9s barely had any effect," Forge said. "Carrington must have some kind of energy deflection tech implanted into the holo-graphene."

Hawk saw more of his soldiers further down the corridor, crouched and armed, but quite rightly loath to enter combat with the Dronik. One of them was carrying a tablet. Hawk pulled his way slowly along the wall, noticing the gravity shifting a little.

"Get me access to one of the parked OIVs, soldier," he said.

"Isn't that dangerous, sir?" Forge said. "If he has access to our systems—"

"He is using a superior algorithm," Hawk said, speaking through gritted teeth. "But we can keep him locked out temporarily – that we know."

The marine keyed the necessary commands into the pad. Hawk turned to Forge. "The OIV is housed in the lower bay. If we can focus its weapons directly upwards and onto this floor, maybe we can bring that damned thing down – ideally, without damaging the space elevator."

"And what if it reveals our presence to the world?" Forge asked.

Hawk took a deep breath. He didn't like it – the time and resources that had gone into the space elevator had been huge, but the alternative was that Carrington would become the victor and that everything would come to nothing. "We blow the whole thing and claim we were fighting alien tech all along," he said. "The Maneuver will continue, I promise you that."

The marine passed Hawk the pad and he entered his authorization code.

"Now, keep him busy, Colonel," he said to Forge. "I'm going to make that demented maniac wish he'd never been born."

***

Bradley followed the gantry to a corridor leading to the hallway elevator, gun in hand. He'd left Shana at the Gallery in the center, where she'd gone up to the Programming Suite in search of answers. The room had been amazing in its size and design, with a spectacular view of Earth seen through its transparent walls.

312

Yet all Bradley could think of was what lay ahead: a brutal assault, the possibility they'd never leave this place alive, or that he might survive, but that Shana wouldn't. He wasn't sure which was worse.

He had every right to be confused after all that he'd experienced, and having a bullet pass through his shoulder certainly hadn't helped, but the situation with Shana had made him even more uncertain of where he stood. His thoughts oscillated between confidence and doubt, hope and despair. *Fuck. Can this get any more complicated?*

The station shuddered as Bradely tightened his grip on the trigger. There was an electronic squawk from somewhere below, and he moved quicker, ready to shoot at any moment. When he saw the hall elevator in front of him he felt a cold sensation in his stomach. It was like the time he'd tried parachuting, and his instincts had tested his nerve, deliberately undermining his brain. But his brain had won that battle, and it would win this one. He took a deep breath and stepped into the elevator, the automatic female voice politely asking what floor he wanted before he could change his mind.

It descended slowly, much more slowly than the main space elevator, allowing him to watch the Earth through the transparent walls as he went, seeing what he was fighting for – his beautiful home. He could see the light of distant cities further to the west and wondered at the scale of human civilization. It had spread over the entire globe, but in terms of time it was a mere blip. He wondered if the world as he knew it would last in his lifetime or if mankind was about to be blown away like a flickering candle. If they won this battle today, would it really make a difference? Or would humanity return to its old ways and business as usual? Were they but a flash in the great scheme of things? Was all of this for nothing?

The elevator stopped on a gantry, but the door remained shut. A red light flashed on the side. He looked around for something to open it, when a voice crackled over his headset.

"Atmosphere lost! Engaging airlock now! Ensure your suit is environmentally sealed!"

The voice was robotic and Bradley's gut felt even colder. *Atmosphere lost?* Then he heard a noise and saw a metal hatch close overhead, and a hissing sounded. His palms were sweating and he wondered if there was an imperfection in his suit, but as the elevator depressurized, he saw a new icon appear over his visor displaying oxygen levels and temperature. The door opened and he took a deep breath. God, he could use a drink.

***

The internal elevator had taken Shana all the way to the top of Orbit Station, where the programming suites and laboratories were located.

Bodies lay strewn across the floor – scientists, and marines, together with the damaged parts of mini-Droniks – and the only sound was that of the environmental systems quietly purring in a strange low hum from behind the metallic walls. She located a terminal and glanced at it to double-check her route. It wasn't far.

She followed the corridor, stepping over the bodies, her weapon at the ready in case she ran into anyone unfriendly or, worse still, one of those killer machines, but she encountered nothing and reached the room unscathed. Inside, rows upon rows of compact computers lined the walls. She sat in front of the nearest terminal and it activated automatically, immediately asking for ID. She used the algorithm and opened the computer, watching intently as a variety of icons instantly displayed: Algorithm Functions, Dronik Models, Orbital Insertion, Weapon Development, Advanced Technologies, Classified Operations. She tapped the last icon and watched as the computer demanded proof of identity. From the look of it, even the algorithmic coding wouldn't suffice.

There was a noise from the next room. Shana spun in her chair, her weapon aimed in the direction of the sound. She got up and stepped over a fallen chair, its dead occupant slumped to the ground, moving silently to the door. She slid it open and stepped quickly into the next room, sweeping it with the barrel of her gun until the figure of a woman in a white lab coat was in her sights. Her face was white, her eyes wide, and a bloody scorch mark on her right arm revealed she'd been injured.

Shana was about to warn the woman not to move, but she barely reacted to Shana's sudden appearance. Her eyes were as vacant as the scientists she'd previously encountered at the Tombside facility.

"Are you okay?" Shana asked, lowering the gun.

"My computer is damaged," the woman said, frowning. "I need access to saved files."

"I think your work's been put on hold," Shana said.

"I won't be able to meet my deadlines," the woman replied. "I need codes and access to another terminal. Have you seen the coordinator? I can't reach him."

They'd obviously utilized mind-altering drugs to make her more pliable, more efficient. "Where's the coordinator's office?" Shana asked. "Maybe we can find what you need there."

The woman, frowning, turned towards the door without a word. Shana followed her to the corridor and up some steps. The walls became transparent again, revealing the massive Gallery where she and Bradley had previously separated. Shana prayed he was okay.

He was a good man, brave and honest, although somewhat naïve when using a gun. But in this crazy, inconceivable situation when two total strangers were thrown together, she had fallen in love with him. And now he was about to meet Hawk, an incredibly dangerous man. She had to get access to the computers if he was to stand the remotest chance of coming out of this alive.

They reached a door, which was scorched and torn open. Inside the room, Shana could see a computer with multiple monitors, a cup of cold coffee and a half-eaten grilled cheese beside it. "This is the coordinator's terminal?" she asked.

"Can you inform him I can't access the programs," the woman said, staring at her. "My passcodes aren't working."

Shana sat in front of the computer, watching as the screen erupted into chaotic static. The mass of pixels gradually coalesced into a clear picture. But unlike the other terminals, this one had allowed her access.

"I wonder why this terminal is open," she said, smiling at the woman who was standing just beside her and receiving a blank stare in return. Shana shrugged. Something had to go right, she supposed. "Let's see what we can do about those programs of yours."

Forge's ears were ringing as clouds of dust obscured his vision. He took a couple of deep breaths to clear his mind while he scanned the icons on his visor. His suit was still intact, oxygen was okay.

He got up, lifting his E-7 rifle, and saw the large hole Carrington had just blown in the wall.

"Ronald?" Carrington's voice sounded on his headset. *"Ronald? You haven't run away, have you?"*

Fallen debris and damaged infrastructure meant the Dronik would have difficulty leaving this section, but it was still capable of inflicting serious damage. The marines had by now pulled back to avoid its weapon fire.

Forge gritted his teeth. He'd be damned if this scrawny lightweight would be the death of him. He edged closer to the wall and fired a quick barrage of energy at the machine. While most of the ray bounced off its protective plate, he did see an external sensor crumple, and quietly hissed with satisfaction, ducking back a second before the wall dissolved into a puddle of molten metal and flame.

"Colonel Forge. I know you and Hawk are planning a nasty surprise for me, but I'd like to point out that I have taken every precaution. There's nothing you can do now."

Was the little bastard really expecting a conversation? Forge shook his head in disbelief.

He signalled for the men at the other end to lay down cover fire. They couldn't risk communications with Carrington listening in, but Hawk would be at the OIV by now and Forge didn't want to be quite this close when the bay collapsed.

The marines hesitated but obeyed his orders, firing streams of energy into the bay. Forge was already running, propelling himself across the distance with every ounce of strength he could coax from the exo-skeleton. He thought he was prepared for Carrington's response, but the speed with which the damned thing turned on him was a real surprise. One of the marines dissolved into a mess of bone and metal, then Forge felt an incredible heat envelope him, blowing him straight across the corridor on a searing wave of scalding flame. He would have been dead – he should have been dead – but then Hawk's plan came into effect, and Forge found himself smiling despite the pain coursing through his body.

"You weren't expecting that, were you, bitch," he mumbled, watching as the Dronik vanished through the collapsing floor in a billowing haze of smoke.

***

Walking in near-vacuum, Bradley was struck by the silence, but every now and again he felt a tremor run through the structure, and the occasional voice broke over his headset, issuing urgent orders, screaming. Something bad was most certainly happening.

Had Hawk's technology genuinely gone rogue or was he fighting real aliens up here? Either way, Bradley was beginning to think he hadn't needed to come this far after all.

He followed the corridor further, passing another body crumpled in a ball. He bent to examine it and saw that the man had suffocated. He nervously checked his O_2 supply, but the gauge revealed he still had two hours' worth oxygen consumption.

Bradley took a deep breath, suddenly conscious that the exo-suit was the only thing keeping him alive, then shook the thought away. He couldn't panic, not up here. Mankind's future depended upon him, as did Shana's.

He'd only taken three more steps before the entire structure started to shake. He felt the panic return. The lights flickered, then went out. He heard a rushing noise in his ears. Had a seal in his suit broken? No, but something very large had just blown away close by. He had a sudden thought that the main elevator shaft had been cut in two and that he was floating within one section as it was flung from Earth's orbit by its own centrifugal force, doomed to drift forever in space, a metal coffin full of dead men and cold technology.

Just as the fear and apprehension was proving insurmountable, he heard a voice over the intercom, calm, cool, and authoritative: Hawk.

"All available troops to converge on Bay Gamma. The threat is down – I repeat, the threat is down. Repair teams immediately report to your superiors. Emergency communication protocols are enacted. Elevator and life support functions are a priority."

There was a brief pause, and then Hawk's voice again, but now passionate... triumphant, even. *"The orbiting station has just endured its greatest challenge, and with your help and expertise we have managed to prevail. Be assured that our cause is just. Our great country needs us. Our world needs us. We will not fail in this noble quest. God Bless America."*

Bradley sighed. The crisis was over, and so was the distraction. Hawk's troops were trained, disciplined, and totally loyal to him. He would have no chance of defeating them in a straight fight – hell,

Hawk would probably make short work of him alone – but something had to be done.

He continued walking until he reached the lower section of the Gallery, stunned by the immense interior, with Earth shining so beautifully through the gigantic panoramic windows. If he was going to make it back home, he'd have to go through Hawk, one way or another, so it may as well be on his own terms.

Bradley found himself walking back towards the central chamber. He held the rifle steady – knowing that other troops would soon come – and gazed at the levels above. Layers of synthetic walls separated the labyrinth of galleries, while sliding doorways were spaced at defined intervals so as to safeguard against decompression. Shana was up there somewhere, but where?

He was contemplating his route when he noticed a cloud of white smoke billowing from a corridor on the other side of a catwalk which spanned the chamber. Bradely walked across to it. The base of Orbit Station wasn't too far below him, and he could see bodies through the glass, though he barely considered them now.

"Bradley!"

He froze at the door, the smoke curling slowly in the still air.

"Brad! I have you in a closed communication! Answer if you can hear me!"

"Shana?"

Her voice came over his headset, brimming with relief. *"Oh, thank goodness. I've accessed a terminal up here and I can see you and other exo-suits on the mapping display. You're heading towards Hawk, but there are at least four other suits near him."*

"So I'm going in the right direction," Bradley said, continuing through the smoke. "Do you know what caused all this carnage?"

"The scientist, Oswald Carrington. I'm in his office. I think he may have lost it, big time."

Carrington? Bradley's mind flashed back to the story of the ruined house and abducted programmer. "So those Dronik things are his invention?"

"Maybe, but those machines aren't the only thing Hawk has lurking around up here. There are other blips on my monitor."

"Where?"

"They're near the space station and heading towards it. Whatever Carrington was doing that kept Hawk busy seems to have gone quiet for the moment, but whatever those things are, Hawk's now bringing them in."

"Meaning there'll be more troops to deal with."

"I think so... and oh, the main elevator's back online. I've managed to cut the feed to the surface, but Hawk is trying to restore communications. He'll know we're up here soon if he doesn't already."

***

After reaching the lower hangar, Hawk had fired off the OIV's first and secondary pulse guns, aimed directly at the upper bay, and then focused both beams on Carrington's Dronik the moment it crashed through the weakened structure.

Carrington had engaged the engines, but Hawk knew where its fuel cell was located and cut out its primary drive system, which in turn triggered a meltdown in the machine's energy core. The Dronik had shuddered a couple of times, then seized up as the thing cooked its own electronics. Carrington was smart, but he was no soldier.

"Open communications to Tombside base, Colonel," Hawk said. "We need more personnel and security up here."

Forge replied with an affirmative, and Hawk powered down the vessel's engines.

"Get the OIVs in. Open all bay doors. I want the station locked down and repaired."

"*Well played, Ronald. I'm so impressed with you,*" Carrington's voice erupted over Hawk's headset. "*I have to admit I didn't see that coming.*"

"I wouldn't be so blasé about it if I was you," Hawk said, dropping through the OIV hatch, weapon drawn. He directed the nearest marine to open the Dronik. "I didn't want it to end this way, Oswald, but you will pay a heavy price for this."

"*Of course I will, and it will be with my life. Do you plan on torturing me first?*"

Hawk didn't reply. Carrington's flippant words would end with a gun to his head. He'd soon learn that staring into death was torture enough.

"It's locked, sir," the marine said. "I'll need tools—"

"Get them, dammit!" Hawk snapped. "And what's the status on the elevator?" He looked to the other marine and saw his eyes widen in concern through his visor. Hawk narrowed his eyes. "What now?"

"Sir, we're trying open a line to Tombside, but it's being blocked intentionally."

"From where?"

322

"Would you like me to tell you, Ronald?"

Hawk looked at Carrington's Dronik. It had only residual power; enough for Carrington to communicate with, but surely not enough to interfere with Orbit Station's main network.

"I'm waiting, Oswald."

"You have an intruder, Ronald," Carrington said, his voice brimming with amusement. *"I deliberately let her peer into my computer. I thought that might be amusing."*

Hawk quietly cursed, then turned to the other soldier. "Go check the Programming Suites."

The marine left. Hawk looked down at the damaged Dronik.

"Care to make this easy on yourself, Oswald?" he asked.

"Oh, I'm quite comfortable in here, thank you, Ronald."

"You don't think that you're getting out of this alive, do you?"

"Yes, indeed I do."

Hawk bit hard on his lip. He wanted Carrington dead, but was painfully aware that vital repairs were needed. And this cold feeling he felt deep inside, that the situation wasn't playing out as expected, refused to leave him.

***

The marine passed Bradley at a fast jog, not even acknowledging him as he headed in the direction of the main gallery.

"Someone's coming your way," he said, adjusting the comm to the frequency Shana was on.

"I'll deal with it. You just get down there. I'll have a distraction for you, Brad. Trust me."

Bradley trusted her, but that didn't mean her plan would work. His hands were sweating in their gloves by the time he'd finally reached Bay Gamma. The smoke was thick down here, and the metallic walls were scorched and cratered. So, this was where the action had happened.

"Marine." A man in an exo-suit was limping toward him. "Where the hell have you been?"

Bradley's mind raced as he searched for a response, but the other man spoke before he could say anything.

"The threat's been dealt with, but Carrington is still at large. Get down to the lower bay. Take these tools."

He passed Bradley a metal case.

"Yes, sir," Bradley said, hoping his nerves wouldn't sound over the headset. He turned for the elevator, but was stopped by a snarl from the soldier.

"There's a fucking great hole in Bay Gamma, you idiot!" he said, grabbing Bradley by the arm and spinning him around. "We don't have time to take elevators!"

Bradley apologized and made for the bay, case in hand. He felt his hands shaking, but the suit disguised his nervousness as he made his way, noting a dead soldier on the ground. From here he could see the breach in the inner hull, where smoke was pouring into the room. He could also see pipes and electrical cables exposed and crackling where a massive explosion must have torn the corridor apart, a steady stream of coolant and gas vapour was still venting, filling the interior with smoke even as it emptied somewhere else into space. He watched as the continents slowly drifted below, eyes wide, and felt suddenly cold. Was he outside? He might as well be. What if he slipped – would he fall to Earth, or spin away into space? He didn't know.

He realized he was staring at the hole when he was supposed to be getting nearer to Hawk. He made for the collapsed metal plate at the center of the room, casting a nervous glance back at where his "superior officer" had just ordered him to go, but the officer was busy checking dead bodies.

Bradley looked down through the hole and saw it: a gigantic metal creature, insect-like, with multiple eyes, motionless, dead. He dropped through the hole into the compartment, and saw the shadow of a man who turned and faced his way.

It was him. The very man Bradley had come all this way to seek out. The man who had initiated all this – the conqueror, the mutineer, the destroyer of countless lives.

Ronald Hawk was wearing an exo-suit, carrying a laser weapon, and looking at Bradley with clear gray eyes. Behind him, one of the UFOs Bradley had seen on the internet hovered just above the floor. A hatch in its underbelly was open and twin barrels on either side glowed with an unearthly light. Bradley froze as Hawk lifted his gun to point it at the dead Dronik. His voice was cold and steady – focused.

"Come on, man. Stop your staring and get that case open."

Bradley placed the case on the ground, his mind racing. Shana hadn't contacted him yet. Was she okay? What the hell was he supposed to do now?

He laid his rifle down, and pressed two buttons on each side of the case, watching it slide open to reveal a variety of tools, some familiar, some not. He glanced at the rifle. Could he use it before

Hawk could react? He caught sight of another shape as it dropped through the hole. It was a man in an exo-suit, also heavily armed. *Fuck.*

"What's the sit-rep, Colonel?"

"The elevator's A-okay and we should have word back soon on the communication issue. The OIVs are coming in as we speak."

Bradley's breath caught in his throat. *OIVs?* He realized that they must be what the UFOs were called, and once they were inside, Hawk would have further reinforcements to hand. Bradley lifted a motorized wrench and looked at the side of the Dronik, praying that Shana's distraction would happen soon.

***

Shana watched in awe as the last OIV slowly moved into Bay Delta. It was staggering to see such complex machines being so expertly piloted so high above the planet. Hawk was a true commander, and the way he utilized all this incredible technology demonstrated that all too well.

She glanced sideways at the female scientist tapping away at a terminal, the woman totally oblivious to anything that was going on. Nothing could be done for her now.

Shana glanced at the map on the monitor and immediately saw an electronic marker coming her way. They must have figured that the communications problems were coming from up here. She watched as the final OIV was locked in place, then the exterior shutters slammed shut, sealing the bay off from the vacuum of outer space.

326

Now it was time for her distraction. She locked the shutter with a keystroke, then yanked the computer from the wall and threw it back through the monitor, watching it disintegrate into a shower of glass and sparks.

"Thank you for all the preliminary work, Mr Carrington," she said, leaving the room, gun in hand. "I couldn't have done it without you."

***

Looking at the complicated circuit boards, Bradley was reminded of the calculus exam he'd taken in his first year of college. He'd stared at the paper, at the meaningless symbols, and felt that every eye was trained upon him. But back then, no one was about to kill him.

He glanced behind him and saw the Colonel glaring at him. Bradley's eyes strayed to the rifle on the floor, but when he looked up, Forge was in front of him, his hand reaching for his collar. Bradley grabbed the gun without thinking, but he was sent flying through the air before he even got close, crashing hard into the wall. He struggled to his feet, staring at the barrel of the weapon now trained directly upon him, and felt panic rising again. He could see Forge's finger on the trigger, saw it tense, but a word from Hawk stopped him.

"Well, I'll be damned. If it isn't you? The God-damned fake news reporter from California."

Bradley's mouth was dry as he forced his eyes away from the gun barrel to look directly at Hawk. He tried to say something but his tongue wouldn't let him.

"I knew you were on your way here." Hawk walked over to one of the dead soldiers, and bent to retrieve the weapon still clutched in the corpse's hand – it was different to the one Bradley had, and was still attached to a pack on the dead man's back. "Of course," Hawk continued, disconnecting the pack with a push of a button, "you'd never have made it up here if it wasn't for Carrington and his damned rebellion."

Bradley swallowed. "You have a lot of adversaries."

"Who doesn't?" Hawk aimed the gun towards him. "America has adversaries. The world has adversaries. But I stand for a better model, and may I say my one real adversary is a friend of yours, Mr Wilcox."

Bradley was surprised he even remembered his name. "You're insane, Hawk," he said. "So, what now? I mean, I suppose you're going to…" His voice faltered.

Hawk glanced away from the soldier to the machine lying inert on the floor.

"Oswald Carrington is a gifted man, Mr Wilcox – far brighter than you'll ever be. Look around and see what he has done. Disabling the Droniks he created, sabotaging the space elevator, and taking down my best men, while at the same time allowing you access to my secret project. But then, look at you – an anti-American news blogger, more interested in spreading cheap rhetoric than working towards the greater good of your country." He shook his head. "But now you're both my prisoners. Our plan hasn't failed; in fact, it's only just begun. With us, the Earth still has a future."

Bradley looked at his gun lying on the floor. He wouldn't have a chance to reach it before he was shot down. "So everything you've done was for the greater good, is that what you're saying?"

"There are seven billion human beings consuming more and more of Earth's fast-dwindling resources," Hawk said. "Every ecosystem is now on the verge of total collapse, and the growing menace from the Far Eastern bloc has resulted in the wilful destruction of our planet and many of its creatures." He pointed his gun at the hatch Bradley had been ordered to open. "Ignorant people like you allow such atrocities to carry on with impunity." Hawk shook his head. "We have no mercy for your kind."

He pulled the trigger. A blazing light coalesced into a burning yellow beam of intense energy which focused on the machine. Hawk kept his finger on the trigger, pouring more and more energy into the metal until it burned red, then white-hot, until the metal dripped like water onto the floor.

Bradley could see Hawk's face through the transparent mask. He was staring at the machine, his lips moving in silent speech as he burned through the plate. Carrington must be cooking in there, roasting alive within his creation. Bradley's eyes went once more to the gun.

"Go on, try it," a voice crackled over his headset. It came from the soldier behind him, who was watching Bradley intently. *"Try it and your fucking death will be very painful."*

Bradley clenched his fists. They were going to kill him! Where was Shana? Where was her promised distraction?

He heard a curse over his headset and realized it had come from Hawk. The soldier didn't take his eyes off Bradley, but he shifted uncomfortably on his feet.

"Mr President, sir?"

Hawk shoved the half-melted plate free of its fixing with the butt of his gun and it hit the ground with a loud clang. Inside, the sizzling and smoking remains of a control panel sparked with residual energy. It was empty.

Hawk's words were calm. "Where is he, Colonel?"

Colonel Forge momentarily looked away, and Bradley took his chance. He leapt for Forge, knocking his gun aside with his arm, but the soldier was well trained and, with lightning quick reflexes, he hurled Bradley back, slamming him into the wall. Bradley rolled behind the OIV, feeling the intense heat of the energy beam as it struck the wall behind him. He looked around for an exit, but there was no way out.

As he lay there, helpless, Forge approached. He was dead. After everything he'd done, this was it.

Chapter 18

Hawk stared in disbelief at the empty compartment where Carrington should have been sitting, letting the fact that he'd been fooled slowly sink in. So, the Dronik had been operated remotely after all, and the scientist had made his escape. Despite all his considerations, Hawk had underestimated the man once again.

When the reporter had made his move, Hawk had barely noticed, confident in Forge's superior strength and skill. But when the high-pitched whine of the OIV's launch rail started up, he felt his heart rate rise, while a cold sickness spread through his stomach. He remembered the very same feeling from Vietnam – a feeling of impending doom.

Hawk spun around. The bay was vibrating violently as the magnets beneath the ship built up to the necessary hyper-velocity as it prepared to hurl itself along the rail and out into space. With growing horror, Hawk noticed that the main shutters were still closed, but how could that be?

No! Carrington couldn't have!

"Colonel!" he shouted, as the vibration intensified under his feet. "We need to get the f—"

His words were lost in the force of the OIV hitting the wall, and he was blasted backwards by the sheer force of the impact. But even as he felt the weight of wall beams collapsing around him, the fear left him.

It couldn't end like this. He wouldn't allow it.

***

The noise was deafening. Everything went black, then emergency lighting activated, illuminating the hangar with a pale red glow. Bradley was lying in a pile of rubble. His shoulder was screaming and he could feel a sharp pain in his temple, then his surroundings came back into focus and he almost choked.

The OIV was gone. So was the wall and half the floor. His feet were hanging over the edge of nothing, and the darkness of space played out before him. The gravity magnets in his boots kept him steady as he pulled himself upright and looked for his gun.

"Shana?" He heard desperation in his voice, but a low crackling noise over his headset meant the comm was down.

On the other side of the chasm, a figure was staggering to its feet. Colonel Forge stood shakily, rifle still in his hand. He aimed it at Bradley before lurching backwards, barely keeping his balance. Bradley thought he detected a thin stream of gas being expelled from a crack in Forge's neck plate. His armor's enviro system must have been breached in the OIV's launch.

Suddenly Hawk was beside Forge, helping him back from the edge of the precipice. Bradley backed away, his moves sluggish and his head cloudy and confused. The crackling gradually died away, and he heard Hawk say, "It seems Carrington wasn't finished after all."

Bradley knew it had been Shana's doing, not Carrington's, but there was no point filling Hawk in on that account.

Hawk lifted the Colonel's arm over his shoulder. He was looking into space, and Bradley saw the remains of the OIV floating in the distance.

"The elevator's compromised and everyone on that vessel is dead," Hawk said calmly. "But the remains will detonate automatically. No trace of our alien ships will remain."

"It seems your plan is over, Hawk," Bradley said, mustering as much confidence as he could.

Hawk looked back at Bradley and lifted his weapon, then lowered it again. "You will die, Wilcox, but I'll let the environment finish the job for me."

Bradley noticed the flashing red light in his visor and the gauge declaring 5% oxygen remaining.

"You'll suffocate slowly," Hawk said. "But don't worry, I'll be back. And I'll make sure your coffin gets fired directly into the sun."

"You caused this, Hawk," Bradley replied, hearing the desperation in his voice. "What kind of a monster are you?"

"You're as much to blame as me," Hawk replied. "We all have to live and die by our actions."

He turned and helped the hobbling Forge.

Bradley realized he was trapped with only the elevator shaft as a means of escape. Beneath him, the Earth shone in the light of the rising sun. There was no way out. His mind raced. "Fuck you, Hawk. You did all of this to save the planet?"

Hawk paused to look back at him. "See you in hell, Mr Wilcox," he replied, nodding at the hole in the floor. "Enjoy your last view of Earth. Oh, and I forgot to mention, your suit is rigged to detonate in case of capture. It will blow precisely one mile from this base, though you may be out of oxygen by then. Die slowly, or die in a ball of fire. Your choice, reporter." He walked behind the charred remains of Carrington's Dronik and out of view.

Bradley felt himself shaking. Only 4% O_2 left now, and it would decrease faster given his panicked state of mind. He walked to the edge of the elevator shaft and looked out through the shattered window, watching the debris from the crash silently flowing away and into orbit. *Fuck.* He doubted he'd even make it out of here, let alone the long fall to Earth. The gap in the floor spanned several yards, way too far to jump, and the wall was smooth and without any handholds.

A voice crackled over his headset. *"Brad!"*

"Shana!" He looked around to place her voice. "Where are you?"

"Over here! Look up!"

He looked up and saw Shana, clad in an exo-suit with helmet, standing on the opposite floor of the elevator shaft.

"You're alive! I was worried you might have got caught in the blast. I wasn't sure where you'd be, so I launched that ship in the hope that it might help you."

"I almost got blasted into space," Bradley said, wondering how many people had died because of her distraction. "But I definitely would have been killed otherwise. You found an exo-suit?"

"Yeah," Shana said. *"Took it off that soldier that Hawk sent up. A good thing too, 'cos there's not much air on this level."*

"Not much in my suit, either," Bradley said. "I'm running out of oxygen and I can't see a way out of here."

Shana said nothing, then asked, *"Where's Hawk?"*

"He's gone," Bradley said. "He must have headed for the escape capsules on the lower level. I saw six of them on the schematics."

"I have to go after him."

Bradley felt like he'd been punched in the gut.

"The mission, huh?"

"This won't end if Hawk survives," she said, her voice quiet. *"He still controls most of our military. If I can stop him..."*

"So you're gonna leave me to suffocate," Bradley said. Strangely, he didn't feel angry. Shana was ruthless. She'd proven that when she'd launched that ship, killing everyone on board. He thought back to when he had compared her to Helen of Troy, the face that launched a thousand ships. But Bradley was no demigod. "Am I just another death on your doubtful conscience?"

She sighed. *"You really don't understand, do you, Wilcox? It's for the greater good."*

"Then you had better go. I'd hate to die for no reason."

She looked at him, her eyes blank through the glass of her helmet, and then she was gone. Bradley looked down on the beautiful Earth, down at the continent of America. Was he about to die for the United States, or the world? And what about Hawk? He'd said he was fighting for the entire planet, and not just for his own country. Was he right? Did the human race really need a mass culling? Hawk had caused so many deaths, but then, so had Shana, and Bradley himself had also killed.

"Brad."

"Did you have a change of heart?" he asked, still looking down on Earth.

"I think I've found a way out," she said.

He looked up to see her on the upper level, way above him. "What about Hawk?"

She shrugged.

"So how do we get out of here?" he said, looking around.

Shana's voice was cold. *"You're not going to like this, Wilcox."*

***

Hawk opened the security door using a voice recognition code, then checked Forge's vitals. He was low on oxygen and, judging from the cerebral scan, was suffering from concussion, but they were at the escape capsule.

All six capsules were there, which meant Carrington hadn't got out this way, but Hawk had to assume the scientist had somehow escaped. He tried communications again, but only static reigned on the airwaves.

"Sir—"

"Save your strength, Colonel," Hawk said, starting the launch procedure on the terminal beside the capsule's door.

"Is the elevator lost, sir?" Forge asked. "Has the Maneuver failed?"

Hawk sighed. With communications down, there was no way of knowing how badly the elevator's structure had been compromised. And he couldn't even be sure whether reinforcements were coming. What he did know was that if Forge wasn't treated soon, he wouldn't last long.

A number of the OIVs were disabled, as were the Droniks, but the elevator was still cloaked, the reporter should be dead by now, and Sheen couldn't hide forever. No, the Counterweight Maneuver wasn't done. On the contrary, it was merely entering a new phase.

336

"I think the elevator will need some minor repairs, Colonel," he said, unlocking the capsule. "But you'll be back in business after a week's rest."

"I'm... gratified... to hear that, sir."

The door to the pod slid open and he pushed Forge in, climbing through after him and sealing the pod shut. He settled Forge into one of the three seats so that the power ports automatically connected to his suit, then he activated life support. He disconnected Forge's helmet and pulled it off before removing his own.

"Thank you, Mr President," Forge said. His eyes were a little glassy. "You didn't have to risk yourself for me."

"You're a good soldier, Colonel," Hawk said, powering up the control terminal. "I don't let good men die. Now sit tight. We're going down the alien road."

***

Bradley focused on the graphene plate of the elevator shaft and shifted his foot. He felt cold fear – nothing else – but all he could do was keep climbing with the help of his magnetic gloves and boots.

He could just make out the edge of the floor above through the hole that had been rent in the elevator shaft's polished wall, and beyond that, Bay Gamma. He didn't dare look down.

"The elevator's just above us, Brad. You're almost there." Shana's voice urgently crackled over the headset. *"Just six more feet, but you need to hurry. I think it's about to move."*

Bradley swallowed. "And how many feet down?" he said.

"Don't think about that, Wilcox."

He reached up to where the graphene plate had been twisted. It was a perfect handhold – hardly a challenge if it had been a climbing wall at the local gym, but far more difficult when one considered what lay below. If he should lose his grip now, scaling a smooth surface over 22,000 miles above the surface of the Earth, and with his oxygen supply getting lower by the second... he pulled himself up, resisting the urge to groan.

"I can almost reach you," Shana said. *"Just a bit further. Come on, come on."*

Bradley reached up and grabbed the edge of a narrow ledge, slowly pulling himself upwards while he searched for purchase with his booted feet. A loud boom sounded above him and he began to feel extremely heavy as he slipped backwards. He looked up, transfixed in horror as the bottom of the elevator started moving downwards. With the Earth behind him, he knew that it would soon pick up speed, gaining the velocity of a projectile which would strike with the force of a locomotive, taking him down to Earth the hard, painful way.

He heard a scream, then felt Shana's hand firmly take his, pulling him up swiftly with the aid of her suit's mechanical muscles.

Bradley was barely inside when the elevator whooshed past them with only inches to spare, accelerating downwards at lightning speed. He was breathing so hard he knew the O_2 would be gone any second. "Please tell me that wasn't me screaming," he said, gasping.

They both looked down the open shaft as the elevator screamed a high-pitched wail on its way down.

"No, it wasn't you," Shana said, her voice shaking as she pulled him to his feet. *"Boy, that was close. I had no idea you liked elevator surfing."*

"Is Hawk still aboard?" Bradley asked.

"An escape pod jettisoned, but Hawk will have communications once he's cleared the station. After that, who knows what he'll do."

"He'll have free rein down there if we can't get off this thing," Bradley said, feeling tightness around his throat. Every breath was an effort.

"I checked the route to the escape pods," Shana said. *"Once we're past the next bulkhead, we'll have breathable atmosphere all the way."*

Bradley couldn't reply. He just let Shana lead the way as he tried to slow his breathing.

The debris and the bodies on the floor meant little now, and the momentary glimpses he caught of the Earth through the transparent sections of the stations walls were just foggy blurs of blue and white.

This epic journey had originally started from a newspaper article, but now, after traveling halfway across America and to the edge of the stratosphere and beyond, he could see just how simplistically he'd viewed things. The financial economy was just a tiny fragment of something much bigger and far greater, and this capitalist idea was in many ways just a massive con. Perhaps people like Hawk were needed to stop those who wouldn't think twice about consuming the planet in a final, gluttonous act of destruction.

And what was Bradley Wilcox in all of this? A force for good? Or was he just another Earth avenger desperately clinging to his role in a fast-decaying system?

"We're here."

Shana's voice sounded miles away as she helped him through a door. There was a hissing noise as the airlock pressurized, and he let her lead him into the next room, his head faint. He almost felt like he wasn't human anymore, but rather a strange alien life form holed up inside some gigantic machine.

And then his helmet was gone and clean, oxygenated air filled his nostrils. His strength came back almost immediately and his thoughts returned, crisp and clear. He felt like he'd just had an extremely vivid dream, but then he saw Shana's face and remembered how serious things were.

"Come on, soldier," she said, a small smile flickering across her face. "We're not out of this yet."

Bradley hurried alongside her, breathing deeply as he went and feeling more relaxed by the second. "I thought you were going to leave me down there, you know," he said, once he'd caught his breath.

Shana looked at him out of the corner of her eye. "My instinct said I should have cut and run, but you do have a strange effect on me, Wilcox. I can see why Sheen decided to trust you."

"I don't think she ever expected me to do much more than expose Hawk," Bradley replied.

"Yes, but you're part of this now, and the world will never be the same again. Neither will we. Hawk hasn't been stopped yet, and he's not going to take this lightly. However, the good news is that he now thinks you're dead, and that makes you very useful."

"Are you saying I've been conscripted?" Bradley said, following her through into another airlock.

340

"We're gonna need some help. Your social security number's not going to be much good now that you're dead, and Hawk will snuff you out if he ever discovers you're still alive."

Bradley cursed under his breath. She was right. He was a marked man.

They left the airlock through the other door, and Shana motioned for him to be quiet. They were beneath the great Gallery, and a long metal corridor stretched out before them. They headed to the end, where another corridor curved around the space elevator's interior shaft. Shana pointed to the left and Bradley heard voices.

"That way!" she hissed, pointing to the right.

They moved as quickly and as silently as they could, hearing the sound of barked orders and handset communications echoing around them. Hawk's pod had already jettisoned, but more of his soldiers must have traveled up from the Tombside base, and now they were systematically closing down all the exits.

Bradley kept looking behind them and almost bumped into Shana. She pulled a lever in the wall, and a hatch opened with a soft whirring hum. A green light flashed brightly in the ceiling.

"No time for subtlety now," Shana said, ducking through the hatch.

Bradley heard shouting and the clank of armored boots, and followed her in, noting the three seats built around a central column covered in screens and dials.

"Just sit back," Shana said, scanning the controls. "The armor should link itself."

"You know how to use this fucking thing?" Bradley said, sitting down and feeling the armor lock smoothly into place.

341

Shana pressed a button and the hatch closed with a whooshing sound. "I familiarized myself with what I could upstairs, but no, not really. I've never been one to follow precise instructions, but I'll figure it out." She checked her sleeve and held it up to the ship's terminal.

Bradley couldn't hear anything on the other side of the door, but in his mind's eye he could see armored soldiers carrying heavy weapons, ready to burn a hole through the door. Then as if on cue, a voice rang out over the pod's speaker;

"Attention, unknown occupants! You must exit the escape pod now or we will engage the self-destruct sequence! You will never make it down to the surface of the Earth!"

"Shana?" Bradley said, feeling sweat building on his forehead.

She fell back into her seat, letting her armor connect. "I've got control of the pod's computer."

"Attention, unknown occupants—"

Shana kicked a pedal built into the base of the control column, and before Bradley could say a word, they had dropped away from the space station.

The booster rockets immediately kicked in and the speed at which the ship accelerated away from the orbiting space station was truly incredible. Bradley couldn't help but think of how far they had to fall, and he tried to focus on Shana's face as the vibration increased, hoping for some sign of confidence, but she looked as scared as he was. What now? Would they go into orbit? Would they explode? Or would they hit the planet at full speed?

Suddenly the vibration calmed. "The engines," Shana said, her face white as a sheet. "I don't know how they exactly work, but they're slowing us down and keeping us on a smooth trajectory. We're on the orbital freeway."

"For where?" Bradley asked, surprised at how calm he sounded.

"Hopefully Mexico."

Bradley sighed. "Oh, nice. Our very own vacation spot. Try to put us down next to a Jacuzzi, will you?"

"Hawk will know where this pod ends up," Shana said, her smile fading. "I've already contacted Sheen for extraction."

"Time for a beer, at least?"

"I'd kill for a cold beer."

Bradley stopped smiling. They'd killed, all right.

He sat back, contemplating the world he'd left behind and the world he was returning to, the person he'd been before the Oakland article, and the person he was now – a reporter with the biggest scoop the world had ever known, and with no chance of telling it to anyone.

Fuck it. He'd earned that beer.

***

Hawk stepped from the pod, immediately hearing the sound of tiltrotor blades. He saw the Osprey approaching low over the hills and waved his arms until he was sure it had seen him.

"Come on, Colonel," he said, helping Forge out of the scorched pod, which was half-buried in the sand.

"Should I speak with the General?" Forge asked.

"You'll be debriefed," Hawk said, watching the Osprey land a few yards from them. "I've already initiated protocols. We have time."

"So much damage," Forge said, shaking his head. "I'd kill Carrington with my bare hands if I could get hold of him."

Hawk sighed. None of the escape pods had registered jettisoning prior to their departure, but he still knew the scientist had escaped somehow.

Soldiers descended the ramp in the aircraft's underbelly, and Hawk watched as they connected a winch to the capsule. General Morgan appeared last.

"We need to get you airborne, Mr President," Morgan said. "The elevator's still cloaked, but a lot of explosions were witnessed. All hell's breaking loose at the United Nations. It's all I could do to dissuade the major foreign powers from crossing our borders."

Hawk loosened the armor around his neck and followed Morgan back to the helicopter. "We were prepared for this scenario, General," he said, raising his voice over the sound of the propellers. "I just need a shower and I'll take care of it."

"Sir, it was noted that another escape capsule was launched," Morgan said, seating himself in one of the helicopter's chairs. "Not long after yours. We scrambled fighters but it disappeared from our sensors."

"The holo-graphene frequency should have showed up," Hawk said, with a vexed frown.

"Unless they're using an advanced maverick algorithm," Morgan said. "The cat could be out of the bag, Mr President. Sheen's still eluding us and if she goes public with the evidence—"

344

"We have got to put it out that Sheen is collaborating with the alien menace, General," Hawk snapped. "Fortunately we destroyed their initial invasion fleet using technology stolen by undercover US operatives and we now have the means to counteract them. This is the story I want fed to the media, and once I'm done, there won't be a place on Earth she can hide."

The Osprey took off and they were on their way. Morgan said nothing for a few minutes, and then asked, "Sir, what about the elevator and the space station?"

Hawk smiled. "It doesn't exist, General, and nobody can prove otherwise."

***

The landing had been a blur, and Bradley couldn't actually recall leaving the escape pod.

He'd found himself floating face-up in water and then mysterious men in scuba gear had hauled him up onto a boat. Sheen was standing there in a suit, her face a picture of concern as she snapped orders at the men to get the boat moving. She looked at him and took his hand. By the time he could compose his thoughts enough to ask Shana what was going on, they were below deck, their armor removed and replaced with white robes.

They'd showered. Bradley had the wound in his shoulder dressed and a shot of antibiotics administered. Now he was sitting opposite Shana, alone but for the assurances of a petty officer that they'd be spoken with soon.

"What about that beer?" he said, his voice slightly hoarse.

She passed him a bottle of water and shrugged. "Think we'll have to wait until we get to Mexico."

He drained the bottle. "What then?"

"We both get drunk," Shana replied, laughing.

"I don't know if I can wait that long."

Shana pushed her wet blond hair back from her eyes and Bradley immediately saw the same sensual woman he'd met on the streets of DC. The computer nerd, the waitress. He'd been oblivious back then, but now it was different.

She caught his gaze and her face softened, and before he knew it, his lips were on hers, the wet curls of her hair in his fingers. She kissed him back hungrily, and he pushed her up against the table. When their lips parted, he knew he wasn't an innocent bystander anymore. He'd just been witness to the greatest secret the world had ever known and he could either act upon it or be totally consumed.

Shana let her robe drop to the floor and looked back at him over her shoulder as she stepped into the shower. He followed her in, leaving his own robe behind him, careless of whether anyone would intrude, and stepped under the warm water, letting her draw him close, feeling her soft skin against his.

They'd traveled to the frontier of deep space together, and now he needed her like there was no tomorrow. Perhaps there wasn't a tomorrow. He felt her warm body beneath his hands. For a brief moment, the world didn't matter.

***

President Ronald Hawk stood behind the podium, flanked by the secret service, with the Stars and Stripes rippling behind him. He felt calm, despite everything that had happened.

The elevator and most of the Orbit Station had survived the damage caused by Carrington and remained outwardly concealed, while even the destruction of the OIVs had played into his hands somewhat. Yes, the cost was enormous, but with Russia and the East now devastated, national debt and securities were things of the past. The Chinese President, Sheng Zhenshen, had personally called Hawk to thank him for his help in stopping the alien threat, explaining that he would be most honored and grateful for any aid the United States could provide. Hawk would, of course, graciously allow this – under his terms, naturally.

His aide approached him, a look of awe on his face.

"It's time, Mr President," Jenkins said, smiling nervously. "You're going out to every nation on the planet. I'm proud to be here for such an historic moment."

"Thank you," Hawk said, looking at the younger man. "Just remember what we have sacrificed, and the tasks that will confront us in the years ahead."

The aide nodded thoughtfully and retreated out of shot. Hawk looked directly at the camera and waited as the man behind it counted down with one hand.

"Citizens of the United States and the world," he began. "Today, American forces, with the help of our allies, have successfully defeated an extra-terrestrial fleet from an unknown world that was intent on destroying our planet and the entire human race. The casualties have been immense. The damage to the great nations of our planet has been incalculable." He paused. "But with this victory, we have shown the will and the combined strength that all the peoples of this world can possess when we act as one.

"For far too long we have been at each other's throats, needlessly destroying our precious planet, its eco-systems, and its creatures, all for the sake of selfish gratification. We now know that we are not alone in this universe, and with that knowledge, there comes a degree of responsibility.

"I ask all of you to join me in a momentous victory, the celebration of life, and a celebration of our beautiful planet. The future is uncertain, and we will need to be on guard for any further invasion, but I will tell you now that we do have a future. So let us take this momentous opportunity to act as one world and build a better home for future generations."

***

Oswald Carrington had managed to land his escape pod on the edge of a dense forest close to a small town.

During his time on the Orbit Station, and with the vast resources at his disposal, he had correctly theorized that Hawk would have never guessed he was able to fabricate a special 3D-printed escape vessel. This single cloaked machine was launched undetected from the trash extraction unit situated in the subsection of the space station.

Carrington had also been quietly innovating and devising a range of miniature Hornet Grifters, propelled by advanced thrusters. Once these things were set loose by voice command, no human could survive the lethal revolving lasers that were comprised within them. And with these weapons safely secured inside the metal case he held in his hand, he would soon become unstoppable.

The short road from the forest led to a small but noisy bar. Carrington approached the neon-lit establishment and entered through the double-fronted doors into the main bar room.

An old 1960s song, "Sukiyaki" by Kyu Sakamoto, was playing on the jukebox. But now everyone was silently watching the big screen fixed to the wall.

Carrington could hear Hawk's televised voice talking over the hushed crowd. The moment he finished his speech, everyone was on their feet, applauding triumphantly. The excitement echoed across the room as per the screen. Hawk stood very proud, his fist raised in acknowledgement, a benevolent smile cracked across his face. The guy was a true hero.

The volume of the music increased as the bartender, a burly man with a shaved head and a thick beard, greeted Carrington with a massive grin.

"This round's on the house, fella. What can I get you?"

"What's the occasion?" Carrington said, placing his case down on the bar top.

"Where you been, man?" the bartender said, looking at him incredulously. "The aliens! We kicked them back to fucking Alpha Centauri or wherever they came from!"

"You know the enemy lies much closer than you think," Carrington said. "It lies within all of us. It always has."

The bartender frowned. "Whatever, man. You want a drink—"

His words faded as the case slid open and the Hornet Grifters ascended with a low hum.

Kyu Sakamoto's song kept playing out loud. But Carrington was already thinking of his next step as the panicked screams started. Humanity was done, and Hawk, even with his heightened supremacy, would not be hindering him much longer.

The world was about to experience the new age of the Dronik.

Acknowledgements

I first came up with the idea for *Counterweight Maneuver* over six years ago, working on the plot outline during evenings and weekends to fit it around my full-time job.

Once the final chapter was written, many steps remained to get to this stage. Thank you to my editor, Caroline Hynds, for getting the text ready for publication and her additional help and advice. Thank you to Claire Perkins for her innovation and expertise in marketing the book.

And, above all, thanks to you, the reader.

Enjoyed this book? For the latest news and updates, please visit www.richiedebenham.com.

Printed in Great Britain
by Amazon

78542410R00212